SOLDIER IN BUCKSKIN

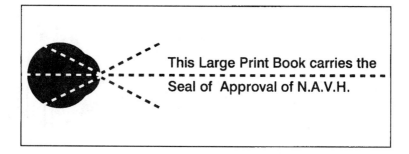

SOLDIER IN BUCKSKIN

RAY HOGAN

Thorndike Press • Thorndike, Maine

Published in 1997 by arrangement with
Golden West Literary Agency.

Thorndike Large Print® Western Series.

The tree indicium is a trademark of Thorndike Press.

The text of this Large Print edition is unabridged.
Other aspects of the book may vary from the original edition.

Set in 16 pt. Plantin by Al Chase.

Printed in the United States on permanent paper.

Library of Congress Cataloging in Publication Data
Hogan, Ray, 1908-
    Soldier in buckskin / Ray Hogan.
      p. cm.
    ISBN 0-7862-0620-9 (lg. print : hc)
    1. Carson, Kit, 1809-1868 — Fiction. 2. Frontier and
pioneer life — West (U.S.) — Fiction. 3. Scouts and
scouting — West (U.S.) — Fiction. 4. Pioneers — West
(U.S.) — Fiction. 5. Soldiers — West (U.S.) — Fiction.
6. Large type books. I. Title.
[PS3558.O3473S59 1996b]
  813′.54-dc20   95-47969

SOLDIER IN BUCKSKIN

Chapter One

Rifle ready and at his side, Kit Carson lay quietly in the rocks above the trail and listened. The muffled cries and scuffling sounds that had brought him to an alert a few moments earlier were growing louder.

For the past week he had been visiting with the Martínez family on their ranch near Arroyo Hondo, but that morning he had said his farewells and set out for Taos. Above him the April sky was a clean, unbelievable blue marred only by a cluster of fleece-like clouds lurking above the towering peaks of the nearby Sangre de Cristos, while all around him the winter-starved trees, sage, and other native shrubs were greening out to match the sage color of the prairie grass. Somewhere off to his right a mockingbird was filling the warm, spring air with his musical imitations and, over in the Indian pueblo to the left, dogs were barking frantically for some reason.

It was all familiar and welcome to Kit Carson. He had returned but a short time from a trapping expedition with Ewing Young and his party — one that had taken them into southwest New Mexico, on to California, and back. Being again in the comparatively civilized clime of Taos, where it was not necessary to be continually on the alert for danger, was a pleasure.

The sounds came again — louder scuffling, and this time a more pronounced cry — that of a woman, Kit judged. A moment later he saw the cause: two hard-bitten trappers clad in customary buckskins, moccasins, and low-crowned, flat-brimmed hats came into view. One was half dragging, half carrying a young Indian girl, probably not yet in her teens, toward an arroyo in which was a thick stand of rabbit brush and other rank growth. Evidently they were also on their way to the fandango and had come upon the girl who was undoubtedly from the nearby pueblo.

Carson considered the trappers nervously. Both were strangers. One was a lean, somewhat hunched, black-bearded man with small, bear-like eyes that were also black. His fringed buckskins were worn and stained by grease, and the brim of his hat was ripped — the result of an arrow that had barely missed its mark, most likely. A hard grin of anticipation split the man's mouth as, left arm about the young squaw's small waist which lifted her churning feet clear of the ground, right hand clapped over her mouth to stifle cries, he proceeded along the trail for the brush. His partner, carrying both rifles in order that the black-bearded one might have both hands free to manage the struggling girl, was a somewhat larger individual with a florid face, light eyes, and cotton hair that pushed out from beneath his hat and bunched about his neck.

Carson waited no longer. Gathering his feet under him, Hawken rifle firmly gripped, he rose swiftly and, lithe as a mountain cougar, dropped off the bluff onto the trail a half a dozen strides ahead of the trappers. Both came to an abrupt halt. An oath exploded from the smaller man's lips, but he did not release his grasp on the girl, squirming wildly to break away.

"Now what the hell do you want?" he demanded.

Kit, the Hawken leveled at the larger of the pair, nodded at the girl.

"Turn her loose. She ain't wanting to go with you."

The trapper grinned, took a tighter hold on the girl. "It ain't what she wants that's going to be good for her . . . it's what she's going to get."

The blond man laughed. Carson shook his head. "Let her go," he repeated quietly.

He was smaller than either of the two in height, but his shoulders were wide, and there was a muscular look to him. His hair, worn long as was usual, was a deep brown with a reddish tinge, as was his mustache. His eyes were a cold blue, and as unyielding as the black walls of the cañon through which the rushing Rio Grande del Norte flowed a short distance to the west.

"Well, now, mister, if you're wanting a little of her, too, why you just wait till I get her stripped, and then we can all have us some fun. Me and Zeb ain't hoggish . . . we'll share. Who might you be, anyway?"

"Name's Carson."

"Kit Carson?"

"Right. Now leave her. . . ."

"Heard about you, Kit. I'm Seth Grieg. My partner there's Kidder . . . Zeb Kidder. Why don't you just lower that shooting iron, and we'll get on with the fun."

"Turn her loose, damn you," Carson replied, his voice rising as anger mounted within him. The Indian girl had ceased to struggle, now hanging limply against Grieg, her dark eyes wide with fright, and hope.

"By God, you're a-meaning that, ain't you?"

At Grieg's question, Carson nodded. "I sure as hell do."

10

"You're barking mighty loud," Kidder said, moving a step to one side. "There's two of us, and that Hawken ain't got but one ball in it."

"And it's going straight into your belly if you make another move! I want you to drop them rifles."

Kidder hesitated briefly and then let the weapons fall to the ground. Grieg shrugged, smiled ingratiatingly.

"Just can't see what all the fuss is about," he said. "She ain't nothing but a goddamn squaw . . . a young one that ain't been cut yet, I'm hoping. We can. . . ."

Carson, his stride quick and light, moved up to Grieg. Shifting his rifle from right to left hand, he drew his knife from the sheath hanging at his belt. There was the glint of sunlight on bright metal as he pressed the point into the back of Grieg's wrist.

"You don't listen good, *amigo,*" Kit said.

The trapper yelled, sprang back. The girl jerked clear, stumbled, and went to her knees.

"Damn you to hell!" Grieg shouted and, jerking out his knife, lunged at Carson.

Kit, a wary eye on Kidder, rocked to one side. Grieg slashed out wildly, missed, and Carson countered with a stab that drove the dark-bearded man back. Hunched forward,

11

arms down, and slightly off balance, the trapper was wide open. Kit stepped in quickly. His arm arced. Again there was the flash of sunlight on metal. Magically a line of surging blood appeared on Seth Grieg's forehead as Kit's blade tip cut across it.

"Damn you . . . you're . . . ," the trapper began, as he staggered back. "I'll. . . ."

Carson, watching both men closely, sheathed his knife and shifted the Hawken back to his right hand.

"You ain't doing nothing," he cut in flatly. "You ain't hurt bad, only marked. Now, you and your partner best move on. Won't be healthy for you around here."

Grieg had put away his knife and was now holding a bandanna to his wound. His mouth had become a tight line and his eyes, set deep within the circle of black hair that surrounded his leathery face like a nest, blazed with pure hate.

"We'll be going, all right . . . but this sure'n hell ain't the end of it . . . no, sir! Next time we meet you sure better have your finger on the trigger of that gun because I aim to kill you dead . . . one way or another! You remember that!"

"I'll remember," Carson said indifferently and nodded to Zeb Kidder permission to pick up the two rifles lying nearby. "Head

12

off down the trail and don't be coming back. I ain't sure I'm doing the right thing by letting you go, anyway, so you move fast because I might change my mind. It's your kind that's keeping the Indians all stirred up against the whites."

Grieg and Kidder, the latter still carrying both rifles, moved off in the direction of the river. At once the Indian girl came to her feet, began to tug at the coarse gray dress she was wearing in an effort to straighten it. She was, as he'd thought, no more than a dozen years old.

"You are from the pueblo?" he asked in Spanish, pointing toward the distant adobe brick structure.

The girl nodded.

Kit glanced at Grieg and Kidder. They were diminishing figures on the trail, moving westward. Lowering his rifle, he swung it about and rested it on a shoulder.

"Go home, now," he said to the girl.

She nodded and managed a thin smile. There was no word of thanks, but Carson could read her appreciation in her dark eyes as she turned and, running lightly, started for the pueblo. After a few moments she slowed, half turned and, raising her eyes, waved hesitantly. Kit responded and, with a final look at Seth Grieg and his partner, Zeb

Kidder, now well in the distance, resumed the trail for Taos.

The first face he saw, when he reached the plaza where several of Taos' more enterprising merchants had laid out displays of their wares to tempt visiting mountain men, was that of Thomas Fitzpatrick, known to most as Broken Hand — a name given to him by the Indians after he had injured himself in an accident.

"Good to see you, Kit!" the trader boomed. "Was hoping you'd show up! Heard you'd been with Ewing Young's outfit."

"Was," Carson replied, looking around.

There were at least a half a hundred trappers present, all easily identifiable in their fringed buckskins, among twice their number of Mexican men and several braves from the pueblo. There were only a few women to be seen. They would put in their appearance that night when the dancing began.

"Sort of like a rendezvous," Fitzpatrick, a tall, craggy faced man, said. "Just ain't as big."

Carson continued to glance over the milling crowd in the plaza. He had never witnessed one of the gatherings in which trappers, traders, and Indians all got together for a few days in summer to renew acquaintances, trade, make new friends, and in general have a good time, but he was looking forward to the experience.

"Like one hell of a big fiesta, I guess," he said.

Fitzpatrick nodded. Then: "You eat yet?" he asked, pointing toward a long table where bowls and plates of food had been set forth by the merchants.

"Not since morning."

"Well, come on. Man can't do no talking if his belly's empty," the trader declared and, grasping Kit by the arm, propelled him to the nearest table.

There were other trappers there helping themselves, some of whom Kit knew, others who eyed him in the wary, quiet way of men forever cautious in the presence of strangers. Carson, taking up one of the tin plates, began to work his way along the table with Fitzpatrick behind him, ladling out portions of savory *chili* stew with the wooden spoon provided, choosing two of the large, corn husk-wrapped *tamales,* a helping of *posole,* several blue corn *tortillas,* and for dessert two *empanadas,* or fried fruit pie made up in tart form. Thus loaded down, and with Fitzpatrick still with him, Kit made his way to one of the young cottonwoods, sat down, placed his back against the tree's trunk, and began to eat.

"You willing to talk?" Fitzpatrick asked, hunkering before him.

"Sure."

"Heard you done right good with Ewing Young."

Carson nodded and continued to eat.

"He pay you good?"

"Enough."

"Well, happens I'm looking for some good men to work for me and Jim Bridger. And maybe a couple other fellows. We're calling the outfit the Rocky Mountain Fur Company."

"Milton Sublette one of them other fellows?"

"Yep, along with Henry Fraeb and Frenchy Gervais. Seems you've heard about us."

"Word's got around," Carson replied, looking off into the center of the plaza where some sort of disturbance had broken out. A trapper and one of the Mexicans had gotten into a fight, it appeared. "Was thinking about doing some free trapping myself."

"One way of making a living, I reckon," Fitzpatrick said. "But it's hard going, and you'll need money for a stake."

Kit nodded thoughtfully and then, setting the plate aside, he rose, crossed to the nearest table, and helped himself to a dipper gourd full of the water from one of the buckets. He started to turn away when a man standing behind the table spoke.

"Whiskey's a dang sight tastier than water, friend. Now, I've got some right good bourbon I can sell you for five dollars a quart . . . or maybe you'd like good Mexican wine, or maybe *aguardiente*. Got some Taos lightning, too."

He wasn't much of a hand for liquor of any kind, most particularly the powerful local brandy, or the concoction of various ingredients that went into the making of the whiskey used for trading with the Indians, but he reckoned it wouldn't hurt to celebrate a mite.

"Whiskey," he said, reaching into a pocket for a half eagle and dropping it onto the table. The price was high, he knew, but on such occasions they always were.

"Yes, sir," the merchant said, a small, slender man in a dusty blue suit and collarless shirt, picking up the coin. Placing the bottle of liquid in front of Kit, he added: "I'm obliged to you, friend. Could tell you were a quality drinker when I first spotted you. Now, if you're wanting a jug of the same when you leave, just you holler. I'll make you a right special price."

Carson nodded, returned to the tree, and sat

down. Broken Hand Fitzpatrick was still there, resting on his heels as before. Kit handed the bottle of bourbon to him and then resumed eating.

"Job with us'll be good for ten, twelve years," the trader said, pulling the cork and having a deep swallow of the bourbon. Smacking his lips, he glanced approvingly at the bottle, added: "Sure is fine liquor. We aim to trap every stream and river between here and the Canadian border. They'll all be good men, ones you can ride the trails with and not be worrying about your hair. Now, Young told me you was one of the best he'd come across in years. I sure would like to have you sign on with us."

"When you pulling out?" Kit asked, having a drink from the bottle. The disturbance in the plaza had ended, he noted, and all was again gaiety and good fellowship on the surface. Underneath, however, there would exist, as there had always, the simmering resentment the Mexican men harbored for the *Americanos.*

"It'll be early fall," Fitzpatrick said, brushing at his beard and mustache. "You interested?"

"Reckon so. Where can I find you?"

A grin of pleasure cracked the trader's

mouth. "I'm real glad to hear that. Can sign my book over at Ewing Young's place."

"Good . . . got my stuff over there. Figured to have myself some fun tonight. I'll drop by tomorrow."

"Tomorrow'll do fine," Fitzpatrick said, getting to his feet. "And if you've got a friend or two looking for work . . . and that you'll vouch for . . . bring them along. I'm hoping to sign up a big party."

Carson nodded. "I'll just do that, if I can," he said and continued to eat.

Fitzpatrick headed off toward the crowd in the plaza and shortly, his plate finally clean, Kit drew himself upright and crossed to the table where he deposited the circular bit of tin into a pan where several others had been placed. Then, grasping the bottle of whiskey by its neck, he sauntered off toward a group of trappers gathered in front of the building where the fandango would be held. The sun was almost down, and the dancing, which he much enjoyed, would begin shortly after that.

Taos had been Carson's home, more or less, for the past five years, and he was fairly well acquainted with the thousand or so residents of the settlement. But his time there had been intermittent since he pursued a life of coming and going that never permitted him to settle down or even remain in one place for long.

However, now as he strolled through the confusion of persons, hearing snatches of conversation, nodding to those he knew, he began to feel more at home. Several times he encountered men he had trapped with in the past and paused to share a drink with them from the bottle. There were a few of the Spaniards and Mexicans who called him by name and exchanged pleasantries over a swallow of the good bourbon.

Dust was now hanging in the motionless air and, shot with fading sunlight, it assumed a golden glow that spread over the village, turning it warm and friendly. Children were playing in the shadows of the trees and buildings, and dogs wandered aimlessly about. The smells of cooking were tantalizing odors in the advancing night, further enhanced by intermingling smoke from numberless piñon wood fires and, over among the low, flat-roofed adobe houses, a mule brayed raucously.

Suddenly a church bell began to toll in measured beats, and the noise in the plaza subsided to some extent but for only a brief duration. A cheer went up from the trappers gathered around the doorway to the hall where the fandango was to be held and, throwing his glance to that point, Kit saw that the musicians — a man with a guitar, another with a fiddle, and a third with a drum — had arrived. They entered the building, one occupied in the past by a merchant of some kind but now vacant and taken over for the occasion, and were immediately followed by the shouting, laughing, noisy mountain men.

Kit continued his leisurely approach. It would be another half hour or so until dark and the time when the *señoritas* would make their appearance — some with their boy friends, some chaperoned by an elderly relative, but all anxious and ready to participate in the fandango. Kit always enjoyed the spirited dances, held primarily for the benefit of the trappers, and never failed to attend if he happened to be in Taos when one was scheduled.

Reaching the doorway he halted, struck up a conversation with two elderly Mexican men, replying in kind to the cool nods of several younger natives who eyed him quietly. He knew well what was filling their minds at that moment — the all too often hated *Americanos* would monopolize the women during the dance, and some would even carry their intentions further by inducing their sloe-eyed partners to go outside

21

with them where they would seek a cool, dark place in which to press their attention.

Usually a fandango ended up in a brawl, not to mention the several individual encounters that were certain to result, but maybe this time would be the exception. Some of the rowdier mountain men like Bear Foot Johnson and Haskie Smith were not around — or at least he hadn't spotted them — and that could make for a more pleasant if less exciting evening.

He wondered then if the two he'd come up against on the trail near the pueblo — Seth Grieg and Zeb Kidder — would show up. No doubt they intended to, but Kit figured he had changed their minds for them. Of course, they just might ignore his warning and show up anyway. He reckoned it would be real smart to keep a sharp eye out for them.

Light was now showing in the windows of nearby houses as well as in those of the hall. More people were moving up to the doorway and entering, men in loose-fitting white shirts and cotton pants tied at the waist with a wide sash in which reposed the inevitable knife, women and young girls wearing fringed shawls, colored dresses that flared from several petticoats, and snowy white shirtwaists so thin from many washings that the nipples of their imprisoned breasts seemed about to burst through the fabric. There were mountain men and traders in buckskin and satin shirts, merchants in business suits, and finally a priest in the usual somber attire.

"Ain't you going in, friend?" a deep voice at Carson's elbow asked.

Kit turned, faced the speaker — a man of about his own age, he guessed. He had a broad smile and eyes that were bright with excitement. He was wearing buckskins and moccasins. He had removed his jacket revealing a new red-and-blue striped calico shirt.

"Name's Monte Rinehart. Heard somebody over there call you Kit Carson."

Kit took Rinehart's offered hand into his own, welcoming the firm clasp which was so different from the customary limp greeting of the native people.

"I'm Carson sure enough. Don't recollect seeing you around here before."

"Ain't been. This here's my first time in Taos," Rinehart said, his eyes pausing on the bottle in Carson's hand. "Seems you sort of live here."

Kit smiled. He had taken a liking to Monte Rinehart immediately, something he seldom ever did. Usually it was only after a lengthy association that he would admit another person into his heart.

"Yeah, I do," he replied, offering the bottle of bourbon to Monte. "Where do you hail from?"

"Up Colorado way," Rinehart said, taking a deep swallow of the whiskey. He smacked his lips, added enthusiastically: "I'll say this for you, Kit Carson . . . you sure do tote around good liquor! I. . . ." Monte's words broke off abruptly, his eyes fastening upon a smiling, young Mexican girl with extravagant charms clearly on display approaching the doorway. "Thanks, partner," he said, handing the bottle back to Kit and turning away. "I see me somebody I sure have to get real good acquainted with!"

Carson grinned as he watched the trapper hurry off, intercept the girl, and endeavor to make himself understood with gestures and stumbling Spanish. He was successful, and together they entered the hall, arm in arm, just as the musicians broke into their initial tune.

Kit moved then to the doorway and stepped inside the hall, now filling with noise and smoke from the *cigarillos* being smoked by men and women alike. Standing his rifle in the corner designated for such, and hanging his powder horn and jacket from its muzzle, he came about and faced the room.

The arrangement was always the same and of no surprise to Kit. The musicians were at the far end of the rectangular hall, while the women and girls, some standing, some sitting on the benches provided, lined one wall, the men strung out along the opposite wall. A dozen or so couples were in the center — the male partners all trappers, he noticed — whirling and hopping furiously to the beat of the music which was being all but drowned out.

Carson spotted Rinehart with the girl that had so taken his fancy and, as they spun breathlessly by, he heard Monte shout: "Get yourself a woman, friend Kit . . . and join the fun!"

Carson smiled and nodded, having that exact purpose in mind. Crossing over, he started along the line of women searching for one in particular — Rosa Lucero. He had met her in the plaza, not at one of the previous fandangos or *bailes,* but during a warm summer evening when the customary after supper stroll by *Taosenos* was under way. The pleasantries exchanged had developed into a lengthy conversation which in turn led to a meeting later on at her house where she served thick hot chocolate and crisp, spicy *biscochitos,* a delicious cookie, and sang Spanish and Mexican songs for him while accompanying herself with a guitar.

He saw Rosa near the end of the line. A young Mexican was standing beside her, hand resting on the back of the chair in which she was sitting. She smiled a welcome to Kit as he approached, her full lips parting and revealing twin rows of even white teeth.

"*Señora Lucero,*" he said, "will you do me the honor?" His Spanish accent was near perfect.

"It shall be my pleasure," the woman replied and got to her feet under the glowering eyes of her escort.

Kit nodded to the man and, with Rosa in his arms, spun away, moving into the circling couples and becoming a part of the stomping, sweating, whirling parade in the hazy room.

"It is good to see you again, Kit Carson," Rosa said.

She had several small, silver bells attached to a narrow belt that she was wearing about her slim waist, and their light tinkling sound was a constant accompaniment to the music being offered by the men at the east end of the room.

"And it is much too long since I have seen you," Carson replied, skillfully guiding the young widow past one of the more energetic

26

mountain men. "I have thought often of you and of that night a time ago."

"And I," Rosa said. "The house is still there, and waiting."

"Then I shall come again."

Carson started to say more but hesitated. A shout had lifted above the music. He swung his attention to the source of the confusion then swore softly. It was Monte Rinehart. The trapper, nearly to the door with his girl, had halted. Two young Mexicans, knives in their hands, were poised threateningly before him, evidently having taken offense at something he had done. Monte would know nothing of how things were in Taos insofar as relations between the natives and Americans were concerned, and the incident bid fair to turn serious.

"Your pardon, Rosa," Kit murmured politely, thrusting the bottle of whiskey into her hands to hold for him. "That man is my friend. I must help him. If I do not return, I will meet you later at your house."

Rosa, accustomed to such sudden interruptions, merely smiled. "I shall be there," she responded and backed toward the wall.

Carson quickly started for Rinehart. The music had not stopped, and there were many couples still unaware of the tension that had sprung to life and were continuing to dance.

But a number of trappers, like Kit having heard the shout, were moving in hastily to stand by Monte Rinehart, a stranger but one of them nevertheless. A like situation had hastily developed for the two Mexicans blocking Rinehart's way. A dozen or more of their friends, dark features set, eyes glittering, hands resting on the hilts of the knives in their sashes, were assembling behind the pair.

Abruptly Rinehart lashed out with a moccasined foot. It struck the hand of the nearest Mexican, dislodged his blade, and sent it skittering across the floor. The other man jabbed with his weapon. Monte jerked back, barely avoiding the thrust, but in that same fragment of time swung a balled fist at the Mexican's jaw. It connected solidly. The man staggered and went down. Instantly the men backing the pair, thrusting the girl aside, began to close in. Kit, knife out and parrying thrusts, shouldered his way to Rinehart and, with the help of the trappers coming to their aid, drove a path through the Mexicans to the door. Reaching the entrance, Carson paused long enough to retrieve his rifle, coat, and powder horn and then, with the wall of mountain men blocking the doorway preventing any pursuit, he followed Monte out into the cool night. Almost immediately Rinehart caught himself and wheeled. "Hello, I ain't letting nobody run me off! That little gal's out for a real good time, and I aim to show it to her."

"Best you forget this . . . leastwise for a spell," Carson warned sternly, pulling on his fringed jacket. "Let's go down somewhere for a bit and do some palavering. We need to wait a spell, maybe an hour or so, to let them *hombres* simmer down a mite. After that you can maybe go back inside if you're of a mind . . . but if you do, watch yourself! Them Mex boys are real handy with a toad stabber."

Monte grinned, nodded. "Seen that myself, old son. But that little girl . . . name's Dolores . . . would be worth spilling some blood over."

"Could be, but you'd be smart to pick yourself another woman for right now . . . let everybody cool off. This Dolores'll still be around." Kit moved off through the soft darkness for a bench a short distance away.

"I sure hope so," Rinehart said, following. Then: "I'm thanking you and them other boys for stepping in when you did. Would've got myself gutted if you hadn't."

"Most likely. Expect a lot of this is my fault, though . . . you being a stranger in these parts. I should've warned you about cozying up too much to the woman in front of the men . . . even if they ain't married or fiancéed."

They reached an adzed log placed upon two large rocks.

"Can't expect you or nobody else to raise me . . . I'm full grown," Monte replied. "Them Mex fellows always that touchy?" he added, sitting down beside Carson.

"Always, and I reckon a man can't blame them much, us coming in here, throwing money around like it was dirt, taking over the town and the women, highhanded as you please. I don't suppose it would do any good . . . for the sake of peace . . . to ask you to forget about this Dolores?"

Monte gave that but brief consideration. "Nope, sure wouldn't. I ain't seen nothing like her since I left home."

Carson shrugged. It was the answer he had expected. "Home," he echoed after a bit, "where exactly was that?"

Chapter Two

"New York," Monte replied, brushing at his mouth with the back of a hand as he gazed at the doorway to the dance hall. "You ain't got that bottle of good whiskey in your pocket, have you? I could sure use a drink after that little fracas!"

Carson shook his head. "Sure don't. Gave it to a friend to hold and didn't have time to get it back."

Matters were in full swing inside the hall again. The music and the stomping of the mountain men as they spun and twirled their partners around the floor was a definite sound in the starlit night, and it was most unlikely that any of the souls living in Taos were unaware of it.

"New York," Kit said frowning. "As I recollect, you said it was Colorado."

"Yep, sure did," Rinehart explained, settling back with a regretful sigh. "Was born in New York . . . a little town on the Hudson River . . . near Albany. Just couldn't get along with my folks and took off running when I was about fifteen. Had a notion I wanted to become a riverboat captain."

31

Monte paused, studied two men who had emerged from the doorway of the smoke-laden hall, and halted near the step to talk. "Ain't them the two jaspers that jumped me?"

Kit considered the pair. "Appear to be. Probably the girl's brothers . . . or maybe one of them's the man she aims to marry."

"Maybe," Rinehart said doubtfully, "but the way she was acting and pulling at me, I don't figure she's wanting to get tied up with any man . . . not ever."

"They all want to get married," Carson corrected. "It's a big disgrace to them and their family if they don't. Sooner or later your Dolores'll tie up with somebody."

"Well, it won't be me!" Monte stated decisively. "I'm aiming to do a sight more traipsing around before I settle down."

Carson grinned. "Then you best be a mite more careful about cozying up to these girls. Them and their family's liable to take it as being engaged. What made you give up the river?"

"Just plain didn't like it . . . was tied down too damn' much. Just wasn't cut out for that sort of work and, when I finally got that through my head, I quit and tied in with a bunch of fellows heading for Colorado territory. You think that little gal . . . Dolores

32

. . . is the kind that'll expect me to marry her?"

Carson's shoulders lifted and fell. "Couldn't say because I don't know her. She mention her last name?"

"My Mex ain't so good, but I did find that out. It's Valesquez . . . Dolores Valesquez. You know the family?"

"There's several Valesquezes around here. Don't know any of them personally."

"Ain't you lived here for quite a while?"

"Yes, off and on. Can do some asking around about them if you like."

Rinehart gave that thought, again transferred his attention to the exit of the dance hall. The music had stopped, and a few couples were wandering out into the open for a breath of fresh air. It would be breathlessly hot inside Kit knew and, even from where he sat some distance away, he could see the thick cloud of smoke hanging from the ceiling.

Finally Monte stirred, swore. "Naw, just you forget it. I reckon I'm growed enough to do my own finding when me and Dolores gets together again. How long you aiming to hang around here?"

"A while," Carson replied and fell silent.

The soft pad of footsteps off in the darkness behind them had caught his attention.

33

Easing forward slightly, he cast a look into that direction. Monte had heard the quiet scuffling also, Kit saw, and was casually shifting his attention to that area. Presently two Indians, blankets draped about them, emerged from the deep shadows and crossed to where they could see the entrance to the building where the fandango was in progress.

"They up to mischief?" Monte wondered.

Kit watched the pair take a stand alongside a nearby hut. He shook his head. "No, they're just wanting to see the whites and the Mexicans cavorting around, I expect. They think it's a real funny sight . . . our kind of dancing. What did you do in Colorado . . . dig for gold?"

"Some. Didn't have no luck so I threw in with some trappers. Was one, an old-timer named Amos Tuttle . . . he sort of took a liking to me. Taught me what I had to know to trap beaver . . . about putting the traps just so far under the water, five inches, no more and no less, and using beaver scent . . . castoreum . . . to kill off our stink, and a lot of other little tricks that made taking peltries easier. I owe old Amos a powerful lot."

"You and him working for some company?"

"Nope, was free trapping. I've been won-

dering why we didn't bump into you somewhere along the way."

"Mighty big country . . . the Rockies 'specially. Could be we did pass, one heading
one way, one the other."

"Likely. Heard you'd seen the ocean with
Ewing Young. You do good with him?"

"Sure did," Kit replied. The music in the
hall had ceased again, and several men had
come outside and were taking drinks from
bottles and jugs while conversing. "There's
plenty to be said for free trapping like you've
been doing," Carson continued. "Done a
spell of it myself, but signing up with a fur
company and letting them supply everything
. . . horses, mules, traps, provisions and such
. . . and letting them do the worrying about
getting the skins out of the mountains to the
market while at the same time they're paying
a man for what he does is a good arrangement, too."

"What I've been told," Monte agreed.
"You figuring to hire out this coming season?"

Kit nodded. His liking for Rinehart had
grown stronger, probably because Monte's
life somewhat paralleled his own, but there
was also the big, square-faced man's unde-
niable charm, his way of speaking, of smiling, his sense of humor. He'd be a good

man to have as a partner.

"I'm signing up with Broken Hand Fitzpatrick and his outfit . . . the Rocky Mountain Fur Company," Carson said. "Grand bunch and the kind a man ain't a-scared to trail with. If you're interested, I expect Fitzpatrick'd be real happy to have you sign up, too."

"Sure something to think about," Monte said. The music in the *sala* had resumed, and dancing had begun once more. "I've done told you all about me . . . how about you? If we're maybe going to be trappers together this winter, I'd sure like to know the howdy-do about you so's we'll have something to talk about."

Carson smiled, brushed at his mustache. He wore no beard and only occasionally permitted the mustache to grow, although there were times in extremely cold weather when he allowed both as well as the hair on his head to go unchecked.

"Can say my home was in Kentucky . . . leastwise that's where I was born," he said. "My pa was a *compadre* of Daniel Boone, and he brought him and what family there was then into Madison County. I wasn't around. Showed up on Christmas Eve. Was in 1809."

"Makes us about the same age."

36

"Figured as much. Well, Pa was kind of fiddlefooted in those days, and we didn't stay there long. When a couple more families moved into the valley, Pa loaded us up, and we went to Missouri. I wasn't no more'n a couple of years old at the time. Went to farming, and then Pa got killed when I was about nine."

"You have any brothers or sisters?"

"Could have loaned you some if you was needing any! Was fifteen of us . . . ten boys and five girls, all told, the last one . . . another brother . . . being born right after the tree fell on Pa and killed him. We managed all right without him, though. He'd picked a good place there in Howard county to farm, and Ma kept us all in school and working the place so that we got by."

"Times was hard everywhere."

"For a fact. I was the littlest one of the boys . . . Pa had hung the name of Runt on me . . . so I was apprenticed out to a saddler by the man Ma married a few years later. It didn't take no six footer like my other brothers for that, but I didn't let it bother me."

"What kind of work did they do?"

"Teamsters, lumber hustlers, jobs like that."

Monte considered Carson speculatively in

the half light. "Expect it did bother you some, and you set yourself to proving you was big as they was in other ways."

"Maybe so. Don't recollect thinking about it much. Anyway this saddler, name was Workman . . . Dave Workman, was plenty good to me."

"I don't figure you was too happy working leather."

"No, hated setting there on a bench using a mallet and an awl and such, but I did learn a lot not only about making saddles but fixing them and harness and making buckskin clothes and moccasins and the like. Right today I can sew together a pair of breeches and a coat good as anybody."

"That's a right handy trade for a trapper."

"Sure is . . . and it got me out of that saddle shop and out here where I was wanting to go all the time. I kept thinking about it every time I saw a wagon train heading west, and I done a lot of practicing with my pa's old rifle, loading and firing and reloading until I got pretty fast at it. I guess Workman could see where my heart was all the time I was with him, so he probably wasn't surprised when I up and left one day to join a party pulling out for Santa Fé."

"When was that?" Rinehart asked.

Kit frowned, rubbed thoughtfully at his

jaw. "Was late summer of 'Twenty-Six, I think."

"Was about the time I got to Colorado," Monte said. "You have any trouble lining up with that wagon train? You must've been kind of little seeing as how you ain't much for size now . . . meaning no offense . . . and that was in 'Twenty-Six which'd make you about seventeen."

"Was some trouble, all right. A couple of my brothers were teamsters on the train. I figured they'd stand by me. Didn't. Sent me back, but I only went part way and joined up with another bunch. When we got to Santa Fé, an old friend of the family's from Missouri named Matt Kinkead took me in and helped me get started trapping."

"It's a wonder some jasper didn't grab you and take you to this fellow Workman . . . you running out on your apprenticeship like you did."

"Can thank Dave Workman nobody ever did. He posted a reward all right, but he offered just one cent for my return. Wasn't nobody going to go to a lot of trouble for one copper."

Monte laughed. "I reckon that proves he was a real friend. You ever go back home?" The music in the hall had stopped once again, and couples were coming out into the

39

yard in search of fresh air and coolness.

"Started a couple of times . . . last time I got as far as the Arkansas, run into a fellow named Campbell who was headed for Mexico and was looking to hire on somebody who could speak Mex. I took the job and, when that was over, signed on with a mining outfit in the Gila country."

"You tried your hand at digging with a pick and shovel?"

"Nope, not that. Was working as muleskinner, but I didn't much like the country, so I quit and came back up here." The musicians had resumed, the twang of the guitar, the thump of the drum, and the squeal of the fiddle riding the night air in a wave of sound. "Tied up with Ewing Young that winter, and we headed south and west. Had nothing but hell, thanks to the Indians and the Mexicans, and finally got back here with my hair this month. Can tell you now I was plenty glad to see that hunt end!"

"Expect you was. I hear you say it paid good?"

"Got me several hundred dollars, besides found a lot of good experience that I won't soon forget. Young's a fine fellow to work for."

"I've met him," Monte said. "Bunking over at his place now."

"Me, too," Carson said. "I. . . ."

Monte Rinehart had come to his feet, his gaze on several persons standing in the flare of light outside the entrance to the dance hall.

"Ain't that my gal . . . Dolores . . . there looking around? Could be she's trying to spot me."

Carson pulled himself erect also and centered his attention on the girl. "Expect it is."

Monte settled his squirrelskin cap more firmly on his head and started toward the girl.

"It sure is her . . . and she's looking for me."

"It'd be smart to hold off a bit longer," Kit warned, taking up his rifle. "Ain't likely them friends of hers has cooled off much yet."

"The devil with them!" Rinehart declared recklessly and struck out across the hard, sun-baked ground toward the girl.

Carson, coat in one hand, rifle in the other, followed quickly but, as they drew near the building, the two Indians abruptly moved away from the wall along which they were standing and, stepping out in front of him and Rinehart, blocked their way.

"Now, what the hell . . . ," Monte began, hand dropping to the knife hanging from his belt. "I. . . ."

"It's all right," Kit said hastily. "They're from the pueblo up the trail a piece. They ain't looking to start something." Then nodding to the two blanket-wrapped men, he said in Spanish, *"¿Que paso?"*

The younger of the pair began a reply immediately in like tongue, speaking slowly. He apparently was just in the process of learning the language either at the church mission or from one of the Spanish families where he would be employed in some capacity. It was a lengthy, labored speech and, when it was over, the older Indian drew a horsehide leather belt with a hammered metal buckle from beneath his blanket and solemnly presented it to Kit.

"Gracias," the old man murmured.

Kit bowed slightly. *"Gracias a usted, abuelo."*

Both Indians turned and, saying no more, faded into the night.

"Now, what the hell was that all about?" Monte asked. "I savvy some of the lingo . . . all that thanking and you calling the old one grandpa . . . but why? What did he give you the belt for?"

Carson, examining the leather strip, buckled it about his waist. It would come in handy for carrying a pistol, if ever he decided to get one, he thought.

"The old man was thanking me for helping his granddaughter."

"Helping her? Where? How?"

"Was on my way here. Came across a couple of trappers dragging an Indian girl . . . was only a kid . . . off into the brush and made them turn her loose. Wasn't nothing much."

"Nothing much! That old redskin didn't seem to feel that way about it . . . giving you a real fine leather belt like he did. You know the trappers?"

"Strangers. One named himself to be Seth Grieg, the other'n Zeb Kidder. I gave Grieg a cut to remember me by."

Monte whistled softly. "Grieg! He's a plenty bad customer. Run into him up on Green River once. You watch him close, or he'll kill you." He was staring at Kit. His voice had taken on a note of respect and admiration. Then: "Them Indians seemed to know you right good."

"Just seen me, I expect. I've been out to the pueblo a few times and done them a turn or two when things were bad, and they needed help . . . like going hunting for them and bringing them in fresh meat . . . deer and elk. Your gal's gone back inside."

"I see that. Leaves me just one thing to do . . . go in after her. You coming?"

Carson sighed, swore softly. "Yeah, I reckon I will, but I ain't sure it's a good idea, just kind of hate to see a fellow I've taken a fancy to get himself all carved up."

Rinehart patted the knife hanging from his belt. "Can do a bit of carving myself if I have to. Anyway, if things get a mite tight, I'll borrow that Hawken from you."

Kit laid a hand on his friend's shoulder. "No, forget about shooting. You kill one of them with a rifle, and the whole town'll be on your back. Do your serious fighting with a knife. They figure it's honorable that way."

Monte laughed. "Staying alive's honorable, the way I see it, but I'll hearken to what you say."

They reached the door, paused there as a flood of hot, smoky air heavy with the smells of sweat, *agaurdiente,* and perfume of some sort met them head on.

"Sure looks quiet enough," Kit commented, letting his glance sweep the hazy interior of the noise-filled room. "If you get yourself in a tight spot, sing out, and I'll come running."

"Fair enough. Where'll you be when this is over?"

"Lady I know's got a place. . . ."

"The one I seen you dancing with?"

"That's her. Aim to go to her place . . .

44

but don't come looking for me. Just meet me on the west side of the church in the morning, and I'll take you over to shake hands with John Fitzpatrick."

Monte's head bobbed, his smile widening as he located Dolores somewhere in the confusion that milled about in the hall. "Can bank on it, partner," he said and hurriedly entered the building.

Carson watched the man, towering well above the shorter, slightly built Mexicans and matched only by some of the other trappers, shoulder his way determinedly through the whirling and stomping dancers toward a distant corner where Dolores apparently awaited him. Kit stirred and, also entering the building, deposited his rifle and other gear in the corner as before. Monte Rinehart would be lucky if he didn't run afoul of the girl's friends or relatives again, he reckoned, and he guessed he should be ready to pitch in and help the man out again when, and if, trouble developed.

But right now, he'd forget about it and, seeing Rose coming to greet him — the bottle of bourbon whiskey in her hand — he moved forward. It was high time he had a little fun.

Chapter Three

"When I cash in," Kit said as he and Monte Rinehart rode slowly along the river searching for beaver sign, "I reckon it'll be from a rifle ball or an arrow. It ain't likely I'll die in bed like city folks do."

Monte nodded. "Same here . . . and that's how I want it. But I ain't much on thinking about tomorrow. Fellow once told me . . . he was a Frenchman . . . that today is what counts. 'Today is right now,' he said, 'and a man's a fool to worry about tomorrow,' and living the kind of life we do, never knowing for sure whether there's a redskin hiding in the brush waiting to put his knife in your heart and then lift your hair, I figure old Frenchie had the right idea."

"For certain," Carson agreed and swung his mount in nearer to the water for a closer look at what appeared to be a beaver lodge.

Monte had met Kit that next morning after the fandango in Taos behind the thick-walled church and gone with him to meet John Fitzpatrick. The two men had so taken to each other that Rinehart had signed on to go with the Rocky Mountain Fur Company party that fall. They had spent the summer in the area surrounding Taos, Santa Fé, and Santa Cruz de la Cañada, the province's largest settlement, devoting most of the time while in Taos to Rose and Dolores. The Valesquez family had finally got around to accepting Monte as a suitor for the girl's hand — although reluctantly — and he had no more difficulty with her brothers and the other young Mexicans who had resented his attention to her.

Monte still had no plans for marrying anyone and settling down but conceded that one day, perhaps, if he survived and, should that day come, it most certainly would be the beautiful, dark-eyed Dolores he would take as wife. Until then, however, they would remain no more than very good friends. Kit and Rose had much the same understanding, although there definitely was no thought of marriage in the minds of either of them. A young widow, Rosa enjoyed Kit's presence. He was always polite and considerate and never failed to favor her with a gift of some sort when he returned after a lengthy absence — a piece of jewelry, an embroidered shawl, a pair of silver slippers — and once he had given her a dashing low-crowned, flat-brimmed hat of the type worn by the *señoritas ricas* that he had bought in Albuquerque. It had been a pleasant summer for both men, and it was with a certain amount of regret they rode out that fall with Fitzpatrick and the rest of the trapping party he had lined up.

"Tomorrow Fitzpatrick wants to head up the Sweetwater branch," Carson said. "Pickings've been a mite too slim along here. You trapped this country before?"

"Been up and down the Platte a few times," Monte replied. "It'll get better as we go along. He say what he aimed to do when we get to the headwaters?"

"Nope. I reckon that'll depend on how things are."

"Likely head for the Green," Monte said. "I can say this for Broken Hand . . . he does things up right. Can't recollect ever being with a company that's organized good as we are."

It was true, Carson agreed. Each man was provided traps, three mules — one for riding, two for carrying packs — blankets, a shelter tarp, and minor equipment for cooking. His own personal equipment was of his own choosing, and in this most hewed pretty close to the same line — heavy drawers worn under buckskins, thick woolen shirts, tough parfleche moccasins, leggings, and either a knitted or fur cap, or one of the wide-brimmed, round-crowned hats. Each had his rifle, usually a Hawken flintlock which was considered the best to be had, powder horn, bullet pouch, wiper, bullet mold, extra flints, and a supply of lead. A Green River knife hung from his belt along with a steel head tomahawk, and there were a few who carried a Springfield flintlock pistol to give them added fire power in a close-quarter engagement.

Monte Rinehart had been right about Fitzpatrick. The party trapped its way up the Sweetwater branch of the North Platte to its headwaters and, upon reaching that point, cut west to Green River. After a few days there with only fair success, they went on to Jackson Hole, a beautiful valley lying between the Teton and Wind River mountain ranges. Prospects there looked good to Kit, but Fitzpatrick was anxious to join the rest of the Rocky Mountain Fur Company party that had gone on ahead, and he led his brigade on to the headwaters of the Salmon River. The men were there, as expected — and dug in for the winter.

"Any trouble with the Indians?" Carson asked Hugh Garrett, a member of the preceding party, as they sat in the warmth of a cabin that night.

"Nope, ain't been none yet." Garrett, a man well into his sixties, scarred and grizzled by years in the mountains, shook his head. "This here's Nez Percé country, and they're friendlies. Right smart people, too . . . but them goddamed Blackfeet . . . they're prowling around."

"Blackfeet!" Rinehart echoed. "Thought their range was over in Yellowstone country."

"Blackfeet don't follow no rules when it comes to hunting," Garrett said, tamping fresh tobacco into his pipe. "They been deviling folks up here right along. We're aiming to go meat hunting now that your bunch has got here and, if you're along, you sure best keep your eyes peeled."

Two days later the hunt for buffalo got under way. It was snowing steadily, and the ground was covered, making it difficult for the mules to move. Carson, leading a party of five men, two of which were Rinehart and Garrett, finally called a halt.

"Getting no place with the animals," he said. "We'll leave them here, hunt on foot."

Garrett nodded his approval of the idea, and the men continued. Almost immediately, Rinehart called a soft warning.

"Deer . . . over this a-way."

Kit and the others swung toward Monte, a short distance to their left. Shortly the herd of deer took flight, lunging through the snow as they sought to disappear among the trees. The hunters brought down three before they were out of range, gutted them, hung them from limbs to be picked up later, and pressed on.

Several hours later Kit spotted buffalo. They were a mile or so east, grazing out on a plain where the snow wasn't deep, and he and his party began to work their way toward them.

"Was along here some of the boys seen a Blackfoot hunting party," Garrett said as they proceeded. "Buffalo sort of favor being out on a flat. Expect that's what got them savages hanging around."

Blackfeet! Kit muttered a curse. "When was that? When was it they seen them?"

"Four or five days . . . maybe a week ago."

"Means they're probably still around," Carson said, studying the surrounding country closely. "Let's move out to the north. We won't get within rifle range from this side of the herd, anyway."

A half a dozen gunshots sounded somewhere off to the west. It was a flurry of firing and then silence.

"I reckon some of the other boys got lucky,

too," Monte observed.

Kit had turned his attention to the buffalo wondering if the shots would send them thundering away. The reports were well in the distance, but buffalo were hard to predict. Sometimes men shooting within only a hundred yards or so failed to disturb them; on other occasions a single gunshot a half mile away would send them charging blindly off into the opposite direction. This herd seemed undisturbed, however, and continued to graze indifferently on the flat. Carson and his men moved slowly and carefully on, following a circuitous approach that brought them eventually to a spur of woods and placed them within easy rifle range of the animals.

"Spread out," Kit directed. It seemed natural and acceptable for him to have put himself in charge although Garrett and two others in the party were older, and no one showed any resentment. "Don't want all of us shooting the same bull."

"Indians!" Garrett warned suddenly, dropping to his knees behind a clump of wild berry bushes. "It's them Blackfeet, sure'n hell!"

Kit and the rest of the party hunched low, their eyes following Garrett's pointing finger to a dozen or more Indians who had broken out of the trees some distance on ahead. It was evident that they, too, had spotted the buffalo herd and were preparing to charge it.

"Some's got rifles," one of the trappers noted. "I count seventeen of them."

"Too many for us to take on," Kit said. "Best we set it out right here, see what happens."

Garrett spat. "What's going to happen is they'll run at that herd hard on, knock down as many as they can with their first loads and arrows."

"Buffalo could come this way," Monte said. "It'd be just fine setting here in the brush and picking us off some of them redskins along with a few bulls."

"There they go."

The Indians spurted suddenly from the fringe of trees and in a wide line rushed toward the herd. They were well out on the plain before the buffalo abruptly wheeled and began to run. At that moment the Blackfoot party loosed arrows and bullets. A single bull stumbled and fell.

Garrett whipping his arms back and forth to ease the cold, spat again, this time to show his disgust for such poor marksmanship. There was another spatter of gunshots. Two more buffalo went down in a flurry of churning hoofs and flying snow. And then the herd was gone, only small, dark spots on the eastern horizon.

"Reckon that's that," Garrett said.

Carson was studying the activity out on the plain. The Blackfeet were gathering around the buffalo, dismounting, and preparing to skin and quarter the animals.

"Just might be we could jump them while they're busy," he said. "I don't figure there's more'n half a dozen rifles in the bunch."

"That ain't all of them," Monte said, pointing.

A dozen more Indians had broken out of the trees ahead and were racing to join those on the flat.

"And I'm betting there's still some more around," Garrett said. "They generally bust up into a bunch of small parties when they're out hunting. I reckon we might as well head on back, get the mules, and pack in the deer we got."

Carson nodded. "Sounds right . . . but I sure hate missing out on them buffalo. Could be we might get some of the men together and come back."

"They'll be gone by then," Garrett said.

"Yeah, expect they will," Carson agreed and, turning, started back along the trail they had made in the snow.

They went first to where they had hung

the deer and, slinging them from poles by lashing their feet together, carried them to where the mules were tethered. Transferring the carcasses then to the backs of the mules, they struck out for camp, taking a more direct route than the one followed earlier. Garrett, being familiar with the country, was in the lead. He pulled up abruptly a time later, raising a hand in a silent gesture for caution. Kit and Rinehart quickly moved up beside the older man.

"That shooting we heard . . . weren't our boys getting mean," he said in a tight voice. "Was them Blackfeet getting them."

Carson's jaw tightened. In a small clearing a dozen strides ahead lay the bodies of five trappers. All had been scalped. There were two dead Indians to prove that the Blackfeet had paid a price for the attack.

"One of the boys got away," Garrett said. "Broken Hand always makes up his hunting parties with six or twelve men in them so's he can keep track. Sure hope that fellow, whoever he is, made it back to camp."

"Can keep an eye out for him as we go," Monte said, and then: "We take the bodies back with us, or are we going to wait and send a party for them?"

"We'll take them," Carson said promptly. "Can't let the varmints get to them."

The party moved forward, loaded the bodies of the unfortunate trappers on the mules and, leading the animals, resumed the return to camp.

"Didn't see their mounts," Rinehart said after they were on their way. "Redskins took them, I reckon."

"For certain," Garrett replied. "Them Blackfeet are real partial to mule meat . . . that and taking the scalp of the man riding one."

The sixth member of the hunting party, badly wounded, had made it back to the camp. About two dozen braves had hit them, he said. He and the trappers with him had been working through the trees and rocks toward a herd of deer when they suddenly found themselves surrounded by Blackfeet. They put up a hell of a scrap, but there were just too many Indians. He'd managed to crawl off into the brush while the scalping was going on and hide until the party left. Then he lit out for camp — bleeding so badly he figured he'd probably run dry before he got there.

"I'm for teaching them stinking bastards a lesson!" Monte Rinehart declared angrily, as they stood around one of several blazing fires. "There's enough of us here to mount up and go after them."

"You ain't going to teach a Blackfoot nothing about the whites," John Fitzpatrick broke in. "They've been hating us . . . and maybe with good cause . . . from the first time they run into a white man. And nothing's going to change that. Besides, we'd not find them. They've moved on for the Bitterroots by now."

Rinehart wagged his head. "Maybe so, but it sure galls me to let them get away with what they done. And it ain't a good idea to let them think they have."

"Don't fret over it," Broken Hand said with a brief smile. "You'll get your chance to even score with them. I doubt if we'll ever see the last of the Blackfeet."

But they did not encounter Indians other than the friendly Nez Percé again that winter and, when the deep snow set in and ice locked tight the streams and ponds, Kit like all the others put in his time repairing equipment and preparing in general for the coming spring season.

When that day arrived, and the trails became passable, Fitzpatrick led his party back through the hills to Green River, hoping to be the first in the area but, as they rounded a bend and struck for a grove in which he intended to set up a camp, the fur company trader signaled a halt.

"Somebody's already there," he said, his voice betraying his annoyance. The area had been a favored location of his for years, and he had looked forward to establishing his camp there again. After a few moments he shrugged, realizing there was nothing he could do about it and continued on.

"Hell . . . that's Alex Sinclair!" someone near the head of the column said. "He's got some of Bean's men with him."

Monte turned to Kit. "Recollect hearing about Sinclair, but who's Bean?"

"Was a fellow that got himself together a big party of trappers down in Arkansas. Was sometime in 'Thirty, I think. Led them into the Rockies, and first off run into big Indian trouble. That was more'n enough for him. He turned tail and headed back to Arkansas, leaving his bunch to shift for themselves. Some of them wound up in Taos. Heard others had gone on north. Surprised you never heard about it."

"Seems I did, now that I'm thinking on it."

The Fitzpatrick party reached the camp and halted, and the two groups exchanged greetings. Sinclair, after passing a few words with Broken Hand, spotted Carson among the others and, breaking into a big smile, hurried up to him.

"Kit!" he shouted, extending his hand. "Sure is good to see you," and after being introduced to Rinehart, added: "Heard from an old friend of yours a time back."

"Who?"

"John Gantt. Was asking about you."

Carson nodded his pleasure. Gantt had been a captain in the United States Army and served his time along the Missouri frontier. Kit had a deep liking for the man who, Sinclair told him, was having a hard time of making a go of the fur business.

"Where is he?"

"New Park, last I know," Sinclair replied.

New Park. It was a fine hunting area up near the Medicine Bow mountains in Colorado. Gantt should do well there if he had men with him who knew their business. Kit turned to Monte.

"Season's done here. Think I'll trail up to New Park, see how things are going for Gantt."

Rinehart bobbed. "Just you count me in. Always liked that part of the country."

Bill Mullady and Tom King, standing nearby, both nodded. Tom said: "Wouldn't mind heading up that way myself, Kit, if you're agreeable. Same goes for Bill here. We was wondering which way to light out."

"I ain't set a foot in New Park in four, or

maybe it's been five year," Mullady said. "We'll trot along with you boys if it's all right."

And it was all right with John Fitzpatrick for them to take their summer's leave, fixing them up with supplies as well as pack mules and horses to ride. They moved out one warm, sunny morning and ten days later rode into the captain's camp — located exactly where Alex Sinclair had said it would be.

"What brings you up here, Kit?" Gantt asked after introductions had been made.

"You," Carson replied. "Heard from Sinclair that you had yourself a small company and thought maybe you could use some extra help."

Gantt nodded, scrubbed at his beard. "That I can! All that talk coming from Fitzpatrick . . . me not having the money or goods to pay for plews and getting undercut by Bent on top of that . . . ain't helped at all. But my partners and I'll make it if we can get enough fur."

Carson had heard it said before that Fitzpatrick was bad-mouthing Gantt but found it hard to believe that Broken Hand would stoop to such tactics. As to the Bents who operated a trading post on the Arkansas, he could not say since he scarcely knew them, but he would not take sides.

Kit with Rinehart, King, and Mullady, although they had not planned on it, went to work for Gantt at once, adding their efforts to those of the men already employed by the one-time Army officer. Carson did not favor spring and summer trapping, believing that it did not give the beaver time to replenish their number, but it was customary and in John Gantt's case necessary, so he made no issue of the matter.

They trapped New Park for a time and then, as results slowed, began to work their way through the high country of the Laramie Plains, down the Platte's south fork, and then to the Arkansas where they set up camp.

"We're running low on provisions and long on pelts," Gantt said once they were settled. "I'll load up and go on to Taos . . . we won't be getting any closer . . . get rid of the beaver and lay in a stock of supplies for the winter. I ought to be back in a couple of months."

Carson, who had assumed second in command of the party, agreed. "I'll keep the traps working from here until you show up. By then it'll be time to move to new water."

Gantt rode out two days later with his pack mules heavily loaded and, as the summer waned, Kit and the others continued to trap unhindered along the river — but with only mediocre success. Then, when the nights had begun to turn cold and the days crisp and brown with the taint of snow on the wind, John Gantt appeared in the distance — coming up as fast as a weary horse and pack mules would permit.

"Something's wrong," Tom King, who had first spotted him, declared. "My hunch is there's redskins on his tail."

King was right. Gantt reached the camp a short time later and, with a vast sigh of relief, swung down off his mount.

"Crows!" he said. "Wasn't sure I was going to make it . . . they been dogging me since daylight. Must be fifty or sixty of them!"

Chapter Four

Tom King swore vividly. "I knew it!" he shouted. "Knew it all the time! Things was too easy. Sooner or later them goddamn savages was bound to show up and spoil things!"

"Yeah," Bill Mullady said with a shrug, "I reckon the ball's over."

Carson was only half hearing. His attention was on the Indians, now ranging out in a line in front of a grove of trees some quarter mile distant. From all appearances they were intending to charge the camp. Wheeling, he faced the brigade, most of whom were present.

"Get your rifles and be ready. Looks like we've got a scrap on our hands."

The trappers responded at once, taking up their weapons, seeing to their supply of ammunition, and then hurrying to station themselves in advantageous positions in the forefront of the camp. Gantt, two pistols now in his belt and a rifle hanging from the crook of an arm, returned to stand beside Carson who continued to watch the Crows.

"They don't seem to have moved," the officer said.

"No, they're holding back . . . but I don't much trust them."

"Can't figure why they didn't jump me sometime during the day. I was alone . . . it would have been a cinch."

"Probably wanted you to lead them to your camp. Pickings would be even better."

Kit glanced at the sun. It was still well up in the afternoon sky, and it would be some time until darkness closed in.

"Then why don't they charge us now?"

"Could be waiting for night, but I reckon it's anybody's guess."

The Crows, fifty or so strong, were still gathered at the edge of the grove. A pow-wow of some sort seemed to be under way and Carson, giving that thought, wondered if the Indians hadn't seen the hasty preparations made in the trapper's camp and were considering the advisability — and possible futility — of mounting an attack in the face of a couple of dozen expert riflemen who awaited them. Abruptly the ranks of the Crows broke, and they began to fall back and disappear among the trees. One of the trappers sent up a cheer, and the tension broke.

"They're pulling out!" Gantt said. "Gone

for good, maybe."

"We won't bank on it," Carson replied. "Best we post guards tonight and tomorrow. When we're out running the trap lines, it'll be smart to go in fours with one man keeping a lookout while the others unload and reset the traps."

"It's whatever you say, Kit," Gantt agreed as they dropped back to the center of the camp.

Carson's precautions proved unnecessary, for they saw no more of the Crows, and the matter was soon forgotten as trapping activities continued with somewhat improved results. By the time the river began to freeze and a move to a winter camp was at hand, many pelts had been taken, stretched, scraped, baled, and made ready for delivery.

"I figured to winter a bit to the north of here," Gantt announced one afternoon late when preparations to pull out had been completed. "Can leave any time."

Carson, hunched by the fire, a cup of coffee in his hand as he discussed the day with Monte Rinehart, glanced up, a frown suddenly pulling at his features.

"North? That'll put us deeper in Crow country. You think that's a good idea?"

"I don't figure they'll bother us," Gantt

said. "They got a look at what they was up against that time they followed me to camp. Could see we weren't about to put up with any foolishness from them."

Carson settled back, shrugged. He didn't agree, but he wouldn't argue. It was John Gantt's company, and the decision as to where they would winter was up to the captain. Later that evening as Kit and Monte stood at the edge of the camp listening to the distant howling of wolves and again drinking coffee laced, this time, with whiskey, Rinehart finished off his cup and turned to Carson.

"I gather you ain't favoring much the captain's choice of a place to winter."

"Could be asking for trouble," Kit replied, "and I sure don't believe in pushing my luck where Indians are concerned."

"I feel the same. Might be a good idea to pull out on our own, head back for the Green, see if we can find Fitzpatrick and join up with him."

Carson was staring off into space. The night was sharp, and overhead the jet black sky sparkled with countless diamonds.

"Yeah, I suppose so. It's a bit late for that, though . . . and, anyway, Gantt's going to be needing all the help he can get, so I can't see pulling out on him now. North

Star's sure bright tonight. Someday I'm going to head out and follow it to wherever it'll take me. That'll be the north country . . . the far end of it. Sure would like to see it before my time comes."

"You ought to be one of them explorer fellows," Monte said, lighting his pipe. "That's all they ever do."

Carson nodded. "Sure'd be fine, all right, only nobody pays a man for doing it. Trapping, I can earn myself four maybe five hundred dollars a year."

"And maybe get your hair lifted one of these here days doing it," Rinehart said dryly.

"Chance we all take," Kit replied. "I'm turning in."

"Same here," Rinehart said, thrusting his filled but unlit pipe in a pocket. "What time's the captain aiming to pull out in the morning?"

"First light," Kit said, "and that ain't far off."

The winter set in for certain not long after the party arrived at the place selected by Gantt for their new quarters. Ice was thick, and snow fell heavily, bringing trapping activities to a halt except those done by some of the men for wolverines whose fur was considered the best for snow boots and leggings.

Buffalo were plentiful, as well as deer, and Kit and Rinehart volunteering to be camp hunters kept the party well supplied with fresh meat. Forage for the horses and mules, however, was a problem, and there were times during the more severe weather when the animals lived on tree bark, chopped and pounded into a meal. But in January a warm wind swept in from the west, and patches of ground became visible beneath the snow that had not entirely blown away. The stock was turned out to graze and quickly began to make the most of it. At sundown the question whether to corral the animals for the night or permit them to continue grazing arose, and Gantt decided, since there had been no sign of Indians, they should be left in the open.

"I reckon the captain knows what he's doing," Tom King said to Kit and Rinehart as they made their way back to the cabins the party had built. "Was me, I sure wouldn't risk it. Would you?"

Carson made no reply. He felt it was unwise, too, but of late it appeared that he was opposed to every decision John Gantt made, and that realization made him uncomfortable. He'd keep his opinion to himself.

"Up to him . . . it's his outfit," he said

finally and went on to his blankets.

Kit had scarcely gone to sleep, it seemed, when a shout brought him to his feet.

"Indians! They've done stole some of the animals!"

Carson hastily drew on his jacket, snow boots, buffalo skin coat, and hurried out into the yard. Many of the other trappers were already there, and a count of the horses and mules was being made.

"Them red devils got nine of them!" the man making the check announced to Gantt. "All horses."

"I'll take a dozen men, and go after them," Carson volunteered. "There'll be plenty of tracks to follow. Don't figure it'll be any big chore."

"Take who and what you want," the captain said. "I guess we should have corralled the stock after all."

"Yeah, I reckon," Carson murmured and, turning, selected his party — Monte Rinehart, Mullady, and Tom King being among them — and struck off into the snow.

"You figure it was a bunch of them Crows that stole the horses?" Rinehart asked as they pushed their mounts steadily over the well-beaten trail in pursuit.

"Just about have to be," Carson said. "We're in Crow territory. Doubt if any of the other tribes would chance hanging around."

They pressed on, having no difficulty until near noon when they were forced to hold back and permit a large herd of buffalo, stampeding madly, to pass in front of them. When the mass of shaggy-headed animals had gone by, Rinehart rubbed at his jaw ruefully. "Well, there goes our trail, old son. Them buffalo plain wiped it out."

Kit nodded as he considered the distant landscape, more definite now as snow had stopped falling. "They would have to keep bearing east," he said after a time. "We'll do the same."

An hour later they picked up the tracks of the Crows and the stolen horses and, relieved that they were again on the right trail, hurried on. But it was near dark as Carson was beginning to look about for a place to spend the night when they caught sight of the Indians. The Crows had halted and made camp in a grove of trees a little more than a mile distant.

Carson studied the Indian camp, barely lit by the flare of several campfires. Vague figures were moving erratically about, and the faint sound of singing rode the cold air.

"Bastards are celebrating stealing our horses," one of the trappers muttered.

"Just what they're doing," Carson agreed, "and that'll make it easy to get them back. They're not expecting us."

Leaving their mounts picketed in a sheltered area of the grove through which they were moving, Kit led the party forward, making use of the brush and trees and the deep snow to mask their approach. When they had drawn within a hundred yards of the camp, he signaled for a halt.

"Looks like they've split into two bunches," he said as they all lay flat in the snow observing the festivities.

"Having themselves a dinger of a time," Rinehart commented. "They're right proud of what they've done."

"Anybody spot our horses?"

"There's four of them there to the left of them first lodges," Mullady said. "Either they've gone and killed the others for eating, or they've mixed them in with their own."

"Stinking redskins!" the man lying beside him said. "I'm for charging them straight on."

"Best we get back our horses first," Kit said, soothing the trapper's anger. "Let them settle down and go to sleep . . . then we'll move in."

"I'm hoping that's pretty soon," another of the party said. "I'm getting mighty cold laying here in this damn' snow."

The time came an hour or so later, and Carson with Monte and four others — the remaining men being left as a sort of reserve with instructions to move in if things went wrong — crawled their way, flat on their bellies, to the Indian camp. They reached the horses without incident and, cutting the tie ropes, drove the animals back toward the waiting trappers by pelting the animals reluctant to move with snowballs. Leaving the camp thus undisturbed, Carson and the men with him returned.

"They still got five horses of ours," Mullady said. "I'm voting we go get them . . . and lift some hair while we're doing it."

"I figure we're lucky to get back them four," someone commented sourly. "And there ain't but a dozen of us, and I'll bet there's five, maybe six times that many of them Crows."

"I ain't worrying about how many of them there is," Mullady snapped. "Them Crows need a lesson, just like somebody said about them Blackfeet. I'm for it, Kit. What do you say?"

Carson glanced around at the men. Almost the entire party seemed eager to do as Bill Mullady suggested, and his own pulses were throbbing with excitement.

"It'll be plenty risky, so you best all speak up, say how you feel."

"I say we got four of them back, and we best quit while we're ahead," one of the older men said.

A murmur of disapproval ran through the party. Monte Rinehart raised his hand.

"Can settle it by taking a vote . . . ?"

The tally was overwhelming for attacking the Crows and shortly, after moving forward a considerable distance to where they would be nearer the camp and leaving the horses in charge of the three men who were not in favor of the assault, Kit again led the way through the snow to the Crow encampment. They drew within a dozen yards of the sleeping Indians. Motioning for all to be ready, Kit raised his head for a better look at the camp now definite in the cold, pale light of moon and stars. Instantly a dog began to bark, and the Crows, alarmed, came to their feet.

"Start shooting!" Carson yelled, and the trappers, raising themselves to their knees, opened fire.

Five Indians went down under the volley. Reloading quickly, the trappers triggered their weapons again, and several more braves fell. Others began a retreat for the second camp a short distance further on, returning the fire with rifles and arrows as they moved. Reaching that point they made a stand, and for a time the trappers and the Crows exchanged shots with neither side sustaining casualties. Kit glanced to the east. They could not keep firing for much longer as ammunition was beginning to run low. The sun, he saw, was beginning to lighten the horizon, and a gray haze was spreading over the land. Shouts went up from the Crows.

"They've spotted us . . . and they see there ain't but a handful!" Mullady said. "They're aiming to charge us!"

"Stay where you are," Carson called. "Let them get close . . . and then open up. Can't afford to let them get in behind us."

The Crows, yelling and waving their weapons above their heads, came on fast. Kit waited silently and grimly until the braves were as near as he dared permit them.

"Fire!" he shouted.

A half a dozen braves dropped. The charge wavered, fell back.

"That it, you reckon?" Monte wondered as they all hastily tamped powder and ball into their muskets and primed the pan.

"Nope . . . they're coming again!"

The woods echoed with the blast of rifles fired by both parties. A man near Kit staggered as a ball drove into his leg, another swore as an arrow slashed into his neck. More Indians went down, but the charge did not slow, and Carson began to fear the possibility of being surrounded.

"Drop back!" he shouted. "Keep shooting as you go!"

The trappers, moving like swift, silent shadows from tree to tree, began to retreat, taking a heavy toll of braves as they did. Shortly they reached the horses, and the three men stationed with them immediately went into action. The Crow charge slowed, came to a standstill as the additional rifles began to cut into their number. Then suddenly the Indians turned and ran, heading for their camp.

With the last of the powder smoke drifting among the naked trees, Carson beckoned his men in. "That's done it. Let's mount up and get back to camp . . . going to be after dark before we can get there."

There was a murmur of assent among the men. Only Bill Mullady expressed any regret. "Sure missing out on a bunch of scalps," he said as they rode off.

"Yeah, we sure are, but one thing for dang certain," King said, "we showed them Crows how the cow ate the cabbage! They won't be nipping at us no more for a spell."

Tom King was right. The Indians gave them no more trouble and, when spring came, Gantt had the stacks of beaver skins they had accumulated baled and cached in a patch of trees not far from the camp. That done, they pulled stakes and began to work their way north, trapping as they went.

Several days later the two men sent in advance doubled back with word that a party was camped in a grove not far ahead. They were not sure if it was Indians or trappers as they were reluctant to get in close. Kit and Rinehart immediately made a scouting tour and returned to Gantt.

"Trappers," Carson reported. "We didn't go in and talk, but they look all right."

The brigade resumed its work and soon reached the camp. The leader of the party — one that Kit felt was somewhat small to be in so dangerous an area — advanced and introduced himself to John Gantt.

"I'm Jacob Klein," he said. "I can't tell you how glad I am to welcome you and your men! The Indians. . . ."

Carson, a few steps away from the pair, drew up stiffly, attention on two trappers coming in from the river.

"Grieg," he muttered.

Rinehart, speaking with one of Klein's men, came about swiftly. "It sure is . . . and that's Kidder with him. Still running together, it seems." He paused, emitted a low whistle. "Old son, you sure did put your work on Seth!"

Tense, Carson made no reply, simply watched the pair draw near. The scar left by his knife on Grieg's forehead was a bright red, white edge line on the man's dark skin. Swinging his rifle about, Kit checked the priming, cradled the long-barreled weapon in his arms, and waited for the trapper to recognize him.

Grieg, a dead beaver hanging by a leather cord slung over his shoulder, came into the camp, head partly turned as he carried on a conversation with Zeb Kidder. Seth was laughing, and he had lost none of his swaggering bravado. Nearby other mountain men noticed the sudden tension that had developed and had fallen silent, their attention on Carson's taut features. Abruptly, Grieg saw Kit and pulled to a quick halt. Kidder stopped also but not quickly enough.

"What's chawing on you . . . pulling up short like that?" he demanded and then, seeing Carson, hushed instantly and took a step away from his partner.

For a long, breathless minute Kit and Grieg stared at each other, neither showing any sign of giving ground. A heavy silence had fallen over the camp, broken only by the restless shifting of the horses and mules in the rope corral and the noisy quacking of ducks somewhere on the nearby river.

"You aim to make your move?" Carson asked, finally. "Can settle up . . . or we can forget it right here, and be friends. It's you that's wanting blood."

Grieg's dark features were flat, emotionless as he gave that consideration. He shrugged. "I don't ever go back on what I say . . . and I sure ain't starting now."

"Then . . . let's get it over and done with."

The trapper shook his head. "This ain't the time or the place, Mister Carson," he said, putting emphasis on the two words and, turning away, walked off toward the far end of the camp. Kidder hesitated briefly and followed.

Kit lowered his rifle. He had preferred to settle the quarrel then and there as there was no comfort in knowing that someday, when least expected, Seth Grieg could take him unawares and put a bullet in his back.

One of Klein's men, the one Monte had been speaking to, pulled off his knitted cap and rubbed at his balding head. "I'll swear, can't nobody get along with Seth! What are you and him grudging over?"

"Little something that goes back a time,"

Kit replied. "He been with your outfit long?"

"Maybe a week. Him and Kidder've been doing some free trapping, they claimed. Showed up one day, and Jake hired them on."

"Best thing he can do is unhire them," Rinehart said dryly as they moved to one of the fires where a large coffeepot was simmering over the flames.

Squatting beside it, Monte poured tin cups full of the strong, black liquid and produced several strips of buffalo jerky to chew on. "Reckon this'll hold us till we get ready to eat," he said, passing the tough, dried meat around. "What are you aiming to do about Grieg?"

Carson was far from dismissing the man from his mind. Seth had made his threat, and he would keep it — all depending upon a favorable time and location. Sitting there by the fire, he watched the trapper unload his gear, skin out the beaver, and insert the willow stretching frame.

"I don't plan on turning my back to him if I can help it," he said. "I offered to make peace, but he was against it. Have to be settled the hard way now . . . I won't again do any talking."

"Ain't no other way you can look at it,"

Monte said, his gaze also on Seth Grieg and Kidder. "I just hope you keep a sharp watch on your hindside."

"Can bet I will," Carson murmured.

Later, after the cooking was over and the meals eaten, the men gathered together to talk — Klein's men off to themselves, Gantt's also in a separate party. The conversations were of beaver and of where they could still be found in plentiful numbers, of the gather that had already been made and the price the skins would bring, of other brigades and where they had been and now probably were, of Indians — the hated Crows and Blackfeet — and where they would likely be encountered, and the Arapahoes, Cheyennes, and Sioux who were considered friendly at the moment.

"Ain't never been no Indian lover," Bill Mullady said, "but, if I had my druthers, I'd pick the Arapahoes. Real fine folk . . . as Indians go . . . and a man'll find the prettiest squaw there is comes from them."

"I'm surprised you ain't got a squaw along," one of the trappers said. "They sure come in handy to do a man's cooking and bed warming."

"Expect I will, come winter this year," Bill replied. "Got me a Kiowa woman back in. . . ."

"Thought you said you was partial to the Arapahoes!"

Mullady stirred, spat into the flames. Taking out his pipe, he knocked the dottle from its charred bowl and began to fill it with shreds of tobacco. "Hell, I never said all of the pretty squaws was Arapaho!" he declared.

Kit got to his feet and, with the intention of discussing the coming day with the officer, moved toward the lean-to shelter John Gantt had thrown up. Abruptly a rifle shot rang out. It came from the brush along the river. Carson felt the hot touch of the ball as it breathed against his cheek. Instantly every man in the camp was reaching for his rifle and leaping to his feet.

"Indians!" someone shouted.

The area within the fire's glow was suddenly deserted. Kit crouched low beside another shelter and struggled to penetrate the darkness along the river bank but could discern no movements. A strong suspicion entered his mind. There had been but one shot fired, and it had been at him. Grieg?

Pivoting, Kit slipped quietly off into the night, circling the shelters and the corralled horses to where he had a view, unhampered by men and the glare of the flames, of the brush along the river.

"Won't be exactly healthy if you're planning on going down there."

Monte Rinehart's cautioning words came to Kit from shadows close by. He had noticed Carson's departure and, realizing what was in Kit's mind, had quickly followed.

"Anything that moves along that brush is going to get shot full of holes. You thinking maybe it was Grieg?"

"Can bet on it. No Indian all by himself is going to fire into a camp of armed men and not get spotted when he tried to get away. And, if there'd been a party of them, there'd've been more shooting."

"Makes sense. There's Grieg now . . . walking up to Klein's fire."

Kit swung his attention to the point Monte had indicated. Most of the men, concluding that all danger had passed, were gathering around the fires again but with rifles still ready in their hands. Grieg and Kidder, Carson saw, were taking their places in the ragged circle. If it had been Grieg who had shot at him, Carson realized, the man was making a great show of having been alarmed just as much as the others in the camp.

Turning, Kit and Monte dropped back to their shelter and shortly crawled into their blankets. Maybe it hadn't been Seth Grieg's attempting to settle his score, Carson thought, but logic assured him that it was. In the days to come, with Grieg being a member of the now combined Gantt and Klein parties, he would need to keep the man in front of him constantly — never turn his back.

"Carson! Carson!"

Kit came awake at the insistent shaking of his shoulder and the sound of his name being hoarsely whispered in his ear. He sat up instantly, hand going automatically to the Hawken lying under the blanket within easy reach. It was still dark.

"It's me . . . John Gantt."

Nearby Monte Rinehart had roused and was also sitting up. "What the hell's going on?"

"Trouble . . . maybe real bad," Gantt said. "Them two free trappers . . . the ones you had trouble with, Kit . . . ?"

"Grieg and Zeb Kidder?"

"They're the ones. They knocked out the man we had watching over the horses, took three of them, and lit out."

"Damned horse thieves, bad as them Crows," Rinehart muttered.

"Not losing the horses that's worrying me," Gantt continued. "Tracks show they headed south . . . and they know about that cache of plews we left at the old camp. Heard me talking about them to Klein. I've got a feeling they're going to steal them."

Kit was already pulling on his overboots and getting to his feet. "No doubt about it," he said, pulling on his jacket and heavy robe coat. "I take it you're asking me and Rinehart to go after them . . . ?"

"I'd be obliged. God, when I think of all that work lost!"

"How long've they been gone . . . any idea?" Monte interrupted, dressing hurriedly.

"Five or six hours . . . and they're riding good horses."

"Means we'll have to hustle right smart," Kit said, collecting his gear.

"That's the truth, but I've got mounts ready and waiting for you," Gantt said. "Do the best you can for me and, if you're not back in a week or so, I'll send help."

Chapter Five

"There's the horses," Carson said in a low voice.

Monte grunted. "I see them."

They were crouched in the thick brush a short distance below one of the cabins they and the rest of the Gantt party had occupied when in camp there earlier.

"No sign of Grieg or Kidder."

"They're around somewhere."

"Maybe," Carson said and began to work his way along the bank of the Arkansas toward the cabin. "If they raised the cache, they could've loaded the pelts in that canoe we used to cross the river in and headed down-stream."

Rinehart made no reply but, keeping a bit to the side of Kit, maintained his position with him. After a few moments he swore softly.

"I expect you're right. The canoe's gone. Was stashed here at the back of the cabin under some brush."

Carson got to his feet, caution no longer necessary. Brushing away the snow clinging to his legs and arms, he said: "There's a chance they didn't take the plews . . . just the canoe to go down river in and get clear of the horse stealing."

"Can mighty quick find out about that," Monte said and, with Kit following him, crossed to the thick stand of trees and brush where the bales of beaver skins had been hidden.

It wasn't necessary to get nearer. They could see the branches and leaves and the saplings that had been cut piled to one side, leaving the pit in full view. Kit shook his head.

"Gantt's sure one for hard luck. This is going to hurt him bad."

"Yeah, I feel real sorry for him," Rinehart said as they followed the tracks of the two men carrying the bales to the river's edge where they apparently had had the canoe waiting.

"Somebody maybe ought to feel sorry for Grieg and Kidder," Kit murmured. "They've got a lot of hostile country to get through before they reach a trading post."

"Was thinking of that. Be lucky if they don't lose them bales . . . along with their hair. Just stand easy. We got company."

Rinehart showed no indication that he had spoken a warning but continued to stare off down the river.

"Where?"

"Them trees off to our left. Three Indians . . . Crows, I think . . . on foot and eyeing our horses. Some of that band we run up against before, I expect."

"You think they see us?"

"Not for certain," Monte answered. "There's a couple more there now. Could be a fair-size hunting party."

"If it is," Kit said, "I sure want to be inside one of them cabins. Turn around slow like, and we'll sort of stroll to that nearest one."

"Let's go."

Together they came about and, moving indifferently, crossed to the nearest of the structures. That the braves saw them was unquestionable, as motion alone would have caught the attention of the Crow warriors even had it not been necessary to show themselves in the open.

"They chasing us?"

Carson, not turning his head, let his eyes touch the edge of the clearing. The Indians had not stirred from where they were, seemed to be having a discussion.

"Not yet," Kit said. "Likely afraid there's more of us around . . . acting real brave the way we are."

"Brave . . . hell!" Monte grumbled. "Every hair on my head's standing on end!"

The cabin was just ahead. Carson began

to veer off slightly toward the brush where they had picketed their horses. The three stolen by Grieg and Kidder were already in the yard between two of the cabins formed by the opposing walls of the structures on two sides and stacked brush on the others.

"Stand there at the corner," Kit said, indicating the cabin by ducking his head. "I'll bring in our horses. Long as them Crows don't think we know they're there, we've got a chance of getting away with what we're doing."

"I'm making out like I don't know they're within thirty mile," Rinehart said. "They're still palavering but, if you hear me yell and shoot, forget them damn' horses and come running!"

"Can bet on it," Kit said.

Strangely, the Crows did not attack. Carson reached the horses he and Monte had left in the brush and, as casually as he could muster, led them back to the improvised corral between the cabins, first removing and then restoring the brush after the animals had been driven inside. He moved them to where Rinehart was waiting, rifle hanging from one crooked arm as he looked off into the distance and, joining the big New Yorker, entered the cabin, closed the door quickly, and dropped the cross bar into place.

"Damn . . . that was close!" Kit muttered, and stepped up to one of the ports that would provide a narrow view of the clearing. "They're leaving! Can see them heading off through the woods," he added in a puzzled tone.

Monte was equally mystified. "What do you reckon they're up to?"

"Ain't sure why unless, like I said, they figured there's more of us inside the cabins. Us acting like we did, and with them three extra horses around, I can understand why they might think that. But I'm not about to question our luck. They've pulled out for now, so let's hustle in our packs and stock up on water . . . and hole up right here until we find out what's going on."

That day passed, one during which Kit and Rinehart maintained a constant watch on the nearby woods, now a bleak, gray line of stark, leafless trees and dense, ragged brush. No more Indians had appeared by sundown and, when darkness began to fall and enclose the land and all upon it, the two men ventured forth to do what they could for the horses in the way of fodder.

There was little difference in the following day, one consumed by a constant watch for the Indians during the hours when the shuttered sun brightened the winter landscape only slightly and then near darkness when they led the animals down to the river for watering and a few minutes grazing. To pass the tedious hours of the days that followed, Carson and Rinehart repaired their gear, such as was necessary, and Kit continued his teaching of Spanish to Monte, a practice they had begun earlier that winter when Rinehart had made known the fact that his thinking had changed, and he intended to marry Dolores when they returned to Taos.

Carson had made no comment when his partner revealed his plans. He had considered marriage to Rosa Lucero at one time, and the matter had gone so far as a serious discussion between them. But Kit had finally convinced both the woman and himself that it was best he not take a wife. He was gone for lengthy periods of time — often for as much as two years — and there was always that possibility he'd run into bad luck and never return at all. Thus it was decided Rosa would lead her life and Kit his, but her door would always be open to him any time he came to Taos.

"This here setting around waiting, doing nothing, is sure twanging on my nerves," Monte said, as they sat warming themselves before the flames in the cabin's fireplace. "You reckon it's worth trying to slip out of here and head back for Gantt's camp?"

"There's Indians all around us . . . Crows for sure, and maybe some Blackfeet. Haven't spotted them, but I feel it in my bones. We'd be fighting for our lives before we got a mile."

"Wouldn't mind doing a bit of fighting."

"We even try what you're thinking, and you can forget about ever seeing that Taos gal of yours again!"

Rinehart swore, spat into the fire. "Then what the hell we going to do, Kit? We're running out of grub, and them horses are starving. How much longer we going to wait on Gantt to send somebody down?"

"Said he'd wait a week and, if we wasn't back, he'd start a party for here."

"Well, they sure'n hell better be showing up pretty soon."

"Seen some deer tracks down along the river bank when I was watering the horses last night. I think I know where they're grazing. You look after the horses tonight, and I'll get us some fresh meat."

Monte agreed, and the arrangement was carried out as planned with Kit returning near midnight, a young doe slung over his shoulder. It had taken longer than he had anticipated as he was reluctant to use the Hawken for fear of drawing the attention of lurking Indians. It had been a matter of creeping up on the herd in the pale night and using his knife, but the effort was worth it. The fresh meat would be a welcomed change in their diet of corn cakes, beans, and coffee.

Three days later several Crow braves, spotting the horses in the make-shift corral, boldly began an approach. One carried a rifle. His companions were armed with bows. Kit and Rinehart, at the ports in the front wall of their cabin, allowed them to draw within range and then neatly dropped two of them.

"Reckon that changed their minds," Monte said as he quickly reloaded.

Kit, also ramming powder and ball into his rifle, watched the braves. They had started to turn and flee, thought better of it and, pausing to pick up their fallen comrades, beat a hasty retreat into the woods.

The Crows continued to hang around, but that was the only attempt to charge the cabin, and it became evident to Kit and Monte that only a small party of braves was keeping an eye on them. That led to a logical conclusion: they were awaiting reinforcements before making an all-out, serious charge.

"I reckon we can stand them off," Carson said, discussing the likelihood with Rinehart. "We've got plenty of powder and lead and can make them keep their distance. And they can't set the place afire if we don't let them get close."

"For sure," Monte agreed. "Ain't no grass or nothing near enough to the cabin to burn. Horses have eaten everything right down to rock."

A shout brought both men to their feet, sent them hurrying to the nearest ports.

"Trappers!" Carson shouted. "Dozen or more coming up. Expect that settles the problem for us."

Monte was already at the door, removing the bar and throwing the thick panel open. At that several of the approaching men — some with their squaws — shouted back.

"Name's Blackwell," the leader of the party, a heavy-set man with dark eyes and bushy beard, stated when he had dismounted and was facing Kit and Monte. "We're looking for John Gantt's camp . . . thought maybe this was it. I'm his partner."

"It was . . . a time back," Carson explained. "He moved on to the south fork of the Platte . . . we're part of his brigade."

"And we're sure glad to see you!" Monte added. "We been forted up here for quite a spell . . . holding off some stinking Crows."

Blackwell nodded. "Seen Indians in the woods as we came up. Didn't jump us . . .

maybe because we were ready for them. If you're with John's brigade, what are you doing here?"

Carson detailed the reason for their not being with the main party and added: "Expect we best move out right away. It looks to us like the Crows are expecting reinforcements, and we'd be smart to rejoin the captain before they get here."

"Four men coming in from the north," someone in the Blackwell party called out.

It was the help Gantt had promised to send, Kit realized. He glanced at Monte and grinned. Rinehart smiled back. It was feast or famine. Either they had no support, or they had more than enough.

Blackwell's group made themselves comfortable in the cabins for the night, as did the men sent by Gantt. The captain had moved and was now at the headwaters of the Platte's south fork in a place called Balla Salado. Kit knew it well — knew also that there had been considerable Indian trouble there in the past. Gantt just could have picked himself a base where he would be harassed continually by hostile braves.

That next morning the party struck out for Gantt's camp, with Kit and Monte serving as guides and outriders. They saw Indians in the distance several times, and it occurred to them that they were actually surrounded, but no attack ever came, and they moved steadily on, taking precautions at night to protect the horses and mules and giving the Indians — Crows or Blackfeet, Kit couldn't be sure — no chance to steal the animals or attack the camp.

Days later, with a light snow sifting quietly down upon the stark land, Blackwell called Kit in from his position in the front of the column.

"Looks to me like good beaver country," he said. "I want you and Rinehart to take a couple of men and swing west, look it over so I can tell Gantt whether it'll be any use coming back this way this spring. You can rejoin us at his camp on the Salado."

Carson said, "Whatever you want, but I'm studying about one thing . . . it'll short you four rifles."

"I've thought of that. I'll still have seventeen men. That ought to be enough to stave off an attack."

Kit shrugged, agreed. The Indians hanging about appeared to be in small bands of a dozen or so and, even if two groups threw in together, Blackwell should be able to hold his own. Of course, if the braves all united to form a large force, that would be a different — and serious — matter.

"This is something that Monte and me can handle ourselves," Carson said then. "That would give you two more."

Blackwell shook his head. "No, it'll be too risky, just the pair of you. Draw whatever supplies you need and move out when you're ready. I'll see you when you get to Gantt's camp."

Within the hour Carson and Monte Rinehart, with two of the men John Gantt had dispatched to find them — Ed Cornwall and Tom Flynn — were mounted and leading the pack horses, pulling away from the main party. They rode steadily up a small stream they located shortly but found little beaver sign.

"This here creek's been trapped out," Cornwall declared that night as they threw up their shelters. "Sure ain't no sense in the captain bringing the brigade back this way."

Kit agreed. "And I'm pretty sure there's nothing much farther west. Tomorrow I figure we can start angling back toward the trail, have ourselves a look-see at the country in between. Way I make it, if we follow that ridge yonder to the right, we'll wind up somewheres close to the Salado."

Monte and the others, leaving it up to Carson, nodded assent, and the next morning all moved off in the direction Kit had

96

indicated. Close to noon, as they drew near what appeared from the distance to be a large valley, they spotted four braves sitting on their horses on the low side of a hogback a quarter mile or so ahead.

"Ain't waiting for us, that's for damn' sure," Tom Flynn said. "I'm betting they're watching another party of whites and are aiming to lay into them."

Kit's jaw tightened, and an impulsive anger shot through him. "Far as I'm concerned, they won't get the chance," he said. "Let's charge them!"

Without waiting for a sign of accord, Carson urged his horse forward and, hammering at the animal's ribs with his heels, sent it into a hard gallop across the fairly level flat. Yells went up from Rinehart and the other men and, abandoning the pack animals temporarily, they raced to catch up with Carson. The braves, startled by the shouts and the sight of four buckskin-clad men, rifles lifted above their heads, rushing toward them, hesitated only briefly and then, wheeling, rode over the rim of the saddle linking the two hills and dropped from sight.

This is a damned fool stunt! Kit thought as he rode on. He did not slow but, with his friends, hurried on. Reaching the lip of the valley beyond the saddle, they topped out almost in unison and started down the incline. The quartet of braves was still ahead but, strangely, had slowed their pace rather than increasing it as would be expected. Instantly, Carson realized what was taking place and, cursing himself for heeding the reckless surge of foolhardy bravado that had prompted him to throw caution to the wind and charge the braves, he half turned and shouted at the men to either side of him.

"It's a trap . . . turn back!" and in that same moment struggled to pull in his horse.

Flynn's mount stumbled on the grade as the trapper sawed on the reins and went to its knees. In that same fragment of time, Kit saw Indians suddenly appear on both sides of the trail ahead, some hurrying out to block their passage, others endeavoring to encircle them.

Flynn's horse righted itself as Kit got his own mount turned about. Rinehart and Cornwall had already succeeded in reversing their animals and were driving hard for the crest of the slope. Monte, lying close to the neck of the bay he was riding, was looking back as if to be sure Kit and Flynn were also coming. The Indians opened fire with both rifles and arrows and, for a long two hundred yards upgrade, it was a headlong race with Kit and the three men with him not returning the shots since none of them wanted to be caught on the ground with an empty gun if their horse should fall or was killed.

Flynn let out a howl just as they gained the top of the saddle and sagged even lower over the back of the horse he was riding.

"Been hit!" he yelled. "But keep riding . . . I can hang on!"

Carson was the last to reach the crest and, with the others a few yards in front of him, sent his heaving, winded horse on down the slight grade in the direction of the pack mules, grazing indifferently on the stiff grass stalks thrusting up out of the snow.

"Rocks . . . over to the left!" Carson raised his voice to be heard above the drumming of the horses' hoofs. "Can fort up there . . . our only chance!"

Rinehart heard, began to veer toward the massive pile a short distance away. Cornwall and Flynn followed instantly, with Kit bringing up the rear. The pack mules, attracted now by the mad dash of the horses, also broke into a gallop for the boulders, losing some of the items in their packs.

Once within the shelter of sandstone, Carson and the others dismounted and hastily prepared to defend their position. Flynn had a bullet in his right thigh but brushed aside all offers of aid from Carson, as he packed his bandanna against the wound to stanch the flow of blood and took his place in line with the rest waiting, rifles ready, for the expected charge.

It did not come. The party of braves — fifty or so — who had chased them up the slope halted a short distance down the near side and considered the wisdom of riding into four rifles expertly handled by men securely entrenched behind a wall of solid rock. Apparently deciding such would not be worth the cost, they wheeled, filled the air with wild yells as they reclimbed the grade and disappeared over the ridge.

At once, Carson turned to Flynn. "Can you ride?"

"Hell yes, I can ride!" the trapper snapped, grumpy at having been wounded.

"Good. We want to be plenty far from here come dark. Can bank on some of that bunch coming back and trying to slip up on us. We'll strike out due east. Should hit the main trail somewhere close . . . could be we'll run into Blackwell's bunch. And while I'm talking and before this gets any older, I'm asking your pardon for doing a damn' fool thing like I did. Knew better but plain didn't pay any attention to my better judgment."

"Happens," Cornwall said, moving to his horse. "Don't go losing any sleep over it."

"We didn't have to follow you," Flynn said, "but we did. I reckon that shows we was feeling the same way about lifting the hair of them redskins."

They rode out a short time later after collecting the pack animals. Moving directly east worked out just as Carson had figured. They located Blackwell's party some distance ahead of them, when they intersected the trail, and quickly caught up.

Blackwell told them that they, too, had experienced a brush with Indians. A large party of what he took to be Blackfeet had tried to run off the horses that first night after Kit and the others had left. One trapper was wounded, an Indian was killed, and several shot during the fight. There were no animals lost.

"Could be we'd best lay low for a day," Carson warned Blackwell after hearing the account. "The band we run into was large . . . a hundred at least. We ought to let them move on. Rest will do everybody good, too, I expect . . . 'specially Flynn. He took a rifle ball in the leg."

Blackwell nodded. "I'll give the order, and I'd be obliged if you'd post the sentries."

Five days later Kit led the party into John Gantt's camp on the Balla Salado. After the reunion was over and he'd reported the loss of the cached skins to the captain, Carson drew Rinehart aside.

"This party's getting too dang big. I'm for striking out on our own, doing a little free trapping, and working our way back to Taos."

"Just what I was hoping we'd do!" Rinehart declared happily, his broad grin expressing his delight with the idea. "You willing to have a little company . . . a couple more fellows that's wanting to pull out, too?"

Carson frowned. "Best we keep the party small. Don't want to attract the Indians. Who are they?"

"One's named Mordecai Adams, other one's Rufus Green. Right nice couple of men, and they know the business."

"All right with me," Kit said and, with Monte at his side, went to talk the matter over with John Gantt.

Gantt was sorry to lose them, but knew he could not prevent their leaving had he wanted to. Paying them off with funds brought by his partner, Blackwell, and selling them back whatever they needed in supplies, he thanked them as they pulled out and expressed the hope that they would some day work together again.

With Monte and their new partners, both large, burly men, Kit headed for the Yellowstone and thus into definitely dangerous Blackfoot territory. But by being cautious, in a small party, and lying low until the Indians had drifted onto the plains for the winter, he figured they would be able to trap and hunt with no problem. He was right and, when spring came, the venture had proved a great success. When they rode into Taos early in the fall, their pack mules were loaded with bales of prime furs, and all were thinking of the gold they would receive for their work.

All but Monte Rinehart. His thoughts dwelt on the lovely, dark-eyed Dolores, and the plans he had for her.

Chapter Six

"What've you got in mind to do now?" Monte asked after they had disposed of their furs and were pocketing the cash.

"Going over to Ewing Young's, clean up a bit, and bank some of this money, then I aim to drop by and say howdy to Matt Kinkead, that old friend I told you about. After that, I reckon I'll go see Rosa. You?"

"Got to clean up, get the stink off me first, too, then I'm heading out for Dolores's. Told me where she lives . . . on the Mora road about a mile from town, she said."

"There's going to be a dance tonight, according to that trader. She'll most likely be there."

"Tonight! Hell, that's a whole half a day off! I can't wait that long. Where's this fandango going to be? Same place?"

"Not a fandango, it's what they call a *baile* . . . a regular kind of a dance that everybody comes to. Doubt if there'll be any trappers there 'cepting you and me . . . and maybe Mordecai and Rufus, if they're still here at dark."

Rinehart scratched at his beard. "That

make a difference, it being real fancy like?"

Carson nodded to an elderly Mexican man and woman passing by and loosened his shirt front. It was warm in Taos.

"Sure does. Ain't no place for a man who can't behave . . . and, if a fellow does start something with the Mexicans, he'll be outnumbered ten, maybe twenty, to one. Can get himself cut up bad."

"I can behave if need be," Monte said. "Can be real polite. I expect Dolores will know where this here *baile* is going to be held."

"She will. They hold them every Saturday night for sure and other nights, too, if they can find a good reason. Probably will be in somebody's home."

"Home?" Monte echoed, surprised.

"Yeah, some family that has a room big enough. Will I see you before the *baile* starts?"

"Expect so, but you best not plan on it," Monte said as they mounted their horses and moved off for Young's inn. "Me and Dolores've got some mighty important palavering to do."

Carson smiled. "I savvy," he said and pointed off to the southeast. "The road to Mora's at the end of town . . . when you start looking for it."

Leading their pack animals, they rode the short distance to the lodgings favored by the mountain men, entered the corral, unloaded their gear, and turned the horses and mules over to a stable boy. As they started for the low, rambling structure, a voice hailed Kit from a side porch. It was Mordecai Adams.

"There's a Captain Lee looking to talk to you," he said. "Making up a company, wants you for a guide."

"Lee? Don't think I know him."

"Understand he's new around here. Army man. Got a load of goods he's figuring to take into the high country for trading to the Indians . . . and trappers."

Adams gestured indefinitely toward the towering peaks to the north. "Have to get back where we belong. Feel kind of pinched in here . . . all those dang people around. You?"

"Aim to stay for a spell. Good luck to you both, and could be we'll come together again one of these days."

"Maybe so, Kit. And good luck to you and your partner."

Monte had gone on ahead. Carson followed, deposited his gear in the room assigned him, cleaned up and, after renewing acquaintances with Ewing Young who had not been present when he and Rinehart first checked in, returned to the stable and rented a fresh horse. He had seen nothing of Rinehart since they had reached the inn and guessed the New Yorker had lost no time getting on his way to the Valesquez place.

Heading his mount north out of the plaza, Kit rode a short distance to the side street where Matthew Kinkead lived. Swinging down from the saddle, he crossed the small yard, edged with wild rose bushes, and tried the door. It was locked. Knocking brought no response and, circling the low-roofed adobe hut, Kit tried again to rouse his old friend. Failing, he returned to the lane. As he was about to get back onto his horse, an elderly woman appeared in the doorway of the adjacent house. Carson removed his flat-brimmed hat and inclined his head politely.

"*Buenas tardes, Señora Mendoza. ¿Como esta usted?*"

The woman smiled, revealing aged, yellow teeth. "*Muy bien, gracias. Tu?*"

"*Bien, gracias. Donde esta mi amigo, Mateo?*"

"Santa Fé," the woman replied.

Kit thanked the *señora* again, mounted, and moved off through the pleasant afternoon for Rosa Lucero's place.

A frown pulled at his features as he halted

at the gate. The house appeared different somehow and, as he sat motionless in the saddle considering lilac bushes that were gone, an apricot tree he had helped Rosa plant at the end of the porch missing, a man came from around the back. He was a stranger to Carson.

"Yes? You look for someone perhaps?" he inquired in Spanish.

"For Rosa Lucero."

"She has gone."

"Gone? Gone where? Into town perhaps?"

The man shrugged in the time-honored manner of the Mexican people. "I do not know for certain where she went. For a time she worked at the great home of Francisco Jaramillo, and then a man came, and she went away with him. To Albuquerque some say."

"But this house, was it not hers? She would sell it to someone, and they would know where. . . ."

"She did not sell it for it was not hers to sell. She lived here as a courtesy of a friend who knew her family. I have purchased it from him."

Carson, disappointment stirring in him, reached into a pocket and felt the small, wooden cross he had spent many hours during the long winter evenings carving as a gift for her. He would have no use for it now. Withdrawing it, he tossed it to the new owner of Rosa's house.

"For you, my friend . . . or your wife," he said and, wheeling his horse about, rode off.

It was hard to believe that Rosa had gone, that she no longer would be there waiting and always ready to welcome him when he returned from the mountains. But a fair man, he found no fault in what she had done; she had a right to security, as did every woman, and theirs had been a relationship of a purely friendly nature. Their understanding had never gone beyond that.

He hoped Rosa and the man who came for her had married; she deserved a good home and children. Kit knew he should not begrudge her that, but he felt a sense of loss, nevertheless. Suddenly restless and at loose ends, and in much the same frame of mind as Mordecai Adams, Carson swung his mount toward the thick-walled church at the end of the plaza where traders making up trapping companies usually camped.

Lee had a fair-size pack train, Carson noted as he rode in and halted. Evidently the man intended to do a great deal of trading. Just where he proposed to go and transact such was yet to be learned but, in the mood Kit was at that moment, it didn't matter; he simply wanted to get back into the high country where he could feel at home.

"You Kit Carson?" a voice called from a canvas lean-to off to the right.

Kit dismounted, nodded. "That's me. You Captain Lee?"

A lean, militarily erect man in woolen clothes and knee-high boots, came forward, hand extended.

"I am. Been told that, next to Jim Bridger, you're the best guide around."

Carson, accepting the man's greeting, had no reply for that.

"I'm in partners with Ceran Saint Vrain and William Bent . . . I believe you know them. Got a load of goods to trade, and I'm looking to hire a guide that can take me up into the Green River country. You interested?"

Kit nodded. "When do you want to start?"

"Soon as possible. I understand there's a chance of running into snow any time now."

"Most likely. Will morning be all right? There's a few things I need to do and I've got a partner . . . ?"

"Morning will do fine. I'm ready to move out right now!" Lee said heartily. "And bring along your partner. I can use him, too."

"Can say the deal's all set, then," Carson said. "We'll be here at first light."

"First light," Lee repeated and, as Kit turned to his horse, wheeled and reëntered the lean-to.

Considering what Rinehart had said where Dolores was concerned, Kit wasn't all that certain that Monte would be willing to leave Taos so soon, but he wanted to be sure there would be a place for him in the Lee party. He'd find out that night at the *baile*. Right now he was going over to Andres Dominguez's *cantina* and treat himself to a drink — maybe quite a few drinks to see if he couldn't get himself in the right humor for the dance.

Monte Rinehart did not have to look hard for Dolores Valesquez. Within only minutes after riding out of the settlement on the road to Mora, he saw her working in a small garden adjacent to a fairly large, one-story adobe house. Pulse quickening, a broad smile spreading across his face at the sight of the girl, the mountain man rode in closer. Dolores, hoeing chili plants growing between head-high rows of corn at that moment, looked up. Her eyes brightened, and her lips parted in a sign of welcome. Both then faded immediately and, turning, she cast a look at the house.

Monte, hurriedly coming off his horse, crossed quickly to her. "Dolores . . . my life!" he said in Spanish. "I have looked forward to this moment since last we were together."

The girl again glanced at the house and then came back to face him. "It is wonderful to see you also, Monte," she said in a restrained sort of way, falling back a step as he reached out for her.

Rinehart frowned. "There is something wrong. I come to see the woman I love, but she greets me as a stranger."

"I fear you do not understand. . . ."

"What is there to understand? I want you to be my wife."

Dolores's full lips parted again into a soft smile, and her dark eyes glowed. Monte took a step nearer to her, and this time she did not pull away. He caught her by the wrists and drew her to him. The hoe she was holding fell to the ground as he crushed her mouth with a hungering kiss.

"No . . . we must not do this," Dolores said, making an effort to free herself. "My mother will see."

"Let her see," Rinehart said. "A man who is to marry her daughter has the right to kiss."

"You do not understand, Monte. There has been a change. . . ."

"A change?"

"Yes. A year ago, my father died. Luis is now the head of the family. It is his will that I marry another . . . one of my kind."

"The hell with Luis!" Rinehart exploded, forsaking his carefully learned Spanish for English and then, reverting again to her tongue, added: "I will talk this over with him and with your mother. Are they in the house?"

"No, only my mother . . . but it will do no good. Luis has given his word." Dolores looked again in the direction of the house. "You must go, Monte."

There was genuine worry and fear in the girl's eyes. Rinehart nodded.

"I shall go, but it is necessary that I talk to you. Tonight there is to be a dance, I am told. We can meet there. Do you know where it will be held?"

"Yes, at the store of Arsenio Lovato. I have planned to be there. Do you know where the place is?"

"No, but my partner Kit Carson will. He is here with me."

"Oh, yes, I recall him."

A dog came from behind the house where it had apparently been dozing in the warm afternoon sunlight and, seeing Rinehart, began to bark.

"You must go," Dolores said anxiously.

Monte turned at once and crossed to his horse. Getting into the saddle, he smiled, bowed slightly and, continuing his stiff, flowery Spanish, said: "Until tonight, my heart."

"Until tonight," Dolores replied and, as Rinehart cut back toward the road, picked up the hoe and resumed her labors.

The dog, emboldened by the retreat of the stranger he had challenged, advanced hurriedly, now barking furiously. Somewhere down the road another of its kind took up the alarm but hushed instantly when a man close by shouted. High above in the canopy of blue a hawk drifted lazily in circles.

Monte reckoned the next best thing to do was hunt up Kit, talk things over with him, and find out where Lovato's store was. Carson had mentioned doing some visiting, and it could be he'd not show up until dark. He'd welcome Kit's advice because he knew the Mexicans and Spaniards well, but there really wasn't much he could do. This was something that he and Dolores — and her family who had once approved of him — would have to straighten out.

Kit was nowhere to be found. Soon after nightfall, wearing a new calico shirt, his fringed buckskin breeches, and beaded moccasins, with hair combed and beard and mustache neatly trimmed, Monte obtained from Ewing Young the location of Lovato's store where the dance was being held and made his way there. He was surprised to find festivities already under way and hurriedly entered.

Carson had preceded him, he saw, and his friend, somewhat the worse for liquor with a plump, young Mexican girl in his arms, was among the couples whirling to the music of a string quartet. Monte wondered where Rosa might be but gave the matter no extensive consideration. Instead he scanned the large square room, not yet hazy with smoke from *cigarillos,* cigars, and briar pipes, for a sign of Dolores. She had not arrived as yet and, disappointed, he backed up and placed his shoulders against a wall to wait.

Carson spotted him a few minutes later and, veering in close with his partner, paused and offered his bottle of *aguardiente* — something of a surprise to Monte who knew that Carson preferred whiskey to the fiery brandy made in Taos.

"How'd you make out?" Kit asked as Rinehart took a swallow from the bottle.

"Just so-so," Monte replied disconsolately. "Got myself a powerful big problem that I'm hoping to fix up tonight when Dolores gets here. Waiting for her now."

Carson passed the bottle to his partner who lowered her head against his chest and, back to the dancers, helped herself to a small drink.

"Where's Rosa?" Rinehart asked.

Kit took his turn at the brandy, shrugged. "Gone! Vamoosed!" he replied and, encircling the happy, smiling girl with an arm, drew her in so tightly that she seemed near to bursting from her clothing.

"Keep your powder dry!" Carson yelled as he and his partner spun away.

Monte barely heard the jocular admonition. Dolores was coming through the doorway — Dolores in a thin, snowy white shirtwaist pulled taut across her breasts, a full skirt of shining red material, and small, flat silver slippers. Her jet black hair was gathered on the back of her neck and her eyes — like ebony jewels, he thought — looked out softly from beneath their full brows, while her skin, a creamy brown, appeared to be velvet.

"God in heaven!" Rinehart marveled as she paused, still not aware of his presence. "I ain't never going to let her go again!"

Dolores saw him at that moment and, taking a deep breath, Monte started toward her.

She shook her head warningly, and he halted, watched Luis Valesquez and the younger brother, José, enter the store, close in, and escort her to the far end of the room, where she joined several girls.

Anger swept Monte Rinehart, and his hand instinctively dropped to the knife hanging from his belt. The hell with her brothers! Who did they think they were — keeping Dolores and him apart? What if her father did die — Luis didn't have the right to take over his sister's life and just force her to do as he wished. And, by God, he'd tell him that right to his face!

Monte's dark thoughts came to a halt. Dolores, in the arms of José, glided by. She caught Rinehart's eye, nodded imperceptibly at the doorway. Happiness welled through the mountain man. Dolores was telling him to go outside, wait, that she would come. He should be careful about it, he realized. José had noticed him when they passed, and he reckoned, for Dolores's sake, it would be best not to arouse the suspicions of her brothers. Leaving his place near the wall, Rinehart approached one of the girls sitting nearby and politely asked for a dance. She accepted immediately and, taking her in his arms, he moved out onto the crowded floor.

The shuffling of feet was making the music

difficult to hear, and now smoke was beginning to collect along the low ceiling, while the odors of the dancers — sweat, liquor, and perfume — were gradually overcoming those of the redolent merchandise being stocked in Lovato's general merchandise store. As far as Monte could tell, he and Kit were the only trappers present, although there were other Americans — one or two in Army uniforms, others in business clothes.

The girl he had picked at random to dance with told him that her name was Louisa and that she did not live in Taos but in a small village along the river. She had come with friends and would be happy to have him visit her and her family anytime he was down that way. Monte thanked her and, after what he considered a proper length of time, deposited Louisa in her chair, managed a meaningful glance at Dolores, and stepped out into the cool night.

The moon was still behind the towering mountains to the east — part of which was sacred to the pueblo Indians, Kit had told him — but a faint glow suffused the land, softening the harshness, altering familiar objects, and creating shadows filled with mystery. Monte, standing off to one side beyond the reach of light spilling through the doorway, waited anxiously. After five interminable minutes, he became fearful that Dolores was not coming, that she had been unable to get away from her brotherly escort. And then suddenly she was there, two other girls with her. Dolores moved quickly away from them and glanced about.

"Here," Monte called and stepped into view.

Dolores murmured something to her friends, who turned to the side and strolled off into the night while she crossed quickly to Rinehart. Before she could speak, he caught her in his arms, drew her close, and kissed her again and again, reveling in the womanly feel of her body pressed hard against his.

"We . . . we must hurry," she managed to gasp. "I cannot be gone long. Come, there is a small hut by the stream that I know of."

Taking Monte by the hand, Dolores led him off into the darkness, halting a short time later at the mean structure she had mentioned standing hard by a small creek. Entering, she sank to the floor and drew him down beside her on the straw matting that covered the packed dirt surface.

"We must talk," she began. "Here no one will see. . . ."

He nodded. "True, but talk will come later. I have dreamed of this moment, and I will not have it spoiled."

He pressed her back firmly until she lay prone. Then, on his side beside her, he leaned forward, pinioned her lips with his and, unbuttoning her shirtwaist, slipped his hand inside and cupped a naked breast. As the nipple sprang to a rosebud-like peak, Monte felt Dolores quiver and heard her moan softly. Caressing and fondling her soft, dusky flesh, he let his head move lower until his lips found the hollow of her throat, traced along her slim, velvet neck, and paused there while his hand strayed down her slender body to the flat of her stomach.

Losing all restraint, Dolores threw her arms about him and, clutching him urgently, held him tight. His hand, restless and probing, forced its way under the waistband of her skirt, began to seek out the smooth curves of her hips, her legs, working finally into the archway between her thighs. Dolores gasped and Rinehart, impatient with the hindering waistband, withdrew his hand. Reaching down he caught the hem of her skirt and pulled it to hip level. Then, using both hands, he removed her undergarment and tossed it aside.

"I ain't ever going to let you go," he said huskily. Raising himself slightly, he rid himself of his breeches.

She did not understand the English words, and he translated them into Spanish. Then, as Dolores made as if to speak, he crushed back whatever she intended to say by pressing his mouth to hers while his hand again began to stroke her soft, responding body and his lips again sought the erect nipples of her heaving breasts. Alternately toying with each for a time, Monte then pulled himself to his knees and, shifting to one side, lowered himself onto the girl's trembling shape.

Later, as they lay facing each other on the mat, he fondling her firm, full breasts, she twining her fingers in the hair on his chest, Monte spoke.

"We shall marry at once . . . become man and wife," he said, laboring a bit with his Spanish. "I shall never leave you but will stay here and work . . . as a farmer in the fields, perhaps."

The faint strains of music coming from the dance seemed to claim Dolores's attention for a moment and then she said: "It cannot be, my heart. I dare not go against Luis."

"Luis!" Rinehart said angrily. "He does not matter . . . only you and I. We can leave . . . go far . . . anywhere that pleases you."

She was silent for a long minute and then: "I fear you do not understand the ways of my people. My brother has given me in

121

promise, and such cannot be broken. It is something difficult for you to see, but I must abide by it, or my family will be in disgrace."

"I do not understand . . . you are right," Monte said flatly. "Nor will I . . . never!"

Again Dolores remained quiet and then, as if just realizing it, she said, "You speak my language with much ease now!"

"I thank my partner, Kit Carson, for that. He spent much time teaching me so that, when you and I married, we would have no difficulties in speaking."

"Kit Carson," she murmured. "He is well thought of by our people. He knows our customs and obligations. Perhaps he can explain to you why our marriage cannot be."

"It is likely, but it will change nothing. I want you for my wife. I will not give you up to another man."

"And I do not want to go to another man, my heart. It is you I love and wish to be with always, but it cannot be, and to that I am resigned. I content myself with the knowledge that you have claimed me and, the Virgin Mary willing, I shall carry within me a part of you that will one day become a child . . . our child. Now, I must return to the dance," she added, sitting up and beginning to dress. "I will be missed."

Rinehart got to his feet, drew on his

breeches, and tightened the lacings. In the half dark of the hut his features were taut.

"A child," he murmured. "More reason why I cannot let you go. I. . . ."

"It is here I find you!" Luis Valesquez's harsh voice cut into Monte's words. "Here . . . lying on the floor with this American dog!"

Rinehart had whirled, anger mounting in a surging tide within him. Beyond the older Valesquez he could see José.

"It is that I love him," Dolores said simply. "I would marry him. . . ."

"That you shall never do!" Luis stormed, his voice shaking with fury. Reaching out, he seized the girl by the arm, shoved her roughly through the doorway into the open.

"Go home, drop to your knees before our mother, and beg her forgiveness, you . . . you whore!"

The epithet was as a knife plunging into Monte Rinehart, opening a gaping wound and allowing the pent-up hatred within him to burst free.

"You'll not call her that, goddamn you!" he shouted, abandoning his Spanish and swinging a rock-hard fist at the Mexican's jaw.

It caught Valesquez squarely on the chin instead, knocked him backward through the doorway, and into his brother. The younger man yelled, jerked clear, and threw himself at Rinehart, knife glittering in his hand. The big mountain man avoided the lunge and drove a sliding blow to José's head, dropping him to his knees.

Sucking for wind, knotted hands hanging at his sides, Monte turned. He had a quick look at Dolores, saw the pain and misery in her eyes, and then she was gone, hurrying off into the night. He started to follow, checked himself as José, on his feet again, was unsteadily closing in. Catching the younger man by both shoulders, Rinehart spun him about, sent him stumbling through the doorway into the open.

He became aware then that men were coming from the store, that they had heard José's yell, and shortly he would be faced with a crowd of angry Mexicans all ready to take up the quarrel with their knives.

"Come on . . . let's get the hell out of here!"

It was Carson's voice, urgent and adamant, coming from the brush below the hut. Monte needed no persuasion. To remain would mean a fight to the death with Luis Valesquez when he regained his senses, if indeed he could remain alive until then — and he wanted no part of killing a brother of

Dolores's. Such would definitely end all hope he might have for making her his wife. Moving quickly through the doorway, he cut sharply left and joined Carson who wheeled immediately and led the way off toward town.

"I reckon I owe you again."

Kit shrugged. "Guess you do."

"How'd you know where I was?"

"One of Dolores's friends told me where you two had gone when I asked. Was a bit worried when I didn't see you and her around. Then, when I spotted the Valesquez brothers heading in your direction, I figured I'd better take a hand."

"You showed up just in time. Was a crowd of their friends coming on the run. Where we going?"

"We're throwing in with an outfit headed up by a man named Lee. We're pulling out in the morning for the Green." Carson came to a halt, aware that Monte was not following. "You planning something else?"

Rinehart dropped to his haunches. Raising a hand, he rubbed at the back of his neck. "Sure am, Kit. I'm obliged to you for everything, but I plain can't leave. I've got to see Dolores again, try and settle things with her and her folks. Back there in that hut we . . . well . . . we sort of got together like man and wife, and I can't leave her to face. . . ."

"Explaining to me's not needful," Carson broke in. "I figure you're the kind of a man who'll always do right. What do you want me to tell Captain Lee?"

"That I'm obliged to him and, if I ain't there by the time you're ready to move out, not to wait but go on. If I'm coming, I'll catch up. Which way are you taking him?"

"Up the Old Spanish Trail."

"Expect I can find that, all right. Whatever . . . good luck, partner."

"Same to you," Kit replied and, shaking Monte's hand, moved on off toward town.

Chapter Seven

Although the two-dozen-member party of Captain Lee's did not move out of Taos that next morning until well after sunrise, Monte Rinehart failed to put in an appearance. Lee, a courtly Virginian visibly anxious to get his pack train of goods under way, had asked Carson if he wished to wait for another hour or perhaps go in search of Monte.

"Nope," Kit had replied. "Told me he might not make it, and to go on if he didn't show up. He's got a little Mexican gal on his mind that he's wanting to marry, if he can get squared around with her family. He'll be coming along when things are straightened out."

They had pulled out shortly after that, Kit in the lead with Lee. They followed the Old Spanish Trail north where it led along the waters of the Rio Grande del Norte, running clearly and swiftly in its high, black-walled chasm to the ford where it crossed, and the route then angled directly for the southwest corner of Colorado. That night, as the party sat about a fire smoking, some drinking coffee, others easing their weariness with a

127

stronger liquid, Lee said: "You mentioned that this friend of yours, Monte Rinehart, was hoping to marry a Mexican girl. This Spanish-Mexican thing confused me when I was in Taos. I had the idea they were all the same."

Kit shook his head, remained silent, listening to the not-too-distant barking of coyotes. It was real, he decided after a few moments, and put his mind to the captain's question.

"Nope, a Mexican is a Mexican . . . and a Spaniard's a Spaniard."

"But weren't they all Spaniards at one time? I remember some of my history from the Point . . . the Spanish came from Mexico and on into this part of the country . . . went on even farther, I believe. Some of those explorers remained, started settlements."

"Not much good at reading history," Carson said, "and about all I know is what I've been told by the folks themselves. Those Spaniards that came from Mexico . . . don't recollect what it was called before they got there. . . ."

"They named it New Spain, I think."

"Yeah, guess that was it. The Spanish took over the country . . . was nothing but Indian people there then. A lot of the soldiers stayed and took the Indian women for wives . . .

and it's their children who are the real Mexicans."

"But there in Taos, the Spaniards. . . ."

"They're the pure bloods from Spain . . . or their direct descendants. Some of them claim to be related to the king, and I expect they are. Usually they're the rich ones . . . the *ricos*. They own big pieces of land . . . grants and hire Mexicans and sometimes Indians to work it for them."

"Much as we plantation owners in the south do the nigras."

Carson shrugged. "Maybe. Don't know too much about things down there, but the Mexican people are a real fine, proud folk, and they'd never think of themselves as being slaves. I figure some of them for my best friends. Same goes for the *ricos*."

"There any slave labor at all in the territory?"

"We're a province . . . still belong to Mexico . . . and not a territory," Kit replied and paused to listen again to the discordant but friendly yipping of the coyotes, now seemingly nearer.

"Guess you could say there's some. They're called *peones* out here, but they're more like what folks called bonded servants back in Missouri. They belong to a *rico* family or maybe one of the Mexican families that have become well-to-do until they've paid off a debt that they've been saddled with somehow. I guess there may be some cases of them being sold or traded off, but I can't recollect any."

Lee refilled his cup from the large pot simmering next to the flames. "I noticed a tribe of Indians close to the settlement. Nobody seemed to pay any attention to them."

"The pueblo . . . the Taos people."

"They ever cause any trouble . . . an uprising or anything like that?"

"It's been a spell . . . more'n a hundred years, I think. They joined up with some of the other pueblo people and drove the Spaniards out. Didn't last long, though, about fifteen years or so, and the Spaniards were back. The Indians tried once more to get them out of what they figure is their country but failed."

"New Mexico has an interesting history," Lee said, getting to his feet. "I'd like to hear more of it."

"Ain't much left that I can tell you," Carson replied, also rising and moving toward his lean-to. "When we get back to Taos, best you look up one of the old storytellers . . . *viejos* folks call them. They're men who've been around for a lot of years and have been passed the history of what happened by *viejos* who came before them. Ask one what you'd like to know."

"Unfortunately, I don't speak the tongue."

"Can find yourself an interpreter and, if I'm around, I'll be glad to do it for you."

Lee smiled, nodded slightly. "Thank you, Kit. That is an offer I shall not forget."

At daybreak they moved on. The smell of snow was in the crisp, clean air, and there was much evidence of it on the towering peaks of the Rockies to the north — on their right hand as they angled across the lower corner of Colorado for the White River.

There was no sign of Rinehart during those days, and Kit wondered if his friend had succeeded in marrying the girl, Dolores, or had instead died, victim of numerous knife wounds at the hands of the Valesquez brothers exacting vengeance upon him for what they would consider a dishonor visited upon their family by him. He hoped it was not the latter. Monte was a sincere man and truly wanted to make Dolores his wife. He hoped his friend had been able to convince the Valesquez family of that fact and that they had accepted him. But the Mexican people, as he had pointed out to Lee, were a proud race who considered themselves inferior to no one regardless of circumstance or material worth and never took lightly what they considered an insult to the family name.

Snow caught Kit and the Lee party not long after they reached the White River and Carson, turning onto the trail running along its right bank, warned Lee that they should increase their pace, that it was important they get to the Green and its tributary the Uinta, where the captain planned to build his trading post, before winter began in earnest.

Lee was wholly agreeable, and they arrived at the desired location — a short distance from the fort-like quarters of Antoine Roubidoux. Roubidoux, it was reported, did a big trading business with the Utes and some of the other tribes, exchanging mountain whiskey — Taos Lightning — for pelts.

Getting busy at once, Lee erected an adobe and timber affair not far from where the Uinta and the Green rivers met and soon had his wares out on display, doing well. Snow, by then, was falling heavily, piling up in deep drifts which made traveling to any extent an impossibility. Kit, keeping the post supplied with meat, had long since given up on seeing Monte Rinehart, contenting himself with the hope that the big New Yorker was still alive and that he would see him again when he returned one day to Taos. He missed Monte's company and, never a man to take friendship casually, he could not help but wish Rinehart would put in an appearance.

"Kit . . . ?"

Carson, at that moment skinning out an elk he had downed earlier that morning, turned at Lee's call.

"Roubidoux's here, wants to talk to you."

Lee's estimation of the trader was somewhat low. Not only did he disapprove of the man's dealing in whiskey, but also it had become known that he furnished squaws for the trappers' entertainment, taking pelts as payment.

Kit beckoned to a young Ute brave standing nearby with whom he had become acquainted and, directing him to finish dressing the elk, walked back up to the post. Antoine Roubidoux was in an angry state of mind.

"Had an Indian working for me . . . a Snake . . . thought he could be trusted," the trader said in his accented voice. "The son of a bitch stole six of my best horses . . . they're worth two hundred dollars or more apiece . . . and struck out for Alta California. Like to hire you to go after him."

Carson considered. It would be a change in his daily routine, which had begun to pall, and trailing the brave and the horses, thanks to the snow on the ground, would be easy. But Lee was his employer.

"Need your permission, Captain."

"You have it," Lee said. "We must not allow the Indians to think they can steal with impunity."

Kit wasn't too sure what the Virginian meant but assumed it had something to do with punishment and agreed. He nodded to Roubidoux.

"I'm ready."

Roubidoux slapped his hands together. "Fine. You can take your pick of my horses to ride . . . and there's plenty of braves laying around to go along if you want."

"Need only one. Gray Eagle, there," Carson said, pointing to the young Ute just finishing up with the elk, "he'll be needing a horse, too."

"Can pick what he wants, same as you."

Within the hour Kit and the Ute brave were mounted and riding south along the Green. The man who had stolen the horses would be striking for California, Antoine had been certain, and such had appeared logical to Carson.

Near dark the following day, Gray Eagle's horse, unable to stand the hard pace, went lame, and the Ute was forced to halt and turn back.

"Have a care," he warned Kit in the language of his tribe. "The Snakes are treacherous. He will kill you."

"I will not give him that chance," Carson replied in like tongue, and rode on.

Kit saw nothing of the horse thief, but the tracks of the animals he had stolen were plain, and he had no difficulty in keeping on the trail. Late the third day Kit spotted the brave at the edge of a grove of trees not too far ahead. Immediately veering into a deep ravine nearby, he began a hurried but cautious approach. The Snake brave, however, was not to be caught unawares. He sensed the presence of the mountain man, some inner instinct warning him of danger, and he went into hiding among the trees.

Kit, knowing well the ways of the Indians, expected as much and, when he came within easy range of his Hawken rifle, he dismounted. Allowing the horse to continue along the wash, he crawled out and stationed himself behind a thick tea bush and waited. Within only moments the Snake showed himself. Musket up and leveled in the direction of Kit's moving horse, he was prepared to shoot the instant the trapper came into view.

"Here!" Carson called and rose from behind the dense brush.

The brave hastily switched his attention and fired. In that same bit of time Carson also triggered his weapon. The Snake's ball missed, but Kit's aim was true. The Indian staggered, clawed at his chest, and fell.

Moving up to the dead brave, Kit dragged him off into the brush, scalped him as was customary, claimed his rifle — one reflecting total neglect — the powder horn, and leather bullet pouch, both of which were well supplied. Making camp then for the night — after securing Roubidoux's horses which the Snake had on a lead rope — Carson rested until daylight and then headed back to the trading post, arriving there four days later.

Roubidoux, jubilant at the recovery, met him in the yard fronting his unwalled premises. "I owe you, Kit! Name your price!"

Kit shook his head. "Ain't none. Any man who won't help another in a case like this is not worth his salt."

Roubidoux smiled broadly. "Ain't never heard truer words!" he said, reaching for Carson's hand and shaking it vigorously. "Now, I want you to remember this . . . if you ever need a favor, all you need to do is ask."

"Might just do that someday," Kit replied and, needing rest, went on to his quarters.

Captain Lee's trading business, intended to be mostly with trappers, proved to be only fair, probably due to the close proximity to

Roubidoux's. Late in winter when a party of trappers came in from the north and in the course of conversation stated that Broken Hand Fitzpatrick and Jim Bridger were camped on the Snake River in upper Colorado and were low on trading goods, Lee immediately prepared to abandon his post and seek them out.

With Carson leading the way, the company pulled out and within two weeks found Fitzpatrick, thanks to Kit's knowledge of the country. Bridger was not there. Lee immediately sold out his entire stock of goods, was paid off in pelts, and made ready for the return journey to Taos.

"Expect I'll leave you here, Captain," Carson said, collecting his pay from the Virginian.

"You joining up with Fitzpatrick?"

"No," Kit said, glancing about. "He's got a plenty big outfit. Aim to strike out with a small bunch on my own."

Lee nodded. "Good luck to you then, Kit. Was a pleasure having you with me."

"Good luck to you," Carson replied.

The three men who felt the same about Broken Hand's brigade as Kit got themselves ready, and the party moved out two days later, working their way up to the headwaters of the Laramie River and trapping there as well as on its tributaries. Hunting was good, and Kit and his partners did well despite the fact that Carson resisted all efforts of the others to venture out onto the plains where beaver undoubtedly were much more plentiful. It was much too dangerous. They were a very small party and could not afford to let themselves be seen by the Indians who resented free trappers. Their belief was that the beaver belonged to them, and only they should trap and trade with the fur companies. The whites were all poachers, as far as they were concerned, and risked death if found in their area.

Kit and his friends spent the summer working out a fine strip of water and, when fall drew near and the beaver became scarce, they moved on, pointing now for the Green where a rendezvous was to be held. Carson had never attended one of the gatherings, a far-sprawling affair attended by all of the fur company representatives, independent trappers, trappers from every region, and Indians belonging to both friendly and hostile tribes.

The men with him had all participated in previous gatherings and, being old hands at it, regaled him time after time with stories of what transpired during such meetings.

"It's something a man oughtn't ever miss!" one assured him late one afternoon when they halted for camp. "Can do plenty of business but, if he ain't wanting nothing but a real good time with all the whiskey he can drink and all the squaws he can last out, then it'll suit him to a T."

"Can run into a lot of fellows a man ain't seen in years," another added. "I recollect the one I went to back in 'Thirty-One. I come across a jasper I thought the Blackfeet had took prisoner . . . was in 'Twenty-Eight. But there that sucker was, big as life and twicet as onery! The Blackfeet had got to him, all right, but he managed to slip away from them and hide in a river till they give up hunting for him!"

"I don't need persuading," Carson said, taking up his rifle. "I'm ready to go . . . but right now let's set up camp. You men do that, and I'll go out and get us some fresh meat . . . I'm a mite tired of having to eat beaver."

Kit, on foot, moved off into the trees toward what appeared to be a large, grassy valley — a place where a man could be almost certain of finding either deer, elk, antelope, buffalo, or all grazing. Coming to a ridge at the edge of the aspens, a mile or so from camp, he hunched low and made his way to where he could look out over the vast meadow.

Satisfaction rolled through him. Fifty feet or so away were several fine elk grazing contentedly on the lush grass. Raising his rifle, Carson lined his sights on a fat young bull and pressed off a shot. The elk dropped instantly, and the others wheeled and raced off for another stand of trees some distance away.

Coming upright, Kit started forward to claim his prize when a crashing in the brush close by sent alarm rushing through him. He whirled. Two grizzly bears — the largest he had ever seen — were charging at full speed. Rifle unloaded and, knowing that knife and tomahawk would be useless, Carson spun and raced for the nearest tree. He could hear the grizzlies — only a few yards behind him — snarling and growling as they came on.

Kit reached the tree, one much too small under the circumstances but his only choice. Dropping the rifle, he leaped as high as he could to reach the stronger branches and hastily drew himself up beyond the reach of the raging bears.

For a good quarter hour the grizzlies prowled about the base of the tree, tearing at its trunk with their claws, ripping up much of the brush and several small trees that grew nearby. Kit, powerless to do anything, waited it out. Finally one of the brutes moved off in the direction of the dead elk to feed, and Carson figured that he'd soon be able to climb down from his place of safety. But the second grizzly wasn't satisfied. He continued to thrash about at the base of the tree, tearing at the aspen's white bark, ripping off large pieces which he chewed angrily into bits. Eventually he, too, wandered off, taking the same course as the first grizzly but pausing frequently to look back as if wanting to be certain the man he had treed was not abandoning his perch.

Carson, only too familiar with the ways of the big, unpredictable bears, had no intention of climbing down the aspen until he was certain that all was clear. That moment came near dark and, descending, he retrieved his rifle, quickly reloaded, and returned to camp.

"Where's that fresh meat you went after?" one of the men demanded as he entered.

"It's a supper for a couple of grizzly bears," Kit replied and related details of the incident.

Elder, one of the younger trappers, swore. "Damn it, elk steak sure would taste mighty good! Being dark like it is, you reckon them grizzlies might've gone and maybe left enough for us to make a meal on?"

"Doubt it. Best thing to do is skin out a couple of them beaver we caught and throw them in the pot. I'm sure not about to go back there looking for that elk . . . just ain't that hungry."

They made the best of what they had and next morning, still hoping there would be some of the elk left, went to where Kit had brought it down. There was nothing but hide and bones. What the grizzlies hadn't eaten, wolves and coyotes claimed.

Chapter Eight

"We going on to Bridger's camp?" one of the trappers asked a day or so later, as they prepared to run the lines.

"No need that I can see," Kit replied. "Hunting's good here . . . and him and his bunch'll be passing by this way going to the rendezvous. Might as well stay put, take all the plews we can. Means that many more to trade when we get there."

The men agreed, and for the next two weeks they worked their traps, taking plenty of beaver. As Carson had figured, Jim Bridger and his party rode in a time later and, packing up, Kit and his partners joined them. All were headed for the Green where that summer's gathering was to take place.

Things were well under way when they reached the last ridge that overlooked a broad plain adjacent to the river where the rendezvous was being held. Looking down upon it, Kit emitted a low whistle of surprise.

"First time, eh?" Bridger, who was riding at his side, remarked with a grin.

Kit nodded. "Looks like everybody in the whole country's here."

"Just about," Bridger said and spat a stream of tobacco juice at a prairie dog eyeing them curiously from nearby. "Reckon I'm kind of used to it now. Been to many a one . . . first one was back in 'Twenty-Five. Got so it's kind of a chore with me."

Carson made no comment, simply continued to stare. There were teepees everywhere — thousands of them, it seemed to him, and three or four times as many Indians. Trappers, too, were more than plentiful, and there were countless traders, all of whom had their goods spread out on display on the ground, in wagons, or on tables.

It was like nothing Kit had ever seen or even imagined, and he sat wordless on his horse looking on while Bridger and the rest of the men moved on down the slope to become a part of the activities. Off to one side there was a shooting contest under way between a dozen or so trappers. Close by a dance was taking place, trappers in fringed buckskins and calico shirts, jackets removed in deference to the warm August temperature, locking hands with each other and rocking back and forth, kicking their moccasined feet high as they circled to the rhythmic clapping of onlookers. Indians were racing about on their ponies, weaving in and out of the teepees, the traders' displays and lean-tos, and the shifting crowd in general. There were several barrels of mountain whiskey being dispensed by traders who demanded and got more skins than were warranted for each cup or jug surrendered, and there were a large number of drunken braves as well as a few squaws staggering about or passed out completely on the ground.

"Hey . . . old son!"

At the shout and the sound of the familiar voice, Carson brought his attention to the slope below. Two riders were racing toward him — one being Monte Rinehart.

Kit responded with a welcoming yell, and hammering his heels into the ribs of the horse he was riding sent it plunging down the grade to meet his old friend. They drew together, both men came off their saddles, and clasping right hands pounded each other on the back vigorously with the left.

"Was wondering what had happened to you," Kit said. "You get yourself married off to that gal?"

Monte sobered and stepped away, shaking his head. "Nope, sure didn't. I'll tell you about it one of these days. First off, I want you to meet a friend of mine. Name's Louie Pineau. He's a Frenchy."

Pineau, still in his saddle, leaned to one side and extended his hand. *"Bon jour, m'sieur,*" he said, displaying a strong set of teeth when he smiled.

A small, lithe, dark man with bright eyes, a heavy beard and mustache, and a friendly way about him, he was clad in the usual buckskins and moccasins and wore a knitted wool cap.

"*Bon jour,*" Carson responded.

Pineau grinned wider. "*Parlez-vous français?*"

"*Un peu,*" Kit said. "Wintered with a French-Canadian one year."

"What did I tell you?" Rinehart demanded, nodding to Pineau. "That there Kit can palaver in a dozen redskin tongues, sign language, and can talk your lingo along with German and Mex. Run into Frenchy down on the White when I was hunting you," Monte continued, turning to Kit. "We went on up to Roubidoux's, was told there that you'd moved on. We been sort of trailing you and trapping beaver ever since. Let's get on down where the fun's going on. Was sure hoping you'd show up here."

Carson swung back onto his horse as Rinehart remounted, and all three men headed toward the sprawling encampment.

"What do you think about this here shindig?" Monte asked, remembering that it was Kit's first attendance.

"Surprising. Just never expected to see the tribes come together like this without tomahawking each other."

"Well, they're all here . . . the Paiutes, the Blackfeet, the Gros Ventres, Utes, Pawnees, Snakes, Arapahoes, the Kiowas, the Apaches, and the Comanches, Navajos. . . . Hell, you name them, and they'll have thrown up a village somewhere around here," Monte said, with a wave of his hand at the broad scene of confusion. "I'm thinking this here one's bigger'n the one in 'Thirty-Two."

"Yeah, I remember you saying you got to that one."

"Sure did, and I ain't ever figuring to miss one long as I can run, walk, ride, or crawl. There's your friend Broken Hand's lean-to over there. Bridger's talking to him."

Carson shifted his attention to the point indicated by Rinehart. The men who had been with him had moved on ahead with the pack animals while he was having his first look at the rendezvous and were now unloading the bales of pelts and stacking them at Fitzpatrick's stand. It had been agreed months previously while they were all on the Snake River that the beaver taken by him and his partners would be sold to the Rocky Mountain Fur Company.

Other companies were in evidence, too — the American Fur Company, Hudson's Bay, several of smaller stature, as well as a few individuals operating solely on their own. All were doing a thriving business from their display of goods which Kit saw at closer range consisted of pots and pans, blankets, ornamental trinkets, knives, hatchets, beads, bolts of cloth in various colors, woolen shirts, drawers, gloves, leather belts, piles of buttons with threads and needles nearby. There were racks of guns — rifles, pistols, and the necessary items that went with them: bullet molds, lead, pouches, powder, and powder horns and flasks. Carson, taking it all in with an encompassing sweep of his eyes, could think of nothing a man might find necessary that wasn't available. Turning then to Fitzpatrick, he checked in his bales of beaver skins, had himself a drink of good whiskey, and then in company with Monte and Louie Pineau moved on.

Kit continued to be fascinated by the monstrous gathering. The thought that the tribes, continually at war with one another and white men, could all come together in peace was unbelievable. But that was what a rendezvous was all about, Rinehart declared. It was necessary so that trappers, fur companies, and Indians could get together once a year and do their trading — buying what they needed and getting set for the months to come.

"It is for that one time a year the hatchet is buried," Pineau added, "but, when it is finish', and they are gone beyond the ridge . . . the truce is also finish'!"

"Frenchy's right," Rinehart said. "The gate's open once the drinking and trading and buying's done. But now, while all that's going on, a fellow can sure have himself a rip-snorter of a time!"

Kit pulled up short as three braves in an impromptu horse race thundered by. All were very drunk and could scarcely manage to stay aboard their ponies. Farther on an independent trader had set up a barrel of mountain whiskey, the same vile concoction as Taos Lightning which consisted of, among other things water, shredded chewing tobacco, black pepper, molasses, and a small amount of liquor. He was doling it out to a long line of braves eager to trade their year's catch for a measure of it. Nearby several squaws were engaged in a trading venture of their own with trappers, willingly going off into the brush or behind a convenient teepee where they surrendered their bodies for a handful of trinkets or a coin or two.

Several trappers were still carrying on the

dance Carson had noted from the ridge, and the shooting contest was also yet in progress, he saw, as they wandered aimlessly through the encampment over which now a pall of dust and smoke was beginning to hang. A fight broke out between a mountain man and a Blackfoot brave nearby, and for several moments there was the flash of steel in the bright sunlight as knives slashed. But it ended almost as quickly as it started when Milton Sublette hurried up and, with the aid of a Blackfoot chief, put a stop to it before either man was wounded.

A trapper in buckskins and wearing a vivid red shirt stumbled up. Although near to the point of falling down from liquor, he was still managing to carry a tin cup of the rank, numbing liquid without spilling any.

"Kit!" he shouted joyously. "Dang me . . . I knowed it was you! I ain't seen you since we went west with old Ewing Young! Can I buy you a drink?"

Carson smiled, having no recollection of the man but inherently polite, accepted the cup and took a swallow of its fiery contents.

"You aiming to stay?" the trapper asked.

"Till it's over," Kit replied, returning the cup.

"Good! Good! Reckon I'll be seeing you again," the man said and, spotting another acquaintance, moved unsteadily on.

The dull, rhythmic thumping of a drum coming from one of the villages along the perimeter of the encampment drew their attention. A number of braves, squaws, and white men had formed a circle inside of which several young girls were performing a dance. All were dressed in beaded doeskin dresses and, barefooted, were moving gracefully about, dipping and twisting to the beat of a drum.

"Arapahoes," Kit said, as they moved in and became a part of the circle of onlookers. "Think they call this the butterfly dance."

"Them's mighty pretty squaws," Rinehart murmured. "I reckon you could say the chief's sort of put them up for sale and's showing them off."

Carson nodded absently, his gaze fixed on one of the girls. She looked a bit older than the others, had a smooth, light-copper skin, large, soft eyes, and a well developed figure that her dress could not conceal. Each time she moved by Kit she smiled, directing her attention only to him. Something within Carson stirred, responded. He watched the girl more closely, marveling at her grace, at the sheen of her braided black hair, at the quiet beauty of her face.

Turning to a squaw standing beside him,

151

he asked, "Grandmother, who is the young one with the blue ribbon about her head?"

The elderly woman nodded. "She is Wahnibe, the daughter of a chief."

Wah-nibe — Singing Grass. "Who is this chief?"

"He is called Running Around."

"Thank you, Grandmother," Carson said and put his glance back on the girl. "Is he among us?"

The old squaw frowned, surveyed the crowd. "No, he is not. Perhaps he is with the traders."

"Perhaps," Kit said and watched the girls, their performance concluded and giggling happily, hurry back into the village.

"Reckon that's done," Monte said. "I'm for going over and trying my hand at shooting . . . and maybe doing a little dancing of my own if I can find myself a pretty little squaw like them we just seen."

"*Bien,*" Louie Pineau agreed as they turned away and then, facing Kit, said: "The one with the blue ribbon, she has eyes for you, *mon ami!*"

Carson grinned. "Seen that. Think I'll have myself a talk with her pa first chance I get."

There was no break in activities at sundown. Bonfires were lit, some of the teepees getting the worst of it, and the drinking and carousing continued unabated. Pineau took his leave not long after dark, his attention being drawn to a buxom young squaw, and Kit and Monte Rinehart drew off to the side a short distance behind the Rocky Mountain Fur Company's display and set up their shelters. After they had laid out their blankets and cooked a supper of fried potatoes, savored by onions, and supplemented with thick slices of bacon obtained only minutes earlier from Broken Hand Fitzpatrick's stock, they settled back, Kit filling their cups with coffee also just purchased from the trader.

"You aim to tell me about what happened in Taos?"

Monte's usually smiling face clouded. "Yeah, reckon this'll be as good a time as any. Had to kill one of Dolores's brothers . . . the oldest one, Luis."

Carson frowned, drew up slightly. "Sure do hate hearing that."

"Just didn't have no choice, Kit. Was next day after the *baile*. I rode out to the Valesquez place. Wanted to talk things over with her mama and brothers . . . see why it was that we couldn't get married. Found them all there, so I sashayed right into them and started speaking my piece. Her mama seemed to think maybe I was all right, after all, but them goddamn brothers of hers, they just bowed their necks and said Dolores was going to marry this jasper they'd picked out for her. Luis and me got into it sort of hot and heavy, and then Dolores gave me the high sign, meaning I'd best go, and let her see what she could do about it.

"That's what I done, but about half way back to town, them two brothers and some other Mex . . . maybe he was the one she's supposed to marry, I ain't sure . . . jumped out of the brush and drug me off my horse. We got to mixing it up right smart . . . me having to use my knife and wishing I had my rifle. I cut one of them on the arm, and that one I didn't know sliced me across the belly. Seen about then that I was a goner if I didn't get high and behind. Put one of my feet on one of them's balls and knocked him out of the ruckus. Cut another'n, the young brother, I think, pretty good and got him backing off. Was then that Luis charged me. I done a fancy side step and stuck my stabber clean up to the hilt in his brisket. He just halted flat footed like, looking kind of surprised, and then fell over. That put a stop to things, and José and his friend picked up Luis and started for the Valesquez house.

"About then I noticed I'd got a pretty deep

154

cut in my arm that I hadn't paid no mind to. It was bleeding bad, so I took out my bandanna and wrapped the place good and tight, and headed for my horse. I got to him and was climbing up into the saddle when I heard somebody say my name. I looked around. It was Dolores. I reckon she'd been scared something was going to happen and wanted to warn me . . . only she got there too late. First thing she said to me when I got down and met her was that Luis was dead. She'd met José and the other fellow as they was toting him back. I told her I was real sorry, but Luis didn't give me no choice. Same went for José and the other man.

"She looked at me with them big eyes of hers, all filled up with sadness, and told me that everything between us was over for sure now, that she couldn't marry me no matter what because I had gone and killed one of her family, and that I best forget about her. I told her again I was sorry, and that we could go away, that we didn't have to live there where she'd be seeing things that reminded her of Luis and her family, and such, but she said that wouldn't help. Luis would always stand between us."

Rinehart paused, stared out over the noisy encampment, alive with the flickering light from a hundred or more fires.

"Well, I hung around a couple of weeks, trying to see her and talk her into looking at things my way, but it was no use, and then she just dropped out of sight. I asked around, was told by one of the girls that knew her that she'd gone to visit relatives, but she didn't know where. I give it up then and headed for the Green after you."

Kit shrugged, finished off his coffee. "Seems we both had bad luck with our Taos women. I'm real sorry."

"Yeah, we sure did. How about us forgetting about this damn slop and getting us some of Broken Hand's whiskey?"

"Suits me fine," Carson said, getting to his feet. "Then we can do some serious talking about trapping this season. Beaver are getting scarce on the Green and all the rest of the regular streams. I've got it in my head that we ought to go up the Missouri and do some trapping along its headwaters."

Monte whistled. "Kit, you're talking about Blackfoot country. They just ain't the friendly kind . . . d'ruther lift a man's hair than eat!"

"I know that," Carson said as they moved toward the fur company's shelter. "Can thank the Hudson's Bay outfit for making them that way. They're wanting to hog all the beaver, so they've got the Blackfeet all

156

tuned up to keep the rest of us out, but I figure, if we can get up a party big enough and make half of them camp watchers, we could go in anyway."

Monte Rinehart nodded. "Well, now, just maybe you got yourself a real smart idea! Let's do some talking around and see what we can come up with."

Late that next morning Kit made his way alone to the Arapaho village. Moving in among the teepees, he asked for that of Running Around and was directed to one of the larger lodges erected near the bank of the river. As he approached, he saw Singing Grass sitting on a blanket nearby. Like all Arapaho women when in their village and weather permitting, she was nude from the waist up and, coming to her feet, stood before him.

Carson had hardly been able to get the girl out of his mind since the previous day when he had seen her dance, and now there before him, her face even more beautiful than he remembered, her skin smooth and silky, looking like a young beaver's pelt — and her breasts, large and firm, the nipples challenging his gaze — he found his breath locked in his throat. Finally he found his voice.

"Your father, Chief Running Around, I would speak with him about you," he said in Arapaho.

A smile parted the girl's lips, and her dark eyes began to glow. She turned as if to enter the teepee and summon her parent but the old chief, hearing the conversation, suddenly appeared. He shrugged at the girl, making it clear that she was not to be present while matters concerning her were discussed, but he did not admit to Kit that he was aware of the purpose for his being there, although he certainly had overheard.

"What is it you seek?" he asked, motioning for Carson to sit down on the blanket.

"Do you know me, Chief Running Around?" the mountain man asked, taking his place.

"Yes. Are you not Kit Carson?"

"I am, and I have long been a friend of the Arapahoes. I would like to smoke and talk with you."

Running Around nodded, reached into a pocket of the buckskin jacket he was wearing, and produced a clay pipe. Making a ceremony of filling it with shreds of tobacco, he took a brand from the small cooking fire close by, lit it, drew a few draughts, and passed it to Carson. Kit took his turn and handed the pipe back.

"It is good," Running Around said. "Now we will talk."

"It is about your daughter, Wah-nibe."

"Yes. She is young and beautiful as the sky at night. She can cook, and sew, and will provide her husband with many fine children."

"Of that I am certain," Kit said, speaking in the Arapaho tongue but falling back on sign language when he could not remember the correct word. "I wish very much to buy her. How much?"

"Ten horses."

Kit shook his head. "The price is very high. I cannot afford to pay it."

"There are others who would buy her."

"I do not doubt that, Chief Running Around, and perhaps they can pay so much. I cannot. But I will be a good husband to her. I will take her wherever I go. I will not let other men molest her. She will be my wife in truth."

The Indian gave that several minutes' thought during which time several braves wandered by, all looking at Kit curiously, and a low-voiced conversation was taking place inside the teepee.

Finally Running Around spoke. "These things you say I know, for I have heard you are a man of good word. How much is it you can pay for my daughter?"

"Five horses."

The chief sighed heavily. "So few! But so be it. It is not enough, and perhaps I should wait . . . but my daughter has spoken of her desire for you . . . and you are a friend. Where are these five fine horses?"

"I do not have them now but must make the money to buy them."

"Then you are not ready to marry my daughter?"

"I am, but I will not ask you to give her to me on trust. It is better that we deal in faith and promise. I will bring them to you at the next rendezvous, if there is one, or will drive them to your village on the Arkansas. That is my word. Do you give me your word that you will not sell her to any other man and let her remain in your teepee untouched until that day?"

The conversation within the lodge had grown louder. There would be Singing Grass's mother and sisters and possibly other relatives present inside.

"So it will be," Running Around stated solemnly. "At the rendezvous you will bring five good, strong horses. Wah-nibe will be awaiting you."

Carson nodded, got to his feet. The Arapaho also rose. Behind the chief, Carson could see Singing Grass peeking through the flap of the teepee.

"It is good that we have an arrangement," Kit said. "My friendship with the Arapahoes will know no ending."

"Nor mine for Kit Carson," Running Around said. "We are now as a family."

"A good family," Kit said and, as he turned away, he saw Singing Grass still watching from the depths of the lodge and smiled. She smiled back, and he moved on. He would find a way to meet and talk with her before the rendezvous ended, but he would honor his promise to her father and take no husbandly privileges until he had duly paid the price required of him.

Chapter Nine

Fitzpatrick, Sublette, and even Jim Bridger had some doubts that Kit's plan — to trap at the headwaters of the Missouri and thus challenge the Blackfeet — was a good one.

"Going to be plenty chancy," Broken Hand warned, "and I ain't all that sure it'll be worth it . . . sure won't, if you and the boys going with you lose your hair!"

"Might be better if you'd work the Mary's River country," Sublette suggested. "Don't think there's been too many trapping around there . . . but it's up to you. We're just hoping you realize how dangerous it is up there."

"Way I see it, hunting beaver nowadays is a dangerous business anywhere. And any man that goes with me will be doing it because he wants to . . . I'm not twisting anybody's ear."

Such wouldn't have been necessary, for when the rendezvous broke up in early fall, a large number of trappers had decided to throw in with Kit on the venture, exacting no other promise from him beyond his willingness to head up the expedition. Carson led them north, an extensive company since many of the men had brought along their squaws, some with children. By the time they reached the intended area, it had become apparent that the brigade was too large to be practical, and thus it was divided, an experienced hunter and trapper well acquainted with the country, Saul Van Buskirk, striking off with half while Carson moved on with the remainder — some fifty men plus a number of camp watchers and, of course, the squaws.

One of the trappers bringing his woman was Louie Pineau. He had taken a fancy to the Shawnee girl he had seen at the rendezvous and struck up a bargain for her.

"Why did you not buy the little Arapaho girl who had such eyes for you?" he asked Kit as he and Monte rode alongside Carson on the trail.

"Did," Kit replied, his thoughts going immediately to Singing Grass, bringing a fresh recollection of her beauty to him.

"You bought yourself a wife?" Monte asked in an incredulous voice. "How's it happen you didn't bring her?"

"Didn't have the price . . . five horses. Expect to make enough this season to buy them, turn them over to her pa, Chief Running Around, at the rendezvous next summer. Gave me his word he'd hold off dealing with anybody else till then."

"Hell," Monte said in disgust, "was no need for you to do that. You got plenty of friends who'd been proud to loan you money to buy the horses."

Carson shrugged. "Just no hand for borrowing. . . ."

"The Blackfeet have many horses, *m'sieur,*" Pineau said. "Perhaps from them you can steal. . . ."

"Sure!" Rinehart declared. "We can pitch in and help! Won't take long."

"Expect it's more likely to work the other way," Carson said dryly. "It'll be the Blackfeet stealing horses from us."

A day short of a week later they reached a place where trapping looked as if it could be good. Halting, they began to unload and set up camp.

"Indians!"

The warning shout came before they had even finished pulling off the packs. A half dozen rifle shots rang out as a party of Blackfeet swept in, discharged their weapons, and rushed on into the woods. They were gone before the trappers could snatch up their rifles and get off a return fire.

"They got Enos Halverson," Rinehart reported a few minutes later. "Shot him dead."

Carson called the men together. "You can

see now what we're going to be up against . . . but I think beaver's plentiful, and it'll be worth taking care. From now on, we go in groups of no less than four . . . and one man's to be on watch all the time. Nobody's to move about, even here in camp, without his rifle. That clear?"

The men agreed that it was but, regardless of such elaborate precautions, four more men were killed and several wounded by the Blackfeet before the month was out. Dissension increased, and again Kit called the men together.

"Not going to tell you that it'll get any better around here . . . could get worse and likely will. But we all knew we'd have trouble with the Indians before we ever started. Now, I'm for doubling up on our guards and being more careful than we are. Trapping's good, and I'd hate to pull out, admit we failed . . . that we let the Blackfeet drive us away . . . but I'll leave it up to you. I led you in here. I'll lead you out if that's what you want. Can take a vote among yourselves."

"Where'd we go?" someone asked.

"Bridger's camping on the Big Snake, up Idaho way. I'd head for there."

The vote was taken, and the overwhelming result was to move on, leave the upper Missouri to the Blackfeet. They broke camp the following day and Kit, disappointed, chagrined by failure, led his party to Bridger's winter quarters.

"Ain't nothing to sweat over," Bridger consoled him when they met and were talking over the unsuccessful expedition. "You ain't the first man to ever make a mistake."

Kit took little comfort from his friend's words and, restless and impatient, he set about working on his gear during the time of ice, repairing and replacing those things that were in need of it, increasing his supply of bullets, sharpening his knife, and the two tomahawks he now carried. He was anxious for spring to come when he could get back to trapping beaver, the skins of which would provide the money and thus the horses needed to buy Singing Grass.

Moody, completely engrossed in his work and hopes, Carson came to attention one morning early as he and Rinehart were eating their breakfasts when Bridger, beside himself with anger, rushed up, shouting Kit's name. Kit, rising quickly and followed by Monte, hurried out of the cabin to meet the trader.

"Them damned Indians . . . they come last night and stole eighteen horses!" Bridger announced in a trembling voice.

"Blackfeet!"

"Ain't sure, but I'm guessing so. Kind of far west for them to be ranging, but they've done it before. Anyway, we have to get them animals back . . . and you're the only man I can trust to get the job done. Pick yourself a dozen men and head out. If it ain't done quick, we'll never see them horses again! I'll follow you soon as I can."

Carson hastily got a party together, one including Monte Rinehart and Louie Pineau who no longer batched with them but lived with his Shawnee bride in a lodge of their own, and struck out across the snowy hills in pursuit of the horse thieves. By next morning they had them in sight — about thirty or thirty-five braves. They were halted on a hillside a half mile distant, apparently resting as the snow had become increasingly deeper to the east.

"No chance of getting up on them fast," Carson said. "Our own horses are belly deep in wet snow, and it's all they can do to walk, much less run. And they're out of rifle range. Leaves us but one thing to do."

"Meaning?" Rinehart wondered.

"Talk."

One of the trappers shook his head. "Hell, them guteaters ain't going to give us back them animals just because you ask for them!"

"Maybe not, but I've been around Indians

since I was a button, and one thing I've learned is that you can't always figure what they'll do. Aim to try walking up to them, ask them for a powwow."

"What do you want us to do if they start shooting at you?" Monte asked, not too sold on the plan.

"I'll leave that up to you. They're stuck in the snow, same as we are. Means they can't get away fast, and we can't do much chasing them. I reckon that adds up to your not doing anything."

Monte shrugged, pounded his hands together to create warmth. "Expect we'll do what we can," he said as Carson began to move away from his party and slog his way through the deep snow for the hill.

"Have a care, *m'sieur*," Pineau warned. "These Blackfeet are . . . how you say? . . . treacherous. You must not trust them."

Carson nodded and, holding his rifle above his head, reached the foot of the slope and began a slow ascent. He could be doing a foolhardy thing, he knew, but he was also aware that Indians respected courage, and it was upon that facet in their character that he was depending heavily. At once he saw a stir of attention among the braves gathered on a windswept strip of the hillside where the snows were not so deep. The stolen horses, he noticed, were in a second clearing a short distance to one side. At that moment two of the Indians separated from the others and, rifles also held above their heads, began to descend the slope. When they were within a hundred feet or so away, both halted.

"What are you called?" the taller of the two shouted.

"Kit Carson," the mountain man replied. "I will talk with you."

There was a brief exchange between the pair, and then the taller one again spoke. "How is it you speak our tongue? Were you once among us?"

"I speak many tongues, for I have long been a friend of the Indian peoples. Why are you not our friends?"

"Who is to say we are not?"

"You have stolen our horses, and that is not the act of a friend."

Again there was conversation, and then the smaller man said: "This talk of friends does not matter. You are unwelcome in our land, Kit Carson."

"And we thought you were Snakes," the brave with him added.

"We are only white trappers, and we were not in your land when you stole our horses. We would talk with you about it and, to show we are friends, we will lay down our weapons if you will also do that. Then we can smoke and talk."

Once more there was an exchange between the two Blackfeet. Finally the taller one said: "My brother, White Hawk, does not trust you, but I am chief and will do as you say. You will come forward a distance, as will I, and we will talk."

"What of my men?"

"They must put down their weapons and come forward with you."

Carson gave that thought, shook his head. "No, this they cannot do. A thief might come and steal their weapons while they were away. I must leave one man to guard the rifles."

The Blackfoot nodded. "This I will do also."

The arrangement was carried out at once, and shortly Kit was facing the Blackfoot chief, a lean young brave in buckskins and buffalo robe.

"How are you called?" Carson asked when the pipe was lit and passed to him.

"I am Red Wolf, chief. Have I heard of you before this time?"

"It is possible. I have moved among the tribes for many years."

"The Blackfeet do not know you."

"Your land is new to me, but I had a friend

170

who lived among your people but later came to live among the whites. It was he who taught me to speak your tongue."

White Hawk spat in disgust at the mention of anyone who would desert the tribe to live among white people.

"Will you give us back our horses?" Carson asked, believing the small talk had gone far enough. "It is not right that you should keep them."

Red Wolf shrugged under his heavy robe. "Yes, I will return them. We believed you to be Snakes. We want to remain friends of all whites."

Half turning, Red Wolf raised a hand, motioned to the braves standing behind him. At once two moved off to where the horses were picketed. Carson watched narrowly. It had been too easy — there had to be a catch to it. A moment later he saw what it was. The braves had selected only five horses and were leading them back to where their chief and Carson were waiting.

Kit gave the animals grudging note, shook his head. "You are not honorable, Red Wolf. You and your braves stole eighteen fine animals, now you return to me five very poor ones. Is this the way a Blackfoot chief keeps his word?"

"I did not give you my hand!" Red Wolf

171

shouted and, wheeling, signaled to his brave to get their weapons.

Carson wheeled to give a like alarm, but Rinehart and the other trappers were already racing for their rifles. Monte, snatching up not only his own gun but that of Kit as well, turned and raced up the now trampled snow trail to meet Carson coming back.

"Charge them!" Kit yelled, waving to his men to fan out, to take advantage of the few trees on the slope.

The Blackfeet had by then reclaimed their weapons and were following a similar plan as they came down the slope. Abruptly the Blackfeet opened fire, and the cold air became filled with the echoes of gun shots, the hiss of arrows, and the smell of burnt powder. Several Indians went down as the trappers triggered an answering volley, and for a few moments it appeared to Carson that, despite the superior numbers of the Blackfeet, he and his men were going to get the best of the encounter.

But it was an illusion. Braves, quietly holding their fire and keeping well in the trees, began to appear to the side, and Kit realized Red Wolf was seeking to draw them into a trap by dividing his warriors and sending small parties to go in behind the trappers.

Suddenly a buck stepped from the back

side of a tree close by. He did not see Kit but was leveling his rifle at a man standing a few paces away, reloading. Kit, with his own weapon, sighted on a Blackfoot hunched low and coming toward him through the snow-laden brush and trees, swung his rifle about, and downed the brave aiming at the trapper. Instantly he began to reload so as to take care of the Blackfoot moving in on him.

There wasn't sufficient time, in spite of the fact that Carson was known to reload a weapon in less than half a minute. As he rammed the ball into his rifle, he saw the brave come to an upright position, sight down the barrel of his weapon. Instantly Kit dodged to one side, hoping to destroy the aim of the Blackfoot, but in the snow his footing was uncertain. He slipped. The Indian's bullet seared across his neck and drove into his shoulder.

"Get back to the horses!" he yelled as he went down.

Getting his feet under him, he turned to follow his own command. The man whose life he had saved suddenly appeared at his side and, supporting him, hurriedly assisted him back into the dense timber where they had left their mounts. Going into the saddle quickly, Carson delayed until all of the party were present and then quickly moved off to change locations in the event the Blackfeet intended to pursue.

"Can expect them to do just that," Kit said, suffering intensely from the wound in his shoulder. "We best keep men posted and on the lookout for them. Red Wolf would like to add our horses to those he's already stolen . . . along with our rifles and our hair."

They waited out the afternoon, being forced to change positions twice to avoid the prowling braves and then, when darkness came and it was safe to make camp, they drew in close to a small pile of rocks and brush and halted. Immediately Pineau and another of the trappers went to work on the wound in Carson's shoulder, doing what they could for it without the benefit of medicine of any kind.

"I would heat water, *mon ami*, to clean the wound before binding it," the Frenchman said, "but a fire would be seen or perhaps the smoke would be smelled by the savages, and so it would be unwise, *n'est-ce pas?*"

Sitting with his back to a tree, Kit nodded. The pain had not let up, and he was cold but knew there was no solution to the problem. The Blackfeet likely were all around them, and they would be fortunate to remain undiscovered.

The night wore on bitterly cold and miserable. The men removed saddles from the horses, wrapped themselves with the blankets as well as they could in an effort to keep warm. But the small oblongs of fabric, while wool, did little to alleviate their discomfort, and by morning all were stiff and sore. Carson, of course, was in worse condition than any. Blood had frozen in his wound, and he could scarcely move. Only Kit's nagging sense of responsibility for the men in his charge gave him a measure of strength and, when the first streaks of daylight brightened the east, he dispatched Monte and another trapper to see if the Indians were still close by or had moved on.

The two men were back within the hour. "Right where we first seen them . . . up on the slope," Rinehart reported. "Horses there where we seen them, too. We're going after them again?"

Kit shook his head. "No, they've not only got us outnumbered, but they're sitting up where they've got the drop on us. Best we leave it up to Bridger . . . he ought to be showing up pretty quick with his party. Quiet, now, we sure don't want Red Wolf and his braves hearing us pull out."

Saddles were put on the horses with care. Few words were spoken and those at low breath. Within a short time they had mounted and were moving off with Carson expecting to meet Jim Bridger and his force of men around each bend of the trail, now being lost under falling snow. But Bridger and the thirty trappers accompanying him were just leaving camp when Kit and his party rode in. They had planned to leave the night before but had been forced to delay — and then, when no word came from Carson, it was decided to ignore the developing snow storm and all else and go in search of the party.

Kit, brushing aside all explanations and barely able to dismount, gave details of the encounter to Bridger, described the location where Red Wolf and his braves had camped, and then surrendered himself to the squaws for needed treatment.

Two days later Bridger returned. The Blackfeet were gone when he and his party reached there and, while they had set out at once to trail them, they eventually were forced to turn back.

It took a full two months for Kit to recover sufficiently for traveling, and by then it was time to start the spring hunt for beaver. Carson, running his traps on the Snake and later Green River — with the aid of Monte and Louie Pineau — accumulated a fair inventory of pelts when the day came to go into summer quarters on the latter stream.

"You aiming to go fetch your little Arapaho squaw?" Monte asked when they had settled down to camp. Supplies were only those being brought in by fur company representatives, and the trappers had not yet done any selling or trading.

"Not sure what I'll do," Kit said. "Got to have those horses to pay for her before I do. No sense going for her until I do."

"You'll sure be needing yourself a woman to sort of look after you . . . that shoulder bothering like it is."

"I reckon it'll cure up all right. . . ."

"It ain't doing too good yet!" Rinehart declared. "I've seen you flinch when you've bumped it against something."

"That will pass," Carson insisted, switching his attention to a large, powerfully built trapper in worn and greasy buckskins and knitted stocking cap, swaggering past their lean-to.

"I twist the neck of any man who I do not like!" he was declaring in a thick French accent to a half a dozen men following in his wake. "No man stands up to Shunar! I am the champion!"

"A bad one, *m'sieur*," Pineau said, coming up at that moment. "He has killed four men

. . . that I know. It is best he be ignored."

Shunar, rifle slung from the crook of an arm, free hand wrapped about the knife hanging from his belt, paused, glared at Kit, and then at Monte and Pineau. Drawing his blade, he made several sweeping flourishes with it and laughed.

"For the little Frenchman there," he said in a loud voice as he returned the knife to its sheath, "I will have no trouble to beat with my hands. For the Americans, the task will be even smaller. With a switch I can make any American beg for mercy like a woman!"

Carson, dejected by his failure to do well that past winter, hopes of claiming Singing Grass for his own growing dimmer, and still pained by his wound, was in a dark humor and in no mood to listen to such reckless talk. He drew himself erect and, ignoring Monte Rinehart's cautioning, stepped forward.

"You are a braggart and have a loud mouth!" Kit said in a voice that also carried well through the camp. "If you say that about Americans again, I will rip out your guts!"

Chapter Ten

Shunar's bear-like eyes glittered. "Ai-eee! The short one! He has a loud bark!"

"And a mighty deep bite!" Carson snapped.

The big Frenchman frowned angrily as laughter broke out among his followers. "This we shall see," he said and, glowering at Carson, moved on.

Louis Pineau laid a hand on Kit's arm. "A mistake, *m'sieur*. This Shunar will not forget what you have said."

"And I'm not forgetting anything, either," Carson replied and turned back to the lean-to.

The confrontation with Shunar had further aggravated Kit's temper and done no good at all for his throbbing shoulder, but he had been unable to let the insults pass. The man was a bully and deserved taking down a few notches. While Carson was not fool enough to think he could match Shunar in a rough and tumble brawl, he was certain he could give a good account of himself with a knife or other weapon. But it would seem the big Frenchman was not interested in a fight where an equalizer was used. He relied on size and brute strength to subdue his opponents.

A yell went up from the center of the camp. Carson gave it no thought, but Monte, throwing his attention to that point, swore deeply.

"It's him again, Kit. He's coming on his horse and carrying his rifle."

Carson made no reply. Turning to his gear, he picked up the Springfield pistol he occasionally used, checked its priming, and thrust it under his belt. Crossing to where the horses were picketed, he mounted one that was saddled and, doubling back to the lean-to, halted.

Pineau considered him with concern. "You, perhaps, could use an ally, *mon ami?* From here I can put my knife into the body of that. . . ."

"No need, Frenchy," Kit broke in. "I can handle him."

"If you don't," Monte, jaw set, declared, "I'll sure'n hell finish him off. Owe you, Kit. This'd be a good time to square up."

"I can take care of him," Carson repeated.

He was thinking of what an old wagonmaster had said to him when he first ran away from home and managed to join up with a train heading for Santa Fé. The bearded oldster had laid an arm on Kit's slight shoulders after noting the uncertainty and nervousness that gripped the boy and given him a reassuring hug.

"It'll be all right, son. Only thing a man needs to watch out for is being afraid of being afraid," he'd said. "When he ain't, he gets careless, and you sure don't want that."

It was a rule Carson never forgot and one that had seen him safely through many tight scrapes.

"Where is the little rooster that crowed so loud?" Shunar shouted, obviously having fortified himself with a cup or two of Taos Lightning. "I have come to pluck his tail feathers!"

"I'm right here," Kit answered and rode out to face the Frenchman. "You aiming to use that rifle on me?"

The horses of the two men were suddenly shoulder to shoulder as they faced each other, placing Kit and Shunar no more than an arm's length apart. Tension had stilled the camp as the Frenchman frowned, seemingly surprised at Carson's belligerent response. He glanced about at the two dozen or more bystanders who had quickly gathered. Abruptly he threw back his head, gestured with a hand.

"You are too small, American! I will not

waste time on you," he said and started to pull away. Suddenly he checked his horse and swung his rifle around to bear on Carson.

"Look out, Kit!" Rinehart yelled.

Carson had anticipated some sort of trick on Shunar's part. Jerking the pistol from his belt, he fired hastily. In that same instant, the Frenchman also triggered his weapon. Shunar howled as Kit's ball drove into his arm, rocking him in his saddle, and causing him to drop the rifle. The bullet from the Frenchman's weapon had clipped through Carson's hair and sped off into space, the only effect of the shot being a slight powder burn on his face and in his eye.

Shunar, clutching his shattered arm, rocked back and forth on his nervously shying horse, cursing wildly. Friends who had yelled encouragement to him were now hurrying up, anxiously voicing questions and Monte, seeing Kit thrust the empty pistol back into his belt, stepped forward and handed him his loaded rifle.

"You had enough . . . or do you want to reload and go at it again?" Carson asked the Frenchman, his voice cold as winter wind.

Shunar continued to swear. "My arm . . . it is broke! *Mon Dieu* . . . you would murder a helpless man?"

182

"Wouldn't bother me none if that man was you," Kit replied indifferently. "All right, I'll let it end here, but I warn you . . . if I ever hear you insult us Americans again, I'll come after you!"

The Frenchman, aided by his friends and still holding his arm, came slowly off the saddle.

"Comprends?" Kit demanded sharply in French.

Shunar nodded. "Understood."

Carson turned back to where Monte and Louie Pineau were waiting. Both were smiling broadly, as were several others nearby.

"You sure fixed his wagon," Rinehart chortled as Kit dismounted. "I bet he won't be pushing nobody around for a spell."

Kit shrugged. "Was about time he was taught a lesson. I'm just hoping he don't forget it."

"Such is not likely, *mon ami,*" Frenchy said. "This day I think you have done many men a great favor."

The fall hunt began that year with the arrival of September. Kit sent word to Chief Running Around that he had suffered an accident and was unable to deliver the five horses necessary to buy Singing Grass, but he assured the Arapaho that he would produce them by the next rendezvous and that he was to consider their agreement still in effect. Carson joined with a party headed up the Snake River.

Trapping was only fair and, when spring came after a winter camp on the Snake, he, Rinehart, Louis Pineau, and a half a dozen other men threw in with Thomas McCoy, an employee of the Hudson's Bay Company who claimed he knew where beaver could be taken in plentiful numbers. It was on Mary's River, he said, and he could all but guarantee a large catch.

"It sure is a good thing McCoy didn't put up no money," Monte said, weeks later after they had worked the length of the stream to its mouth and found beaver far from plentiful. "We'd've sure left him flat busted!"

McCoy could not understand it but Kit, now running in hard luck and more or less becoming accustomed to setbacks, only shrugged. Beaver could have been plentiful when the man was last on the Mary's, some six months or so previously. But a party of twenty or thirty trappers arriving after he had departed could have cleaned out the river in a short time.

"Where d'you say we head for now, Kit?" asked Godey, one of the party who apparently felt it wise to put stock again in Carson's knowledge of the country and its best possibilities.

The men were hunkered around a fire, one stirring the contents of a large pot containing potatoes, onions, and chunks of rabbit meat. Next to it coffee, in two separate blackened containers, was coming to a boil.

"Ain't sure you ought to ask me," Carson replied, "but I'd say the Big Snake. It's always been good there."

"Then it's the Big Snake far as I'm concerned," Godey said, amid several other assenting votes. "We can move out in the morning."

But trapping was no better in Idaho, and after a time even McCoy was ready to quit.

"Been wanting to have a look at the Columbia River," he said one morning. "And there's a couple of things I need to go to Fort Walla Walla about. Figure to pull out today . . . and any of you wanting to come along are welcome."

Monte glanced at Kit who shook his head.

"Not done hunting," Carson said. "I'm for working our way back down the Big Snake. Ought to be able to pick up a few plews."

"Suits me," Rinehart said.

Beaver skins had taken on great importance to Kit because of Singing Grass. Heretofore Carson had trapped simply as a way

185

of life, a means by which he could supply himself with personal needs. That had all changed after he had seen the Arapaho girl and made a deal with her father. Now skins meant horses — and with horses he could buy his bride. Monte sympathized with his friend. He had gone through a similar trying experience with Dolores — only he had lost. Kit still had a chance to win.

The company split, some going with McCoy to the Columbia where it joined the Walla Walla River, while Kit and the men who chose to remain with him struck off down the Big Snake. Trapping continued to be poor, so poor in fact that it was not worth the effort, and in a few days they abandoned the quest for beaver and, low on supplies, began to worry seriously about food. Again luck was not with them. Thanks to earlier parties of trappers and roving bands of Indians game was scarce, and shortly hunger became a very real factor in their existence.

"Can start bleeding the horses, cook the blood," suggested one of the men who had gone through a period of starvation. "Between that and the roots we're managing to dig up, maybe we can make it."

Roots had been their sole diet for the past few days, but the idea of bleeding did not appeal to Kit. If they further weakened the already gaunt horses by doing it and were left afoot in the vast Idaho wilderness, they really would be up against it. Yet, in the end, he agreed.

"How far do you figure we are from Fort Hall?" Monte asked one morning as they worked their way slowly across a vast flat.

Carson paused to look around, get his bearings, and recall landmarks. "Maybe a week . . . could be less."

Monte, face drawn, eyes hollow, shook his head. "I ain't sure I can make it that much longer," he said and glanced back at the rest of the party. "Ain't certain any of them can either. What do you say we kill one of the horses? We've got to have meat."

Kit frowned. He was in no better condition than the other men but was refusing to give in to exhaustion and hunger.

"May have to. Let's hold out for one more day. Could be something will turn up . . . a deer or some buffalo."

"Hell, I'd be right glad to see a polecat," one of the trappers declared grimly. "I'm mighty damn sick of blood and roots."

"You ain't by yourself," the man beside him stated wearily.

They continued on that day without seeing any game, spent a bad night, and awoke the next morning to behold a small party of Nez

Percé Indians drawn up close by, watching them. Kit, and the men with him, greeted the braves with customary dignity and then traded several beaver skins for a horse that they quickly slaughtered. It pained Carson to make such use of the animal, but it was that or starve. He and the trappers rested and feasted on the meat for several days and then, strength returned, they resumed the march to Fort Hall.

Several days later Carson spotted the smoke of the fort in the distance. "We're about there!" he sang out.

Cheering, Monte and the other men crowded up beside him, and a short time later they were entering the compound, as worn and thin as their horses.

Fort Hall, owned by the Hudson's Bay Company, was not only a trading post but a stopover for travelers en route to Oregon. Kit, selling off what furs he had to the post factor, as did the others, settled back to rest for a few days and to decide his next move.

"Can pick yourselves up a couple of horses cheap, if you want," Monte told Carson one morning. "Fellow going through's run short of provisions and's having to sell off some of his team to raise money. Expect you can do real good for yourself."

Kit lost no time bargaining for the animals

and drove them into one of the fort's corrals with three others that were his, quartered there along with Rinehart's and the rest of the party's. As he was leaving the railed-in yard, the post factor called to him.

"Can use some meat," he said. "Be glad to pay you and your brigade to bring in some buffalo. You'll find them plentiful about a day east of here."

A smile broke Kit's mouth — one of the very few he had been permitted in some time. Maybe his luck was finally changing for the better! He'd picked up two good horses at a low price and now was being offered a job to hunt.

"Can consider us hired," he said quickly and, rounding up Monte and whoever among the rest of the party wished to participate, rode out immediately.

The trader had been correct. Within a day's ride they came onto a fairly large herd of buffalo and, killing what they figured would be a sufficient number, headed back to the fort.

"Things are sure looking up," he remarked to Monte when they had turned in the skinned carcasses and collected their pay. "Might be smart to just hang around here for a week or so. Could be I can lay my hands on some more horses real cheap."

But that night it all changed again for him. Camped outside the fort, as was customary for visitors, Kit was awakened early in the morning by the sudden pound of running horses. Leaping to his feet in the half light, he saw a party of Indians — Blackfeet, he thought — driving off several horses. With Monte and the other men, by then awake and on their feet, he hurried into the compound. The corral where they had left their horses was empty.

"You let them redskins steal our horses!" Monte shouted angrily at the sentinel charged with seeing to the safety of the place. "Why the goddamn hell didn't you fire an alarm?"

The man shook his head. "Seen a man come in, let down the bars, and drive the animals out. Figured it was one of you fellows turning them loose to graze."

"One of us! For crissake, can't you tell the difference between a man and a Indian?"

"Was dark," the sentry said lamely.

"That makes about as much sense as saying you thought we were letting the horses out to graze at three o'clock in the morning," Carson said in disgust as he turned away.

"I . . . I sure am sorry about it. Was a bunch of them Blackfeet, I expect, getting even for all them buffalo you fellows killed."

Kit, thoroughly disgusted with the way things were going, headed back to the shelter he and Rinehart shared. He had no horses at all now — not even one to ride or one to use for packing gear. He was completely afoot — and the same applied to Monte and the rest of the trapping party.

"Means we're stuck here for a spell," he said wearily, as he settled down on his blankets.

Monte, shivering from the cold, entered the lean-to and, digging about in his parfleche, produced a half-full bottle of whiskey. Pulling the cork with his teeth, he handed the liquor to Carson.

"Sure seems . . . but I reckon somebody'll come along headed for the rendezvous before long," Rinehart said, watching Kit take a long, comforting swallow. "Can maybe buy something to ride from them, if more pilgrims running in hard luck ain't showed up in the meantime."

Carson, stirred impatiently, returned the whiskey. "The hell with waiting around! Was thinking if we could get our hands on some horses right now . . . borrow them . . . we could go after those damned Blackfeet."

"Suits me," Rinehart said. "Can bet the rest of the company will want to take a hand in it, too."

Kit reached again for the bottle. "I'll talk to the factor, see if he can finagle us something to ride."

The trader was of no help. Horses were scarce, and the men who came by the fort would be unwilling to part with their animals, and he owned none himself. There was nothing to be done but wait.

The party of trappers began to break up after that, some leaving on foot, others throwing in with companies heading back into the mountains. Carson and Rinehart hung on, waiting out the long days and nights until, finally, welcome relief in the form of Thomas McCoy arrived. The trader had with him a good stock of horses, and he not only agreed to outfit Monte and the men who had not departed with mounts at a fair price but made a deal with Kit for two working horses he needed as well as the five he must have for Chief Running Around when they gathered for rendezvous on Green River later on. Kit took a silent vow to himself, when the transaction was completed, that he'd never again bad mouth the Hudson's Bay Company or the men who had or did work for it as long as he drew a breath.

Reaching the gathering a week after leaving Fort Hall, Kit quickly sought out the Arapaho camp and the father of Singing Grass.

With the girl, lovelier than ever, it seemed to him, standing in the opening to their teepee, two other maidens nearby, all giggling and whispering, Carson picketed the horses in front of the shelter and moved off. It was up to Running Around now. He had fulfilled his part of the agreement.

"Don't figure you'll be wanting me around," Monte Rinehart said when Kit had returned after delivering the horses. He was poking about in their combined gear, picking out the items that were his.

"Singing Grass and me getting married's got nothing to do with us partnering. Sure, I'll have to fix us up a lean-to of our own, but I'm figuring on you pitching yours close by."

Monte nodded. "Was hoping you'd feel that way. Sometimes a man changes when he takes hisself a wife . . . like Frenchy Pineau. Didn't go with us to Mary's River . . . and I ain't seen him around here yet."

"Well, nothing's going to come between us. Anyway, I ain't sure I'll be having a wife. I'm a year late bringing those horses, and old Running Around has maybe backed out of the deal."

"You see the little squaw?"

"Yeah, she was there, prettier'n ever and grown some. Don't think she's married, but like I said her pa could have changed his mind when I didn't show up last year with the horses and put her up for sale again."

"When'll you know for sure?" Monte asked, taking up his gear and carrying it a few yards off to one side.

"Sundown, if these Arapahoes are like the others I've been around. I'll either have a bride or five horses back."

Rinehart grinned, slapped his hands together. "Then we got time to do some drinking and looking around. Let's take a *pasear* through the camp and see who all's here."

The rendezvous was much the same as the previous one Kit had attended. Plenty of mountain whiskey, drunken Indians and trappers everywhere, noisy games and contests — those between trappers and braves dangerously serious. The squaws were still vying for the attentions of white men willing to pay for their favors, and traders, more numerous than before, were eagerly hawking the merchandise displayed before their lean-tos and in their wagons, piling the beaver skins taken in payment nearby — their prices as high, if not higher, than before. Bars of lead for making bullets were being sold for a dollar each. Powder came to twice that amount per pound, and coffee was bringing as much as a half eagle for a one-pound sack

— all depending upon how well the man doing purchasing stood with the trader he was dealing with.

"Can use myself a couple of new blankets," Monte said as he approached Thomas Fitzpatrick's stand. "Sort of wore mine ragged last winter."

"Kit . . . Kit Carson!" Bridger, one of Broken Hand's partners standing near the back of the lean-to, called out. "Come here. Got a friend who wants to say howdy."

Carson nodded and, when Monte halted to finger the woolen covers on display, he circled the shelter to where Bridger, a bottle in hand, was standing with a buckskin-clad man who appeared vaguely familiar.

"Lucien Maxwell, Kit," the trapper said, extending his hand. "Seen you down in Taos a couple of times . . . usually at a fandango."

Carson accepted the man's hand, smiled. "Recollect seeing you at the same place. Seems you're from back East somewhere."

"Illinois," Maxwell said. "Making my home in the Taos country, however. You figuring on heading back there any time soon?"

"No, aim to keep on trapping this country."

Bridger, passing the bottle around, smiled broadly and winked. "Kit's got a mighty good reason to stick around! He's taking himself a young squaw today . . . a real pretty one, I'm told."

Maxwell nodded, took a drink from the bottle, and said: "Here's luck to you, Carson!"

Monte appeared at that moment and Kit, now with the bottle, had his swallow and passed it on to Rinehart so that he could participate in the toast. The four men conversed for a time, mostly about the scarcity of beaver during the past season and the corresponding increase in the price being paid for their skins, and then Carson and Monte Rinehart resumed their meandering through the turmoil of the encampment, visiting and renewing friendships.

"Two white women around here somewheres, I was told," Monte said, pausing to glance about. "On their way to Oregon from back in the States."

"Long ride for a woman," Kit commented and thought no more of the oddity concerning two city women being present at a trapper-trader-Indian gathering. He had a more personally important matter to think about — lovely Singing Grass.

He glanced to the sun, dropping low in the west. It would soon go down, and Running Around would either bring Singing Grass and whatever possessions were hers to his lean-to, or else he would return the five horses, signifying that the agreement was canceled. The old chief might, Kit realized. It had been two years since the pact was made, and Kit had agreed to claiming the girl and paying the necessary price within one but, when he had taken the horses to Running Around's lodge and had a glimpse of Singing Grass, he got the impression that all was well. But there was nothing certain in that. Only sundown and the arrival of darkness would tell.

He hoped that Singing Grass, if she did become his, would be happy with him. He would make her a good husband, just as she should make him a good wife. Many of the trappers had squaws as wives and took them along on the hunts, which is what he planned to do with Singing Grass. She would probably like that kind of life but, if not, he had already made up his mind to take her back to her people rather than to let her be unhappy. She was much too young and beautiful to turn into a camp drudge like some of the Indian women he had noticed.

"Where we going from here?" Monte asked when they had exhausted their touring and were back again at the lean-to. "You figuring to stay put somewheres with your little gal for a spell, or you going out soon as the season opens?"

Kit shrugged. "She ain't mine yet," he said. "Either way, I'll be going out . . . I'll just take her along. Heard some talk about a party going up to the Yellowstone."

"Getting into Blackfoot country again. Man stands a good chance of losing his scalp."

"Found that out the last time we traipsed around where they didn't want us. We'll talk it all out when the rendezvous's done. Right now I've got something else to think about."

Rinehart grinned. "You have for a fact, old son," he said, moving off to where he had piled his gear and intended to erect his own shelter. "See you in the morning."

Carson sat quietly in his lean-to, smoking his pipe and waiting. The sun was gone, and darkness was upon the camp. Small cooking fires were springing to life along the flat bordering the river, and some of the trappers — those without squaws — well into their cups were bringing in wood for the night's bonfires.

Abruptly Kit came to attention. Through the late amber haze he saw Running Around, astride one of the horses he had earlier delivered to the chief's lodge, slowly approaching. Behind him came Singing Grass, head lowered, leading a second horse upon which were her belongings — a small bag of miscellaneous items, her clothing, and the skins for a teepee which were customarily a part of the ceremony — a sort of dowry with some tribes. Hung over her free arm was her blanket.

Carson remained motionless where he sat, as was also customary at such moments. Running Around, stoically ignoring the stares and comments of trappers and squaws alike as he and his daughter passed by, pulled to a halt in front of the lean-to and waited for Singing Grass to draw up beside him. Kit's pulse quickened, and his heart lifted with pride as he looked at the girl. She was dressed in a newly made doeskin that was decorated not only with beads but with silver ornaments as well. The moccasins that were on her feet were also new. She had pulled her jet black hair back from her face, braided it, and allowed the two strands to hang lightly across her shoulders. A radiance glowed in her eyes, while the soft youthfulness of her skin took on a pale gold sheen from the nearby fires.

Pausing only briefly, she dropped the rope of the pony she was leading, moved past Running Around. Stepping up to Kit, she laid her blanket in his lap, signifying that his teepee was now her teepee and thus accepting him as her husband. Turning slowly, solemnly, she sat down beside him. The old chief nodded in satisfaction and, moving forward, grasped the edge of the blanket affixed to the front of the lean-to as a flap and let it fall into place, thereby shielding the newlyweds from the eyes of outsiders.

"It is done. I have been true to my word," Carson heard Running Around say as he took Singing Grass into his arms and held her close.

Chapter Eleven

It was hard on midnight and Monte Rinehart, unable to sleep, sat in his lean-to, staring off into the night, his only companion a half empty lard can of whiskey he had earlier purchased from one of the traders. There was still some activity in the camp, but on the whole things had quieted considerably. The sense of loneliness, of desolation, had entered his consciousness when he had seen the young Arapaho girl enter Kit's lean-to and had seen the improvised flap, like a curtain closing him out of his friend's life forever, drop into place. If things had gone right, he thought bitterly, he too would have a beautiful woman to hold in his arms, to cherish and call his own, and make love to. But luck had not been with him. He had been granted only a taste of paradise and then cast into the darkness of frustration.

He wondered if he had a son — or perhaps it would be a daughter. Monte had tried not to think about it, but there were times, as now, when the memory of Dolores crept back into his mind from the deep recesses where it was stored and filled him with a vast emptiness. Had Dolores married the man her brother — *goddamn him to hell!* — had chosen for her? Or was she at loose ends, perhaps thinking of him as he was of her? She too — like Kit's Singing Grass — would still be young, and chances were she had taken a husband, if not the one Luis had picked for her, another of her kind. But she could be waiting for him. Monte savored that possibility as he took a pull from the can. It could be. He reckoned there was only one way he'd ever know — return to Taos one day and find out. Yes, that was the answer, and maybe then he could either get her out of his mind once and for all or have himself the wife he had dreamed of. Taking another swallow from the can, Monte lay back on his blankets. That was the only way, short of death from an Indian's arrow or rifle ball, that he would ever find peace from remembrance.

"Why is your friend sad?" Singing Grass asked a few days later as she and Kit were strolling across the meadow that lay a short distance from the flat where the rendezvous, now approaching a conclusion, was still noisily under way.

A change had come over Rinehart, Carson agreed. There had been times in the past when he had become aware of a quiet, almost sullen dejection in the man and suspected it had to do with Taos and what had occurred there, but he respected Monte too much to pry — and Monte had not been inclined to unburden himself by talking about it. Now the dark moodiness had appeared again, and Kit was certain it was brought about by recollections of Dolores.

"He grieves for a woman he knew and wanted very much, but lost," Carson replied.

"To death?"

"No, to another man. It is a long story. I will tell you of it another time."

"If he is so sad for a woman, why does he not take an Indian girl to wife, as you did? I know of many Arapaho maidens who would be proud to become his woman and make him happy."

Kit gave that thought. "I shall tell him of your words. . . ."

Singing Grass said, her features quiet and serene but mischief dancing in her wide, dark eyes: "Have I not made you happy, Kit Carson?"

"More than any man could hope for," he said as they continued, now barely hearing the hubbub of the encampment.

Singing Grass had not only pleased him but surprised him by her knowledge. The education of an Arapaho maiden, she had explained, began when she was three or four summers old. They were taught by the older women of the tribe how to sew, make garments for herself and her brave, as well as for the children she would bear. She had to become proficient in the art of cooking and must learn to recognize the wild plants and roots in the fields and woods that were edible and could be relied upon in times of famine. It was necessary she also become expert in the handling of hides — cleaning, scraping, and working with them until they were as soft and pliant as cloth.

The lean-to Kit had rebuilt for their use had been acceptable for that first night only. Singing Grass had then insisted they erect her teepee, declaring that it would shame her before her people to live in such a lowly shelter. A teepee was the home of a woman, the center of her life, she pointed out. It was a place for building good memories of many things, for talks with her husband and her friends — a quiet abode for lovemaking and the birthing of children. Too, a woman needed privacy to do her sewing and to take care of personal things — not to mention meditation and communicating with the gods. Although Kit saw little need for putting up a teepee, there being but a few days left before the encampment broke up, he gave in under the plethora of reasons presented him and, going back into the woods, cut the necessary lodge poles and erected the shelter.

There was also the matter of her obtaining the items she felt they would be needing in the days to come when on a trapping expedition. Kit had always traveled light, keeping his gear to an absolute minimum, but he realized that with a wife this could no longer be the rule. For her to improvise, as he often did, would be demeaning in the eyes of other squaws, and he could not permit that. Thus he arranged with Fitzpatrick to give her whatever she wanted, after which he would settle up.

Singing Grass's cooking, while wholesome and nourishing, might involve prairie dog stew and the like and so was not entirely to Carson's liking. However, it came to him that he would — very subtly, of course — have to show her how to prepare the food that was more suitable to his taste. Prairie dog was acceptable only when all else was unavailable, as were songbirds, roasted crickets and grasshoppers, snakes, and the like, along with roots, certain plant leaves, and various tree barks pounded into a meal. He had in fact savored them all — but only in times of dire starvation when nothing else was to be had. As a consequence it was necessary that he lay in a stock of standard provisions sufficient for both from Broken Hand Fitzpatrick's supply which, in turn, called for an extra pack mule before all the preparations were completed. He now had a woman, two horses, and two pack animals. Kit realized this was more personal property than he had owned in his entire life and had incurred with it an equal amount of responsibility.

They had turned back to the encampment after spending an hour or so in the shadowy solitude of the forest and found Monte with Louie Pineau and his Shawnee squaw awaiting them at the teepee. The Frenchman had just arrived from the Brown's Hole country, he told Kit after greeting him and congratulating him on taking Singing Grass as his woman.

"There is poor hunting there, *mon ami*," he said. "It will be wise to go another place this season."

"We're hearing a lot about the Yellowstone," Rinehart said. "Could be we ought to head up that way."

Carson nodded, sliding a glance at Singing Grass. She and Little Bird, as Pineau's wife was called, were eyeing each other warily, the current hostility between the Arapahoes and the Shawnees manifesting itself in that moment. Abruptly Singing Grass turned and entered the teepee, leaving Little Bird to wander over to Rinehart's lean-to and find a seat on his blankets.

"I'm willing to go wherever the beaver are," Kit said finally.

Pineau agreed, bobbing his head vigorously. *"Bon! Bon!* It is settled."

"Sure is," Monte said, smiling. "Going to be like old times . . . us three working together."

It was good to see the New Yorker smile again, Carson thought. Monte had shown little happiness these past days even though he had noticed his friend, well liquored up, participating in the dancing, the wrestling and other games, and on several occasions going off into the brush with one of the squaws. But it had appeared he was doing it all with a minimum of enthusiasm and more as a means for passing the time. Perhaps the Frenchman's presence would now cheer him up a bit.

"Something I've been wanting to tell you, Kit," Rinehart said as they settled on their haunches beside the teepee. "Ought've a couple of days ago, but you've been a mite scarce."

Carson smiled. He had somewhat neglected the rendezvous, preferring to spend his time with Singing Grass. The day would soon come when he would be gone for its entire length, perhaps even longer, and he was making the most of the hours with her while he could.

"And so it should be!" Pineau declared. "Kit is on . . . how you say . . . a honeymoon! Why should he waste time with men . . . *n'est-ce pas, mon ami?*"

Kit nodded, but it grieved him to think that taking a squaw bride had come between him and Monte. It was, he hoped, only temporary.

"Go ahead," he prompted.

"Well, it's that bastard . . . Seth Grieg. We figured maybe he was dead . . . he ain't."

Carson came to quick attention. "You sure it's him?"

"Ain't no doubt . . . and he's here. Seen him down by the river."

Immediately Kit got to his feet. Hanging his rifle in the crook of an arm, he said: "Take me to where you last seen him. Aim to settle with him right now . . . I don't want him trailing along behind me this winter, looking for a chance to put a ball in my back or a tomahawk in my skull. Expect to have my hands full keeping the Blackfeet from doing that."

The three men struck off through the

sprawling camp, now beginning to break up as trappers and Indians alike prepared to take their leave, and made for its upper end, angling as they did toward the river.

"Kidder with him?" Kit asked.

"Didn't spot him," Monte replied, "but you can bet he's around somewheres. I guess they sort of retired on all them plews they stole from Captain Gantt . . . would've brought them a big pile of money."

"They headed off down the Arkansas with several bales in a canoe," Carson explained to Pineau. "Figured the Crows or maybe some other tribe lifted their hair. Seems not."

"It is the way of life," the Frenchman said with a shrug. "The evil ones . . . they survive."

"Don't see his lean-to," Rinehart said, slowing his stride. "Son of a bitch was there by them rocks. Gone now."

Kit swore silently, glanced around. "Could've moved to somewhere else in the camp," he said and, pivoting angrily, started back through the collection of shelters and teepees. It was not likely Grieg had thrown in with any of the Indians who had raised their lodges outside the encampment proper.

Seth Grieg had not only moved but had apparently departed the rendezvous entirely. That became evident after Kit, with the aid of Monte and Louis Pineau, made several fruitless sweeps through the camp and failed to turn up the man.

"Expect when he seen me he figured you were around, too," Rinehart said, "and showed the white feather."

That Seth Grieg was a coward was not news to Kit. It merely disturbed him more. Seth, still carrying a grudge and a scar from their encounter near Taos, would eventually find the opportunity he sought to even the score — and that would be at a moment when least expected and when the advantage was clearly his. Carson had hoped to settle with the man, as he'd mentioned, before the season began — but he could forget that now. He'd simply have to be on the watch for Grieg just as he would be for hostile Indians.

"Looks like some palavering going on over at the Hudson's Bay people's tent," Monte said as they started back, pointing to the gathering in front of the fur trader's display of goods.

He hurried toward it. Kit and Pineau quickly followed. As they drew near, John McCoy, standing in the back of a wagon speaking to the trappers, paused and beckoned to Carson.

"Kit . . . want you to hear this. Just got

210

word that the Blackfeet have gone on the warpath up in the Yellowstone country . . . killing and scalping every white man they can find. Been some talk about a brigade heading up that way. If you're one of them, best you and the others forget about it, leastwise till things settle down some."

"Where'll you be going?" someone in the crowd asked.

"Back to Fort Hall. I figure trapping along the Snake will be good this winter."

Carson doubted that. He had hunted along the deep cañon country in the spring with Monte and several other men and found the take unsatisfactory for the effort involved. The Snake was overworked, to his way of thinking, and it would be at least two years before it could be trapped profitably again.

Moving up to shake John McCoy's hand and thank him for past favors, Carson, with Frenchy Pineau and Rinehart, returned to his teepee where he found that Singing Grass had prepared a meal for them — making it clear that she cared neither one way or another if Little Bird took a place among the guests.

Later, when the supper of stew, corn cakes, and coffee was over, the three men settled down on the folded blankets outside the lodge to smoke and talk. Little Bird had again retired to Rinehart's lean-to, making no comment on the repast provided by Singing Grass who busied herself within her teepee.

"What do you think about them things McCoy said?" Monte asked. "We still going up on the Yellowstone?"

"Still the best bet," Kit observed, "even if the Indians are raising hell. Sure not going back to the Snake."

Pineau nodded as he puffed on his pipe. "I am agree with you. Now, I understand my countryman, Lucien Fontenelle, is assembling a company to go there. I am certain we would be welcome."

Fontenelle — Kit had heard of the Frenchman. He was now a partner in the American Fur Company, it was said, and usually traveled with Andy Drips, a man whom Carson also knew slightly.

"Fine with me," he said. "When does Fontenelle aim to move out?"

"Tomorrow . . . or perhaps the next day. Of this I am not certain, but I will see him, tell him of our wishes, and learn of the departure."

There were over a hundred men in the party, many of whom had their squaws with them. Fontenelle's plan was similar to that set forth by Carson the previous time he had ventured into Blackfoot country: half of the men would run trap lines, the rest would serve as camp watchers entrusted with the job of protecting the horses, mules, provisions, and of course the squaws. The party proceeded with caution, bearing in mind John McCoy's warning relative to the fierce Blackfeet but, when they reached the Yellowstone River, they had seen no signs of the warring tribe and so began at once to work their traps.

As the weather became crisp and the onset of winter became more evident, the brigade intensified their efforts, taking many beaver on the Yellowstone and its tributaries, moving on then to the Bighorn which they worked thoroughly. Finally, when icy winds carrying snow began to sweep down from the north, they went into winter quarters on the Powder River, not far from a village of Crow Indians who, while friendly, needed to be watched closely and kept away from the horses and mules.

That first evening in camp while they were eating, Singing Grass said: "The Blackfeet have gone from here."

Carson stared at her, glanced then at Monte. It had become a custom for them, working side by side, to take their meals together. The arrangement pleased Singing Grass who still had hopes one day of lining Rinehart up with an Arapaho girl.

"How do you know that?" Kit asked.

"Old Duck, one of the Crow women, told me of it. She came to visit."

"You will welcome a Crow woman into our teepee but not the wife of my friend, Louie Pineau . . . ?"

"The Crow woman is not a Shawnee," Singing Grass replied with simple logic.

"Did you watch that she did not steal? It is their way as it is for their men to steal horses."

"Old Duck did not steal. I am aware of their ways, also. It was told to me by my people."

"I am pleased you were watchful. What about the Blackfeet? Where are they?"

"They have moved on to the big river . . . and beyond it," she said.

"The Missouri," Monte murmured thoughtfully. "Explains why they ain't bothered us none. Now, I would like to know what made them move. Sure wasn't because they seen us a-coming and got scared, or because there ain't no beaver or game around."

Singing Grass had done well in learning English from Kit. She understood Rinehart's oblique question, shook her head. "There has been a sickness among them . . . the disease that leaves holes in the skin if it does not kill."

"Smallpox!" Carson said. "That's plenty bad. It still don't seem like a good reason to pull stakes. Couldn't find a much better place than right here."

"The old ones said a bad winter is coming, that they should seek a place of better shelter from the storms, and one where there would be grazing for the animals."

"Guess that explains everything," Kit said. "We ought to tell Fontenelle about it, let him know what we'll likely be up against, and get set for it."

"I'll pass it on to him," Monte said, rising and going off in search of the Frenchman.

The Blackfeet were right. It was one of the worst winters Carson could remember and, while his lodge was warm and comfortable thanks to Singing Grass, the animals all suffered considerably, not only from the intensely cold weather but from the lack of forage which, toward the last of the days when the bitter onslaught swept in from Canada, consisted mainly of branches broken from trees and pounded into a pulp for them.

Spring eventually came, changing the spotless white flats, valleys, and the stark forests into fresh green. Fontenelle ordered an immediate move, and the party struck camp and headed back to the Bighorn River and other streams in its area where hunting had been good, with their ultimate goal being the Three Forks of the Missouri. They traveled slowly, taking pains to do a thorough job with the traps, and it was well onto summer when they reached the country that the Frenchman had in mind and turned up the North Fork. Scarcely had the entire party got strung out along the brushy, winding stream when word came rushing down the column that brought it to a stop.

"Blackfeet . . . a big village!"

Pineau, who had been riding forward with Lucien Fontenelle, hurried back to Kit with a request from the Frenchman that he take several men and go ahead, see what they were up against. Kit, with Monte and Pineau, swung up beside the company leader when they drew abreast. Fontenelle was speaking with a stranger, evidently the person who had warned him of the Indians.

"Not sure the village is Blackfeet," he said in his rich, southern accent. "Like to know for certain about that . . . and if it is, how large? Mister Harden, here, tells me it is very large . . . but that's contrary to what the

Crows told us, so I need to know the truth. Take a good look . . . I'll wait a bit then follow with the rest of the company."

Carson, his scouting party now enlarged by the addition of Harden, rode on at once. He had taken time, however, to tell Singing Grass of what he was to do.

"I do not know how far ahead of us they are," he explained, since this would be the first time that they would be apart. "It is possible I will not return for several days. If that is the way of it, do not fret. I shall miss you."

"I shall miss you also," the girl said. "Have a care, my husband."

The Indians Harden had seen were Blackfeet Kit saw when they reached the camp that next day, and it was a large one, giving lie to the words of the Crows that the dreaded smallpox disease had all but wiped them out.

"Going on the warpath, too," Monte pointed out as from the edge of a band of timber they watched the braves streaking their faces with ocher and breaking into frantic dances while brandishing their rifles or some other weapons overhead.

Kit swore softly. "Means they've already spotted us."

"And plan to be waiting," Pineau finished.

"No doubt about that."

The squaws and the old men, with the children, appeared to be readying the village for a move to a safer place, some distance away probably from where the ambush was to be laid.

"Best we get to Fontenelle quick . . . let him know what we'll be up against," Carson said and, returning to where they had left their horses hidden among the trees, they mounted and rode hard to meet the oncoming party.

Fontenelle listened to the report, nodding his head slowly as Carson, aided by Rinehart and Pineau, outlined the situation. When he had finished, the company leader stroked his beard thoughtfully for a time and then spoke.

"Hunting is too good for us to let ourselves be driven away by these Blackfeet . . . there is plenty here for them and us, too. I say we fight, let them know we are determined to stay."

A cheer went up from the trappers, signifying their approval. Fontenelle turned immediately to Carson. "I am told that you are wise when it comes to such matters as war with the savages."

Kit frowned, shrugged. "Can't say that I agree much with that. I'm willing to do what I can."

"Good. It will be you who is in charge. How many men do you want for your army?"

Carson frowned again at the military implication and then grinned. "Forty or fifty'll do . . . long as they've got plenty of powder and lead."

"Each man can draw what he feels he needs," Fontenelle said. "When will you leave?"

"Soon as everybody's ready. It'll be better to do our traveling at night . . . can keep from being seen by any sentries they may have posted."

At dark that day they left and reached the Blackfoot village without incident. The braves were still making war preparations, and the old men and squaws had yet to finish their moving to the new location.

"Scatter out, a length apart," Carson ordered, motioning to his men to take up positions with six or eight feet or so separating them in a line. "When I give the word, charge. We'll catch them not looking."

They had halted in a thin band of trees just below the Blackfoot encampment and, delaying until he figured every man was in place and ready, Kit shouted the signal. Bent low over their horses, the line of trappers surged out of the trees and began to race across the strip of open ground separating them from the village — firing their rifles as they did. A half dozen braves went down under the first volley, equally as many at the second. But by then the Blackfeet, well over a hundred in number, had recovered from their surprise and were snatching up their weapons, leaping onto their horses, and leveling a return fire, all the while retreating steadily.

More Indians fell as the trappers continued to trigger their rifles, and a few of them sagged in their saddles or fell from their horses when bullets and arrows found their marks. But they rushed on, gained the encampment. Many of the trappers left their mounts and, knives out, began to scalp the dead and finish off the wounded with tomahawks, after which they collected the scalp lock. Carson shouted for them all to press on, continue the pursuit of the braves. Shooting on the part of the trappers had diminished to an alarmingly low volume due to the time needed for reloading by those who were continuing the charge, and those on foot who were occupying themselves avenging past wrongs by Indians, fancied or otherwise.

"Fall back!" Carson yelled when the forward drive stalled for lack of fire power and the Blackfeet, recognizing the change, turned and, filling the air with shrill, nerve-shattering yells, began to mount a charge of their own.

The trappers retreated grudgingly a short distance and then, reinforced by the men who had dismounted and ceased firing while they satisfied their lust for blood and scalps, took up the fight. Again the Blackfeet gave way, but Carson, aware that ammunition was now running low despite the precautions he'd insisted on, did not resume the assault.

Monte, taking refuge behind a rocky mound at the edge of the village while he rammed powder and ball into his rifle barrel, shouted: "We going to make a stand here? There sure is a mess of them redskins!"

"Keep falling back," Kit replied in a voice that could be heard by others. "We'll need help from Fontenelle and the rest of the camp."

Moving constantly, the trappers retreated to the band of trees from which the attack had begun. Kit, cutting his horse in and out of the aisles between the timber and rock, continued shooting, shouting at his men to do the same. Fontenelle would hear the gunfire as it drew nearer, he figured, and, concluding that things were not going well, would come with reinforcements. But the retreat must be speeded up. Kit could now see horses filtering quietly and hurriedly among the trees, not only to the sides but behind him and the trappers as well. Suddenly the buckskin-clad man to his right went down as his horse tripped over an exposed root. The trapper yelled, tried to kick clear, but the weight of the fallen animal was on his leg, and he lay pinned to the ground.

Carson left the saddle in a long jump when he saw the man struggling to free himself with no success — saw also three Blackfeet, knives drawn, rushing in to finish off and scalp the trapper. Not breaking stride, Kit leveled his rifle at the nearest of the braves and triggered a shot. The Blackfoot threw up his arms and fell from the saddle as the ball drove into his chest. Reaching the trapped man, Carson snatched up his Hawken to shoot again, but the braves had veered off.

Turning quickly to the struggling horse, Carson avoided its flailing hoofs and, grasping its headstall, got the animal to his feet. Helping the trapper to rise, he wheeled, picked up his own rifle and, as the rescued man remounted his horse and raced off into the trees, dropped back to where he'd left his own animal. Carson swore deeply. His horse, frightened by the shooting, the confusion, and the pungent smell of gunsmoke now hanging in the air, was trotting off into the forest. On foot, rifle unloaded, he headed for the nearest rocks as two braves, noting his predicament, whirled their ponies about and started for him. Grasping his tomahawk, Kit prepared to defend himself. In that moment, one of the mountain men, seeing Carson trapped and in a desperate situation, rode in close, yelled for Kit to swing up behind him, and then hurried on to overtake the retreating trappers.

The deadly game of shoot and fall back continued throughout the day, and then near dark Fontenelle with twenty or so men arrived. The retreat halted, and the Blackfeet, countering the resistance, moved into a scattering of large rocks and began to snipe at the trappers.

It became quickly evident to Carson that they were wasting ammunition in returning the Indians' fire and regrouping his forces — now considerably larger — mounted a fresh charge. For a brief time it was a matter of furious encounter, with many hand-to-hand combats in which knives and tomahawks took their toll of both sides, while elsewhere among the trees the crackling of rifles was a steady sound. A score of Blackfeet went down to be immediately scalped, while a similar number of trappers met with a like fate.

And then abruptly it was over. The braves,

seeing they were fighting a losing battle, began to retreat. Shouts went up from the trappers, and several hurried off to camp with the report that the fight was over, and in all likelihood they would have no more trouble from the Blackfeet.

Carson, with two dozen or so men still working to drive the snipers from the rocks, was not all that certain. The Blackfeet were not only fierce fighters but zealous guardians of the area they considered their own. He could not see them giving up despite the defeat they had sustained.

He started to call out, warn his over-confident men to use caution as he knelt to reload his rifle. Motion directly ahead caught his eye. A tall brave, resplendent in feathers, bead-decorated buckskins, and war paint, had stepped from behind a tree. Kit dropped his rifle, reached for his knife, and started forward. The Indian coolly raised a hand, palm outward, and shook his head.

"I know of you, Kit Carson," he said, "and that you speak my tongue, so hear this. This is not the end for the Blackfeet. No longer do we think of the white men as gods with great power as once we did. We know now they are only evil. Someday soon we will meet again, Kit Carson, and it will be many of the white men who die."

Abruptly the brave, evidently a chief or a subchief, turned away and, throwing himself onto his horse, rode off into the forest, hazy with smoke. Carson's eyes followed the brave until he was lost among the trees, and then, after he had disappeared, Kit continued to watch. The Blackfoot's words of warning were like a fireball in the night. They foretold what was to come, what could be expected. The first white men had treated the Indian peoples well — *as gods with great power,* the brave had said — but that had changed. A flood of greedy men had come into the country, taking what they wanted by whatever means necessary with no thought as to the rights of the tribes.

Kit, having reloaded the Hawken, swung onto his horse and, cutting about, joined the stragglers now heading back to camp. The brave no doubt had spoken the truth. They would hear from the Blackfeet again as would other parties of whites who came later.

Pausing long enough to accept the congratulations of Lucien Fontenelle and making certain that Monte Rinehart and Louie Pineau had come safely through the fight, Carson continued on to his teepee, a sadness filling him as he considered the plight of the Indians. They could never win, of that he was sure. The tide of people flowing into the

West from the States was inevitable and un-stoppable, even as night followed day. Where it would end for the Blackfeet, the Arapa-hoes, the Sioux, and all the other tribes he could not imagine.

Moving slowly on, the wailing of squaws grieving for their trapper husbands, an eerie, nerve-wracking discord lifting above all other sounds of the camp, Carson made his way toward his lodge. The sight of Singing Grass standing before it awaiting him quickly washed away his troubled thoughts and, hur-riedly dismounting, he crossed to her side. She was smiling, and there was a glow ema-nating from her features that matched the deep softness in her eyes. Throwing his arms about the girl, Kit held her close for a long moment, thanking God above that he was alive and grateful to have returned and then stepped back as she pressed gently against his chest.

"There is this I must tell you," Singing Grass said. "I would have done so those days before, but I wished not to burden your thoughts when there was fighting to be done."

Kit frowned. "What is this you speak of?"

"I am with child. It will come in the sum-mer."

Carson stood motionless for a long breath

as surprise raced through him. Then, pivoting, he threw back his head and yelled as sheer joy and happiness overcame him.

Chapter Twelve

The party resumed trapping immediately, steadily working its way up the North Fork of the Missouri encountering no opposition from the Blackfeet. Notwithstanding, Carson now felt the need for greater caution after being advised of his coming parenthood by Singing Grass and took greater pains to avoid exposing himself unnecessarily. Such applied not only where Indians were concerned but to Seth Grieg, also, who could be anywhere in the area as well as to accidents while trapping. None of the three overtook him. In due course word was relayed by a passing company that a rendezvous would be held at the usual time that summer on the Wind River.

The news was welcome to Kit. The child was due to arrive about the time the gathering would occur, and Singing Grass would thus be in camp, comfortably settled and not on the move. There were, of course, many women with the party who could take care of her should the occasion present itself, but it would be better, Kit felt, if they were in the semi-permanency of the rendezvous which usually lasted for a month or so.

Monte Rinehart, who was as proud of the coming event as Kit, agreed with that thinking and, as the brigade veered from course and began to make its way across the mighty Teton Mountains and on to Wind River, he was as solicitous as Carson himself for the welfare of Singing Grass.

"You got a name picked out for the little button?" he asked one day as they were passing through a thin scatter of trees on the slopes of a mountain. "Or are you leaving that up to the mama?"

"Ain't decided yet, but I reckon it'll be up to me to pick one. Singing Grass tells me it's the custom of her people for the father to do the naming. Maybe I'll call him Monte if it's a boy."

Rinehart's jaw sagged, and his eyes filled with pleasure. "Now, that sure would be real fine, Kit . . . and it'd make me mighty proud!"

Carson nodded. "I figure you for my best friend, Monte, and having a son with your name will always remind me of the good times . . . and the bad ones . . . we've seen together."

"Been in a few of both, all right . . . and I ain't never forgetting none of them . . . 'specially the tights you've got me out of!"

Singing Grass, who was riding nearby,

smiled in her quiet way and asked: "Do you speak of the child?"

Kit nodded. "Monte was wondering what I would name it since it's my job to do it. I said my son would be called Monte to honor him."

Singing Grass smiled again and looked off into the distance. "I fear such cannot be, my husband," she said in Arapaho.

Concern filled Carson's lean features. "Why? Is there something wrong?"

"No. It is that we shall have a girl child."

"A girl!" Kit echoed, a broad grin erasing the lines in his face. "How do you know this?"

"I know," Singing Grass said simply. "Is it to be a disappointment to you?"

"No . . . never! I would like to have a daughter . . . a little one just like you."

The Arapaho woman settled back contentedly, relief in her dark eyes. Then: "How many days until we reach the place of the meeting?"

"Three, maybe four. Are you tiring?"

"Yes, but not greatly. I think that I should no longer ride my pony, however. A drag would be best now."

"You will have one for tomorrow," Carson said and late that day, when the party halted for night camp, with the assistance of Monte and the advice and suggestions of Louie Pineau who was no less taken with the idea of Singing Grass's presenting Kit with a girl child, he made a sturdy *travois* — as the Frenchman termed it.

When they reached the site of the rendezvous, they found it already well attended — even to the presence of an English nobleman named William Stuart whom Carson had met once before. Leaving the custom of cruising through the encampment to renew acquaintances until later, Carson erected the teepee for Singing Grass and saw to her needs which, she assured him, were few. The matter of having a child was a woman's affair, she told him, and sent him on his way to attend to his own business. Anyway, the baby would not come for days, perhaps weeks, and he should not permit the possibility of its arrival to interfere with trading and selling pelts and laying in provisions and other supplies for the coming season.

Kit did as he was bid. Joining with Monte and Frenchy Pineau, he went about the task of preparing for the next expedition. When that was done and Singing Grass continued to rest comfortably — now under the attention of several of the older squaws — they threw themselves into the activities of the gathering, taking part in shooting contests, wrestling matches, foot racing, and the like while all the while drinking their share of Broken Hand Fitzpatrick's good whiskey, leaving the Taos Lightning to those who found it more to their liking.

"Me and Frenchy had a look around for Seth Grieg while you was putting up your teepee," Monte said, as they paused before a display of rifles, powder horns, bullet pouches, and other weaponry. "No sign of him."

The trader behind his improvised counter studied them anxiously. "If you've got skins to bargain, I'll do you best," he declared.

He had arrived early, the man who said his name was Henry Oglethorpe advised them, in order to deal with the Indians and free trappers and get his share of pelts before the big fur companies arrived and set up their displays.

"Done all right, too," he said proudly, pointing to several stacks of baled beaver skins. "Most of these are from Indians."

"Sure seems to me like there's more redskins around this here rendezvous than I've seen at others," Monte observed as they moved on.

The thought had occurred to Kit also, and he wondered at the reason. Was it an omen of peace to come, or of greater resistance?

The tribes could be outfitting themselves to fight more effectively, trading their furs not so much for gewgaws and mountain liquor as for rifles and ammunition. Carson had the feeling that the latter was more likely. He had not forgotten the loathing words of the young Blackfoot warrior back on the Missouri's North Fork and later on that day spoke to Bridger and Fitzpatrick about it. Both agreed that matters were probably going to get worse between the trappers and the Indian peoples, but they had no solution for it. As long as there was a demand for beaver skins in the eastern and European markets, the hills would swarm with men fulfilling that demand. A man would simply have to keep a sharp watch on his backside as well as on the trail ahead of him if he was to keep his hair, Bridger said. The business of taking beaver had to continue.

The rendezvous broke up a short time after that. Singing Grass still was carrying her baby and Kit, reluctant to head back into the upper Missouri country, chose to go instead with Monte Rinehart and a half dozen other trappers to Brown's Hole in Colorado where there was a trading post. There he could leave Singing Grass in good hands while he worked along Green River.

Louie Pineau departed with his squaw after wishing Kit and Singing Grass well, lining up with a party who intended to trap the North Platte. They would meet again, the Frenchman assured them and, if they missed the christening of the child, he and Little Bird — still unforgiven in the eyes of Singing Grass for being a Shawnee — would certainly attend the child's first birthday celebration.

As the encampment gradually disintegrated with the usual conflicts between the exiting tribes, the rivalry of trappers, and the competition that had bordered on warfare involving the independent traders and the large fur companies, Kit struck his teepee. After making Singing Grass comfortable on the drag, he headed south with Monte and the other men, bound for Brown's Hole — a vast, deep Colorado valley some thirty miles in length and a third of that in width in places through which the Green River flowed.

At a point where a small stream generally known as Vermillion Creek junctioned with the Green, the trading post, called Fort Davy Crockett, had been built. It was a solid, low-roofed, three-roomed edifice boasting no stockade, there being only the rustic principal building with corrals and outbuildings hunched on a barren flat, with several small parties of Indians, usually Arapahoes, Utes,

Nez Percés, and Crows camped around it.

Singing Grass well withstood the journey, fortunately one of short duration. After erecting the teepee in a location convenient to the post and settling in his wife, Carson joined Monte who was looking after their animals. Together they went to talk things over with the factor and see if there were any parties being organized.

Kit found Fort Davy Crockett — frequently referred to by trappers as Fort Misery — in charge of an old friend's brother, Prewitt Sinclair, and his partner, Phillip Thompson. They were preparing to head south for northern New Mexico where the plan was to trade with the Navajo Indians. It would be an expedition covering but a short time, and Sinclair told Kit that both he and Monte were welcome to come along as there was talk of Kiowas being on the war-path.

Kit liked the idea very much but, before he agreed to sign on as hunter and guide, he wanted to talk it over with Singing Grass. She assured him there was no need to remain close, that she would be all right.

"The child will not come for a time," she said.

"Of this you are certain? I will not leave you alone if . . . ?"

Singing Grass waved him off firmly. "It has been said before that the bearing of a child is woman's work. You go. Besides, there are many of my tribe who will help me."

Carson, only partially convinced, joined with Monte and several other men making up the Sinclair-Johnson trading party and struck south from the fort for the country of the Navajos. They encountered no trouble, although they had word of Kiowas preying on wagons traveling the Santa Fé Trail off to the east of them.

The venture proved profitable for the two partners, and they returned with a large stock of colorful woolen blankets woven by the Navajo women which were much in demand in the cold Colorado climate as well as with a herd of thirty or so mules. Reaching the fort, Kit went immediately to his lodge. He found Singing Grass had been wrong for, as he entered the warm interior of the shelter, she was sitting on a folded blanket holding a baby. Smiling proudly, she looked up at him.

"You have a daughter, Kit Carson!"

Kit dropped to his knees beside her and took the small bundle into his arms. "You are well? She is well?" he asked, studying the small, round face in the soft wrapper intently. The child's eyes were closed, and he could not determine their color, but she had a wealth of soft, shining black hair, pale copper skin, and high cheekbones that were legacies of her mother.

"We are both well. You?"

"I'm fine . . . better than ever now!" Kit said unable to contain himself and, turning to the flap of the shelter, pulled it aside and stepped out.

"Monte! I've got a daughter!" he yelled.

The shout drew the attention of other persons within range of his voice, and all turned. Several smiled, amused at the sight of the bearded, buckskin-clad trapper, respected and feared throughout the mountains and plains, gently cradling an infant in his arms. Rinehart, talking with two men, wheeled instantly and hurried up. Kit, holding the baby carefully in one arm, drew back the coverlet for Monte to have a look at the child's face. The New Yorker whistled.

"Now, there's a right pretty sight! Fact is, she's prettier'n anything I've ever seen . . . and I've seen a heap of pretty things in my life, like the sun going down on a cloudy day, a whole mountain covered with purple flowers . . . but that little nubbin beats them all! You name her yet?"

"Ain't had time," Carson replied, turning

back into the teepee.

Rinehart, following, greeted Singing Grass and sat down on one of the folded blankets. He sighed, shook his head, and grinned. "Well, you sure can't call her Monte, not that I wouldn't be proud, but it just wouldn't be fitting."

Singing Grass looked quickly at Kit as he returned the baby to her. Some of the expressions used by him and Monte when speaking English often eluded her as her grasp of the language was still somewhat rudimentary. Carson translated, and her lips parted in a smile.

Then: "It is for you to say what she will be called."

Kit nodded to his wife. "I have thought, and I have decided. I have a relative who is very dear to me. She is called Adaline. Such will be our child's name."

"Adaline," Singing Grass repeated slowly, savoring the word. "It has the sound of flowers."

"That her name?" Monte asked, his Arapaho as basic as Singing Grass's English and, when Kit signified confirmation, added: "That's right pretty, too! A fine name for a fine little gal . . . Adaline Carson."

"Adaline Carson," Singing Grass echoed and, with the baby cuddled in her arms, began a low, sing-song chant as she rocked back and forth.

The arrival of a daughter changed Kit's way of life. When Sinclair and Thompson decided to dispose of the mules they had traded from Andrew Sublette, a brother of Milton Sublette who in partnership with Louis Valesquez had established a post on the South Platte, Kit elected not to go with them.

"Ain't hard savvying why you're aiming to hang around close," Monte, who was to be a member of the party, said. "If I had me a pretty little wife, and a humdinger of a baby like you got, I'd sure'n hell stick around my teepee, too!"

Kit nodded. "That explains it. And I figure to keep it that way till spring. I've got myself a job here at the fort keeping the folks in meat, so it ain't that I'll be loafing."

"Not likely if you aim to keep them from going hungry. Game's a mite scarce around here, I'm told. Now, have a care, old son, I'll be seeing you when I get back from this here mule drive I'm going on."

"I'll be here," Carson responded, clapping Rinehart on the shoulder. "Just you see to it that some redskin don't lift your scalp!"

That year's rendezvous was held again in

the Wind River country. While it was going on, Monte Rinehart, having assumed the rôle of a doting uncle, made a project of showing off tiny Adaline Carson to every person attending the encampment. When the rendezvous broke up in late summer, Kit and Monte joined the Bridger party, heading to the Yellowstone where they would set up for winter camp, trapping until thick ice finally prevented them from doing so.

It appeared that the cold months would pass pleasantly with no trouble from the Blackfeet since none had been encountered. But then, just as the new year turned, a group of men out hunting for meat came upon a Blackfoot camp. The word angered Bridger, and he immediately organized a band to attack the hostile tribe and drive them back into the hills before they could create any problems. Kit and Monte, among the forty-man war party Bridger headed up, were directed to take a portion of the force and command the left flank.

"Damn Blackfeet again!" Rinehart muttered as, cold and wet, they pushed on through the snow. "Figured we'd learned them a good lesson!"

Carson made no reply. He was recalling once more the words the Blackfoot brave had spoken that day on the North Fork of the

Missouri. He had not doubted what the man had said, and it appeared now that he had been correct in accepting it not only as truth but prophecy.

"There they are!" Monte called out a short time later. "We best sort of circle. . . ."

Before he could finish, rifles barked over to their right as several trappers opened fire. The Indians, gathered on the bank of a stream and evidently in the process of moving against Bridger's camp, were caught by surprise. They wheeled their horses and, plunging into the icy river, crossed and retreated into a heavily wooded island at its center.

The trappers followed swiftly but not fast enough. The Blackfeet had time to settle in and met Bridger's charge with a volley of bullets and arrows. A man a short distance from Carson fell dead, the one just beyond staggered and went down, badly wounded. The exchange continued for a time with the trappers being unable to tell if their shooting was effective or not, so well fortified were the braves. When darkness eventually began to envelop the country, Bridger called for a retreat to camp.

"We'll go after them again tomorrow . . . first thing before light," he said, when they were all together again. "Meantime, just to be safe, I aim to keep sentries on the job. Don't want none of them red devils sneaking up on us."

There was no need for the precaution. The night passed without incident and, when Bridger and his party reached the island in the center of the Yellowstone that next morning near daylight, the Blackfeet had disappeared.

"I reckon we got a-plenty of them," one of the trappers said, looking about at the blood smeared logs and rocks behind which the Indians had done their fighting, "but there ain't no bodies!"

Bridger pointed to a hole in the ice that covered the river. "Expect they dumped them through there," he said, staring off into the east. "That way they don't have to fool with the dead . . . and they ain't leaving them around for us to scalp. Boys," he added, shaking his head, "them devils ain't gone. They're still around . . . I can smell them. We'll sure need to keep a lookout on the job for a spell."

Jim Bridger knew whereof he spoke. Two weeks later the guard posted on a bluff a mile or so from camp rushed in with word that the Blackfeet were approaching — at least fifteen hundred warriors strong. Kit, at his teepee with Rinehart eating a meal of buffalo steak prepared by Singing Grass, swore quietly.

"Fifteen hundred braves," he repeated, "and there's only sixty of us!"

Rinehart shook his head. "I reckon the odds are really against us this time, old son," he said grimly.

Chapter Thirteen

"Kit . . . Rinehart . . . Owens!" Bridger called out, his dark features set in hard lines. "Want you with me. We'll have a look-see."

Immediately Carson and Rinehart, abandoning their meal, and the third man, Dick Owens, hurried to their horses. With the sentinel leading the way, they rode quickly to the bluff from which the sentinel had observed the Blackfeet. Reaching there, Bridger swore raggedly.

"Fifteen hundred for sure . . . and more coming," he said.

The Blackfeet had halted on the island in the center of the river that they earlier, in smaller numbers, had occupied. They were now busily engaged in erecting more substantial fortifications — an arrangement of poles, brush, and rocks that resembled a large teepee without the upper third.

"Reckon they mean business for sure," Owens commented dryly.

"Ain't no doubt of that," Carson agreed. "Best we start throwing up some fortifications of our own."

"Just what I was thinking," Bridger said

and, leaving the sentinel on the bluff again to keep a watchful eye on the Indians, departed with his party back to camp. "All we're going to have time for are breastworks," he said as they rode. "Kit, you take half the men, start cutting trees, and drag them into that clearing there in the front. I'll take the rest and get to bringing in all the logs and rocks we can find."

The seriousness of their situation was reflected in Bridger's voice and manner and upon their return the men, some assisted by their squaws, immediately set to work. By the end of the day a substantial wall stretched across the front of the camp and extended a short distance down each side. The rear was left open, not from choice but simply because there was not time or available materials to complete a circular fort.

That night Carson outlined to Singing Grass what she was to do if the trappers were overrun — a possibility that was almost a dead certainty.

"I have talked with Bridger," he said. "You and the rest of the squaws are to take the children and be ready to mount your ponies and leave when you are warned to do so."

"How will this warning come?"

"There is a young boy of twelve, one too young to fight. He will be with us. When the time comes when we can no longer stand against the Blackfeet, he will be sent to tell you so. It is then you must take our daughter and flee."

Singing Grass had listened intently. She shook her head. "An Arapaho woman's place is with her husband at all times."

"You are more than an Arapaho woman . . . you are my wife!" Carson said sharply. "You will hear me well, Singing Grass. I will not chance you and Adaline becoming slaves to the Blackfeet! You will go as I order."

The woman bowed her head. "So it will be, my husband. But where can we go? This is not a land I know, and one the other squaws perhaps will not know."

"Bridger told me there is a party of trappers down the river . . . two days distant. Go to them. Tell them of what has happened. They will know what to do."

The camp remained on the alert throughout the night and the following day, during which it was reported that even more Blackfeet had arrived to supplement the already overwhelming forces that occupied the island. Finally, on the third night, the sounds of a war dance reached the trappers, and they knew the attack would come the next morning. Bridger called the men together and briefly outlined what must be done. Well before first light every male in camp had taken a position along the line of breastworks with his rifle, pistol if he had one, knife, and tomahawk laid out before him. Powder, bullets, wadding, and ramrod, along with all other necessary items, were placed within easy reach.

At sunrise the sentry rode in hurriedly with the warning that the Blackfeet were on the move. In the heavy tension that settled over the camp following that, Carson took a moment to be with Singing Grass and their young daughter and then rejoined Monte behind the thick fortifications.

"You reckon this is going to be it?" an unusually sober Monte wondered.

"There's a mighty good chance of it," Kit replied. "I'm wishing now I'd left Singing Grass and Adaline back at the fort. They'd be safe there."

"Maybe," Rinehart murmured, staring off into the cold, gray light of the early hour. The tension had increased, and now a strange hush lay over the land — as if time had been suspended. "There's enough of them out there to overrun the whole damn' country."

"Probably'll try, if we don't stop them," Kit agreed. He threw a quick look along the breastworks, assuring himself that every man was ready.

"You ever going back to Taos?" Monte asked when Carson had resumed his position.

"Figuring on it . . . someday. Like to take Singing Grass and Adaline back there and show them off. Thought I might do it this coming summer if things worked out right. Now I ain't so sure. You?"

Rinehart shrugged his thick shoulders, brushed at his beard. There were bits of ice glistening on the surface of hairs. "Ain't sure I want to . . . but I reckon I'll go if you do."

"Here they come!" Bridger's voice was strong, carrying the length of the fortifications and on back to the squaws in the camp a hundred yards away. "Be goddamn sure you make every shot count! We ain't got no powder and lead to waste."

The Blackfeet, bent low on their horses, charged across the flat at breakneck speed. The riders in the forefront drew near, slowing as they saw the wall behind which the trappers had stationed themselves. At that the mass of several hundred braves came to a halt. Four more daring than the others, no doubt anxious to count coup, suddenly spurted from the ranks of the braves and came racing forward. A spatter of rifle fire, coming from somewhere near Bridger's position, broke out. All four of the Blackfeet reeled on their ponies and fell, their bodies bouncing limply when they struck the frozen ground.

Immediately a half a dozen or so of the men in the front, chiefs and sub-chiefs, drew together. There was a discussion, one well beyond the hearing of the trappers, of course, punctuated by much arm waving and gestures and then, as silence continued to hang darkly over the camp, the legions of Indians began to turn and move, withdrawing at least for the time.

"They ain't done!" Bridger warned. "Don't be fooled by them devils!"

Waiting until there were none to be seen, Bridger dispatched two men to the bluff with instructions to keep an eye on the Blackfeet and sound a warning when they began to return — which, Kit was equally certain, they would do.

"They ain't going to miss no chance to wipe us out like this," Bridger said. "They're over there now powwowing, trying to figure out a way to get at us. I reckon, if they don't think of circling wide and coming in on our hind side, they'll just up and charge us straight on . . . and hope the Great Spirit will sort of look after them."

"Sure going to be a pile of dead redskins laying out there if they do," Dick Owens said with a shrug.

"They can afford it . . . a hundred, even two hundred if need be. Means we best change our shooting habits. I don't want every man firing off his piece at the same time. That'd leave us with a lot of empty rifles and give them a good chance to come rushing in on us. When they charge, I want every other man to shoot while the fellow next to him holds his fire. Then it'll be his turn to pull the trigger while his partner's reloading. Pass that word down the line."

It was a good strategy, Carson had to agree, as they all settled down to await the assault. Under such an arrangement, the trappers could throw a continuing hail of bullets at the oncoming braves.

The day wore on, bitterly cold despite numerous small warming fires. The women cooked up hot meals and brought them to the men, which helped greatly. Around mid-afternoon the wind got up, bringing with it the smell of fresh snow. Still the Blackfeet held off. Late in the day Bridger made the short trip to the bluff alone, placing Carson in charge of the fortifications while he tried to figure out what was going on in the Indians' camp. He returned to report that all was quiet there. The braves were simply sitting and lying around their fires — also waiting.

"For what?" Monte Rinehart wondered.

"Can't be sure, but it could be for more reinforcements," Bridger replied.

A nearby trapper swore and spat. "Hell, they sure don't need no more! Enough of them out there now to eat us alive!"

"Who knows what them blasted redskins think?" another man observed sourly and fell to chewing on a piece of pemmican brought to him by his squaw.

The snow failed to come, and the chill wind died along with the arrival of darkness. Almost immediately the eerie yells and dull thumping of drums announced that another war dance was under way. The trappers remained at their posts throughout the night and, when the grayness in the east began to lighten, they prepared themselves again to repel a charge.

It came as the sun, no more than a circle of weak light beyond a thick overcast, made its muted appearance. The Indians came pouring out of the trees, howling and screeching and firing their weapons as they came thundering toward the trappers crouched behind their fortifications. Suddenly the charge slacked off, just as it had that previous day. A broad flare of light had appeared in the northern sky. It took on the shape of a fan — one of purest silver — and began to grow. Shouts went up from the ranks of the Blackfeet, now milling about uncertainly. Shortly the silver started to fade, and layers of clouds, some yellow, some green, others a pale violet, appeared, draping the sky like shimmering, fringed curtains.

" 'Tis the lights!" one of the Canadians said in an awed voice. "The great colored lights of the North!"

The delicately shaded clouds seemed to fade and then turn to more intense color. A broad band of red became visible, and momentarily the entire breathtaking display climbed higher into the heavens, hung motionless for a brief time, and slowly disappeared.

"The Indians are pulling out!" a voice shouted from somewhere along the fortifications.

Carson, standing motionless and fascinated by the spectacle, shifted his attention to the Blackfeet. They were turning away, moving back toward the island in the river where they had set up their camp.

"By George . . . they sure are!" Bridger declared. "It was them lights that done it. Must've figured they were a bad omen."

A cheer went up from the trappers stationed along the breastworks. Several rose and started for the camp to spread the good news among the women.

"Hold your places!" Bridger shouted in sudden alarm, halting the exodus before it became general and there was total desertion from the fortifications. "That bunch is tricky. They just might come back!"

The men returned to their places, some grumbling, others accepting the order stoically. Bridger waited out an hour and then sent Will Montgomery, one of his close friends upon whom he depended considerably, to the bluff for a look at what was taking place. Montgomery returned in only minutes.

"They're pulling out for dang sure!" he reported exultantly. "Them lights scared them plumb yellow! Seems most all of them've gone already, heading back the way they come, other's lighting out for Crow country . . . and all in a powerful hurry!"

Bridger nodded in satisfaction. "I reckon that's it then. We can get back to work now . . . they're gone for good."

Jim Bridger proved right. They saw no more of the Blackfeet that season and trapped with good success. When spring broke the icy grip of winter and the land turned fresh and green, they moved out, pointing for the summer rendezvous which was to be held this time near Horse Creek on Green River.

Kit was relieved to see warm weather come. Singing Grass had developed a persistent fever during the bitter months which he hoped would disappear in the summer. But it did not and, when Bridger proposed they return again to the Yellowstone country that coming season after the encampment broke up, he declined.

"Could be I'll join you later," he said. "I'm taking Singing Grass up to Fort Hall . . . her people are going to be close by. Aim to stay around for a bit and, if everything works out all right, I'll meet you on the Yellowstone."

"Good enough," Bridger said and glanced at Monte Rinehart. "How about you?"

Monte shrugged, grinned. "I reckon I'll be tagging along with Kit. Hell, somebody's got to look after him."

Singing Grass was happy at the fort and shortly began to improve. When he was certain that all was well with her, Kit with Rinehart and another trapper moved out, eventually located, and teamed up with Bridger. They worked the Missouri proper. It was while they were following its course northward that they encountered two trappers, both worn and harried looking, who stated they were members of the Gale party.

"Camp's about fifteen miles on up the river," one said. "They're in a bad fix . . . Blackfeet all around. We was able to get down in the water, slip by. . . ."

Blackfeet! Carson shook his head. Trouble with them was far from over — that was sure.

Bridger, in the lead with Kit and Monte Rinehart, moved out that same day. When they drew near enough to smell the smoke of Gale's camp, they spread out and cautiously made their way through the thick brush and trees to the clearing where the party had set up its shelters. Gale could not contain his relief when he saw them.

"Indians jumped us . . . got six wounded men."

"Couple of your men run into us downstream," Bridger said. "Told us you was in trouble."

"Ain't no doubt of that," Gale said. "Sure would take it as a favor if we could throw in with you. Maybe them redskins'd back off, leave us alone then."

"Not likely," Carson murmured.

The suggestion was agreeable to Bridger and the other men in his party, and the next day Kit and Monte, in company with a dozen other trappers, began setting traps as they worked upstream.

"Main party'll catch up with us," Carson had explained to his men, "so we won't have to double back."

The work proceeded smoothly, and then around midday a week later two of the trappers who had been somewhat in advance rode hurriedly into the camp that Kit and three other men were setting up for the night.

"Indians . . . them danged Blackfeet!" Tom Edwards, one of the trappers, shouted as he came off his horse. "They're nipping at our heels!"

"Took a couple of shots at us," his partner added. "We best get ready . . . they ain't far behind us!"

Immediately Kit ordered the half-prepared camp abandoned and, with their animals and gear and the remainder of the party which returned at that point, they drew off into the thick brush nearby.

"We ain't got much of a chance," Edwards said. "They got us outnumbered maybe three or four to one."

Kit nodded. "We're pretty well hid out . . . and they've got to come to us. Gives us the edge."

Almost in that same moment the first of the Blackfeet came into view. They were well within rifle range, and the trappers opened up at once. A half dozen braves went down.

Immediately the remainder drew back, fading quickly in behind the trees and rank undergrowth as they sought to get out of sight.

"Change around . . . keep them guessing where you are," Carson said. "They'll be trying again."

The men drifted silently off to new positions. One taking a misstep made a small noise. Instantly the Indians opened fire, aiming their shots in the direction of the sound. Kit cautioned his trappers to wait, to hold back. Emboldened, the Blackfeet appeared again. Carson hissed the signal, and the mountain men triggered their weapons. Several more Indians fell, bringing about another hasty withdrawal.

For the rest of the day, it was a matter of sniping, with each side taking pot shots at any moving target. One or two braves were hit, but so far none of the trappers had been hurt. A lull settled in around mid-afternoon, and Carson, suspicious, unwilling to believe the Blackfeet had given up, sent men off into the dense brush to see what was taking place. He could have spared himself the effort. Hardly had the scouts slipped off into the shadows when Monte yelled to him.

"Fire! The goddamn savages've set the brush on fire! They're aiming to burn us out!"

Kit glanced hurriedly about. They were

suddenly encircled, and the crackling of the flames was growing louder. Nearby, in a small clearing where they had concealed the horses and mules, there was a noisy shuffling about as the animals began to grow nervous. At once Kit sent three men to stand with them, do what they could to keep them calm. The Blackfeet, certain now that the trappers would be driven into the open where they would be easy targets, started to edge forward through the trees and growth beyond the flaming brush.

"Start shooting!" Carson ordered, as the heat from the fire began to make itself felt. "We're done for if we show ourselves!"

"And we're cooked good if we stay here!" one of the men added grimly.

The trappers, keeping well out of sight by making use of the trees, the brush, and the thick smoke boiling around them, began to pick off the braves, unable to see the white men because of their own efforts to dislodge them.

"The fire's dying out!" a voice called through the heavy pall.

Carson, puzzled, dropped back more into the center of the ring and looked around. The report was accurate. The crackling flames were dwindling, with only small pockets of fire visible here and there.

"Them Indians've gone too," another man said, emerging from the smoking brush. His face was soot streaked, and there were places on his buckskins where hot coals had fallen and left their marks. "Heard a couple of them talking. Said Kit Carson was a magic man . . . that you just stopped the fire."

Carson grinned. Whatever, he was amazed at their good fortune and deliverance from what appeared to be sure death by fire or bullet. He spent no time in pondering the miracle but quickly got his men together and rode hard for the main camp, some six or eight miles down the river.

Bridger met them as they came in. "Blackfeet?"

Kit nodded and related the incident. "Ain't no way I can explain why that brush just quit burning," he finished. "I reckon it was the hand of Providence."

Bridger agreed. "That's twicet now that something has come between us and them and turned them back, when by all counts they could've wiped us out. I'm beginning to think there is something magic about you, Kit, like them redskins said . . . but I sure ain't for pushing our luck around here no further. Come morning, we'll move on to Stinking Creek."

But there was no safety there. As they settled in, a Blackfoot sniper killed one of the Canadians that was in the party, and Bridger ordered a continuation of the move, pointing now for the North Fork of the Missouri.

"Doubt it'll be any better there," Carson remarked to Monte, opposing the location. "Way I see it, the Blackfeet are aiming to drive us out for good."

Kit's words proved prophetic, for not a day passed that the party was not fired upon. When it became apparent to Jim Bridger that they were gradually being surrounded by an ever-shrinking ring of determined Blackfeet who kept themselves cleverly concealed in the brush and offered no target for return fire, he elected to push hurriedly on.

"There's a Flathead village about four days on," he said. "They don't have no use for the Blackfeet either so, if we can get there, we'll be all right."

The Flathead village was where Bridger had said it would be, and they greeted the trappers with no show of hostility. He and Carson sat down for a smoke with the chiefs, detailing their troubles with the Blackfeet and asking for an escort to the Big Snake River. One of the chiefs agreed, and shortly the party was again on the move, eventually reaching their destination without interference where they spent the remainder of the season trapping.

By then Kit had become anxious to see Singing Grass again, fully recovered, he hoped, from her illness. Joined by Monte and Jack Robinson, a trapper with whom they had been working, they passed up the summer rendezvous and continued on to Fort Roubidoux, where they disposed of their furs.

"Me and Monte're heading on down to Fort Hall," Kit told Robinson. "Got my family there. You're welcome to come along if you're of a mind."

Robinson shook his head. "No, I think I'll hang around here for a spell. Could be I'll join you later."

At Fort Hall, Carson found Singing Grass better but far from well. Adaline, who scarcely remembered him, had grown even more than expected. Dissatisfied and worried with what he had found and upon the advice of the post's factor to seek better medical care for his wife, Kit loaded up his family and, with Monte and four other trappers who wanted to come along, pulled out on the long journey to Bent's Fort on the Arkansas.

Chapter Fourteen

"She feeling any better?" Monte asked, glancing at Singing Grass several days later when the party reached the Arkansas and were halting for night camp.

Carson, moving up to the drag upon which his wife lay, nodded. He had kept Adaline with him on his horse all of that afternoon to give Singing Grass as much rest as possible.

"Seems so. Be mighty glad when we get to the fort, though. I'm hoping she'll brighten up some then."

Monte nodded. "It'll be nice to see her pert again," he said, taking charge of Adaline so that Kit could get the shelter up. "Sure hoping we'll find a doctor there."

"Same here," Carson replied with a worried frown.

But their hopes were destined for disappointment. After leaving the four trappers behind who had decided to remain and engage in trapping for a time, they hurried on down the river and in a few days reached the walled, castle-like structure known as Bent's Fort. A number of Indian tribes had set up their teepees along the nearby Arkansas, among them, Singing Grass noted, a village of Arapahoes.

Entering the gate, Kit and Monte drew to a halt in the area customarily used by trappers lying over for a time. Leaving Rinehart to erect the shelter this time, Carson went immediately in search of William Bent or Ceran St. Vrain, the factors in charge of the post. Locating Bent, he asked about a physician. Although there was a distinct need for one, Bent told him, there was not one available.

"Have got a woman, a sort of a nurse. Name's Anna Balling. I'll send her over to see your wife, Kit . . . maybe she can help. Where're you camping?"

Carson stepped to the window and pointed to where Singing Grass still lay on the drag, listlessly watching Monte Rinehart get the lodge ready.

"I'll be with her," Kit said, anxiety filling his eyes, and started to turn away.

"Don't fret too much, Kit," Bent said, dropping a hand on Carson's shoulder. "This woman is as good as any doctor I ever saw. She'll be honest with you and, if she can, she'll have your wife up and about in no time. Meanwhile, I'm glad you rode in . . . been looking for somebody like you."

Carson paused. "Meaning?"

"We can use a hunter here at the fort. Pay is a dollar a day and found. Would please me to have you take the job, and I know Saint Vrain would feel the same."

Carson gave it but a few moments' thought. With Singing Grass ill, he shouldn't leave her for any extended length of time, and as a hunter for the fort he would seldom, if ever, be gone overnight.

"Can consider me hired," he said and then added: "That partner of mine, Monte Rinehart . . . can you use him, too?"

Bent nodded. "Sure can. We've got about a hundred people, counting travelers, to feed. Now things are running low. I'd like for you to start tomorrow . . . and there's no use in putting up that teepee. You and your family can live in one of the houses," he added, pointing to several small adobe structures built against the inside of the fifteen foot high wall. "Move your wife into any one of them that's empty. Your partner can stay in the bunkhouse. Now, go ahead while I roust out Anna Balling."

"I'm obliged to you," Kit said, shaking Bent's hand. "Soon as I get settled and my wife looked after, I'll be ready to go to work."

Hurrying into the open, Carson made his

way across the wide, busy yard, cluttered with the big freight wagons that regularly plied the route between St. Louis and the fort, corrals in which were horses and oxen belonging to trappers and pilgrims, many of whom could be seen off to the side bargaining for one thing or another. Squaws were plentiful, some in tribal dress, others favoring clothes imported from the States and traded for by their men. Children were equally plentiful, as were pets — dogs, cats, goats, and the like — wandering aimlessly about the compound.

"We can forget about the teepee," Kit said, moving up to Rinehart. "I've hired on to hunt for the fort. We'll be living in" — Carson hesitated, located an empty hut near the gate, and pointed to it — "in there. You'll do your living in the bunkhouse."

Monte clawed at his ragged beard. "Was just about to go rustle up some lodge poles. You say you've hired out to Bent and Saint Vrain?"

"Did. You've got yourself a job, too . . . if you want it."

Singing Grass had come to her feet and, taking Adaline by the hand, was walking somewhat unsteadily toward the adobe house — no more than one large room divided in half — that Kit had indicated. She appeared pleased with the idea. As was her way, she had said nothing one way or another, but Kit wondered if her pleasure came from realizing she no longer would be living isolated and in the open, or that he would not hereafter be away for long months at a time.

They settled in, carrying into the new quarters what few belongings they possessed while Monte led the horses and pack mules into one of the corrals. The nurse sent by Bent presented herself a half hour or so later, explaining that she would have been there sooner but had been delayed by one of the children who had fallen from the sentry platform along the wall and broken an arm.

A large, rawboned woman with a reddish complexion, large, capable-looking hands, and of obvious German ancestry, she squatted beside Singing Grass who was lying on a pallet of blankets and made her examination. Kit, with Adaline, remained in the adjoining room, which was meant to serve as a kitchen and dining area. When the nurse appeared a few minutes later, he rose quickly to meet her.

"What . . . ?" he began.

Anna Balling raised a hand to silence him. "I do not know. I'm not a doctor, but I recognize what is called female trouble. Your wife is very weak and tired and much in need of rest."

"It was a long trip down from Fort Hall."

"I understand. She told me that she has not felt well since the birth of the child."

Carson frowned. "I did not know that. She never spoke of it."

"She is an Indian. I have been around them for many years, and I know that an Indian woman will never admit a weakness to her husband."

"What do you think I ought to do?"

"Stay here for a while."

"Aim to. I've hired on to work for the fort."

"That's good. Rest will do much to cure her, and I have some medicine . . . a tonic that I had sent to me from Saint Louis . . . that I will bring over."

Kit thanked the woman and, when she had gone, hurried to where Singing Grass was now sitting up.

"It is time to prepare the food," she said. "I will. . . ."

"Not today you won't," Carson said, heartened by the German woman's words. "Tomorrow will be soon enough. It is your daughter and I who will prepare the food."

Singing Grass protested weakly and then lay back down, calling Adaline to be beside her. Kit, looking through their store of provisions to see what was on hand and what was needed, left the house and made his way to the fort's store where he purchased what he wanted. He paid cash for the articles selected but made arrangements with the man operating the business for Bent and St. Vrain to give Singing Grass anything she wished on credit. He would settle up once a month if such was agreeable.

The clerk, apparently already having been informed of Carson's standing, told him it was as he thrust out his hand.

"Name's Rostetter, Mister Carson. Sure is a pleasure to welcome you . . . and an honor. We've been hearing big things about you for a long time."

Kit grinned as he took the man's hand into his own. "Sounds like somebody's been spreading it on a mite thick," he said and, leaving the store with its well-stocked shelves, started back for his quarters — wondering, as he crossed the yard, where Monte Rinehart had gone.

Carson prepared a special treat for Singing Grass: fresh eggs fried with bacon, potatoes, bread, canned tomatoes, and preserved peaches. He fixed enough not only for the three of them but for Monte Rinehart as well — but his friend failed to put in an appearance. When the meal was over and Singing Grass and tiny Adaline — now losing her shyness in Kit's presence so that she unleashed voluble chattering in both Arapaho and English — had fallen asleep on the pallet, he went in search of the man.

He found Rinehart in the rear of the blacksmith shop, starting a bottle of whiskey with three other trappers. Seeing Carson approach, Monte grinned broadly.

"Howdy there, old son! Was coming over to see you. You know these fellows?"

Carson shook his head and accepted the hands of each while their names registered indifferently on his mind: "Gabe Jackson . . . Will Ames . . . Charley Fawcett."

"Glad to meet you," he said and brought his attention back to Monte. "Figured you'd maybe like to go talk about that job Bent's offering you."

Rinehart pushed his round top hat to the back of his head, eyed a young Ute squaw sauntering by. "Well, now, Kit, I ain't so sure I'm wanting the job. Never was no hand to tie down, stay put . . . it just ain't my kind of living. The boys here and me, we're cooking up a little sashay into the country around Fort Walla Walla. Gabe says we can do real good if we get up there early."

Kit made no reply. He could understand

Monte's feelings, but it grieved him to see his longtime friend and partner go. It was their first parting since Taos. After a moment he extended his hand. Rinehart pressed it firmly.

"Sounds like a right good idea, and I expect you'll do plenty good. Now, anything you need of mine, just say so."

"Between us we got a good outfit," Jackson said.

Rinehart, face tipped down, murmured: "Yeah, sure am obliged, Kit."

"When'll you be pulling out?"

"Morning . . . or maybe yet today . . . all in how we're feeling a couple of hours from now," Monte said, his attention again on the Ute girl. "Sure hope your missus gets better. I'll appreciate it if you'll tell her *adiós* for me . . . the little button, too."

"I'll do that," Carson said, the lost feeling still with him, "but drop by on your way out if you're of a mind. I'm saying it again . . . good luck . . . and have a care."

"Same to you, old son," Monte replied as Kit turned away and struck out across the yard for his quarters.

Reaching there and finding both his wife and daughter still asleep, Carson dug out razor, soap, scissors, a change of underclothing, and a towel and made his way to the scrub house he'd noted near the quarters itinerant trappers and other male travelers occupied. There he spent the next hour shaving off his beard, trimming his hair and mustache, and cleaning himself up in general. Finished, he returned the clothing he had removed along with his shaving and shearing paraphernalia to the adobe hut and, finding himself still at loose ends, headed out once more across the compound, this time in quest of a bottle of liquor.

He paused as an expensive-looking carriage, pulled by a fine team of four horses wheeled through the gate and hurried up to the post door. A thick coating of dust covered the vehicle and the animals, lending the impression they might have traveled a far distance that day. There were four persons inside, barely visible from the side through a heavy curtain of some sort of screen-like material.

Bent appeared in the doorway of the post and hurriedly moved to the carriage. The curtain was pulled back, and two Spanish women, one very young and both exceptionally beautiful with large, doe-like eyes and dark hair, emerged. As Bent helped them down, he beckoned to Carson.

"Kit, some folks here I'd like you to meet . . . fact is, they're from Taos, too. I understand you've spent some time there."

Carson stepped in closer. Removing his hat, he bowed politely. Bent nodded to the older of the pair.

"This is my brother Charles's wife . . . Maria Ignacia."

Again Kit lowered his head. "Ma'am."

"And this is her sister, Josefa. They're daughters of Don Francisco Jaramillo. Are you acquainted with the family?"

Kit smiled, eyes on the younger girl, as breathtakingly beautiful as was Singing Grass that day he had gone to speak to her father, only in a more sultry, exotic way. These were *ricos* — and not exactly in the circle of friends with whom he associated in Taos.

"I regret that I am not," he replied, "although I have heard of Don Francisco."

"And I have heard of you, *Señor* Carson," Josefa said, her eyes sparkling. There was an open friendliness about the girl that made her doubly attractive.

"Good things, I hope."

"Such is questionable," Josefa replied airily and, giving him a quick smile, allowed Bent to conduct her and her sister into the post.

Carson moved on, obtained his bottle of whiskey from Rostetter at the store, and once more returned to his new quarters.

Nurse Anna Balling was there. She had brought the medicine — tonic — and had instructed Singing Grass, again sitting up, to take doses of it regularly. When Kit entered the room, the German woman turned to him.

"I have explained to your wife that she must take the tonic regularly with each meal, but I'm not sure she understands."

Kit hunched beside his wife, repeated the nurse's instructions, putting them as best he could in the language of the Arapahoes. When he had finished, Singing Grass smiled.

"It will be so," she said. "It has the taste of rotting meat, but I will take it if I must."

Singing Grass smiled again and, laying back, closed her eyes. Kit studied her worriedly. He had not noticed how thin her face had become, and her body — once so young and full — now seemed little more than copper-colored parchment and bones. Rising, he followed Anna Balling into the yard.

"Will she be all right?"

The woman glanced off toward one of the corrals where a skittish horse was creating a disturbance. "I cannot say, but I think so. It would be better if you could get a doctor . . . she is in no condition to travel and be taken to one."

"I'll speak to Bent about it. Meantime, will you drop by often as you can? I'll have to ride out tomorrow but aim to be back by dark."

"You should make it a point to do that," the woman said. "I'll look in on her and the little girl as often as I can . . . but it would be a good idea to get someone to cook for you . . . one of the squaws perhaps."

"I'll try to get one."

"No need," the nurse cut in. "I know of one . . . a very reliable Kiowa woman. I'll bring her tomorrow and tell her what it is she must do. You might explain it to your wife ahead of time, so there will be no problem."

Kit assured the woman he would do so, thanked her for her help, and offered to pay, but she said such wasn't necessary. Bent and St. Vrain saw to her compensation. Singing Grass, when he told her about the Kiowa woman, wasn't too pleased with the plan and agreed to it only until she was better and could get help from one of her own tribe. But it worked out fine. Both Singing Grass and Adaline took to Yellow Bird, who was large and motherly, and within a few days the Kiowa woman had become an established member of the Carson household, leaving Kit with no worries along those lines to trouble him as he roamed the hills and plains in his search for buffalo and other game.

Time passed swiftly and smoothly for him after that first day, and he swung into his job with great pleasure. He missed Monte, however, and time and again wished his old partner had gone to work for Bent and St. Vrain, but he understood Monte's reason for not doing so. Mountain men were a footloose breed and resisted being tied down or compelled to adhere to any sort of schedule. To live they had to feel free and unfettered, able to do as they pleased, when they pleased. He was that way, Carson realized, and it struck him as strange that he had accepted William Bent's offer of a job so readily. It had to do with his sense of responsibility, he supposed, a throwback to his early upbringing, but he felt no pangs of remorse.

Hunting was good, and Kit had no trouble keeping the fort supplied with meat, although it was necessary at times that he and the two other hunters who worked with him were forced to range wide to locate the drifting herds of buffalo. It was after one such occasion, when arriving home late, that he found Anna Balling awaiting him. Alarm raced through Kit at the sight of the solemn-faced nurse and, moving past her quickly, dropped to his knees beside Singing Grass. Nearby Yellow Bird sat with Adaline on her lap, crooning softly.

"What is it? What's wrong?" he asked in a taut voice.

"I'm afraid it is the worst," the nurse replied. "She has a very high fever. Yellow Bird came for me around noon. I haven't been able to do anything about it."

Anna turned away wearily, shrugged helplessly. "We need a doctor so bad," she murmured.

Carson, crouched beside Singing Grass, leaned forward and took her face in his hands. Her skin was burning hot. When she opened her eyes, they looked deep set and unusually bright.

"My husband . . . Kit Carson," she whispered in Arapaho, mustering a faint smile.

Kit leaned closer, kissed her on the lips. "You must get well," he said, also speaking in the tongue of her people.

"No, I fear the time has come for the Dark Shadow to cover me . . . for I have seen the visions of the past." The words came slowly, haltingly, and were barely audible to Carson. "You . . . have treated me . . . with kindness . . . and care. For that . . . I have always honored you. That . . . I want you to . . . know."

"It is the same with me," Kit replied huskily.

"Have our daughter . . . grow up . . . among your people. Such . . . will be better . . . for her."

"You have my promise."

Singing Grass managed another weak smile. "You were always . . . agreeable . . . to my wishes . . . my husband," she said and closed her eyes.

Wah-nibe, his beautiful Singing Grass, died that night. Sorrowing, Kit turned her wasted body over to her people, knowing that she would prefer the burial ceremony of the Arapahoes to that of the white men. Accordingly, she was placed upon a bier of dry wood, dressed in her white doeskin and beaded moccasins and wrapped in a blanket which also contained all of her worldly possessions. Carson could not force himself to remain once the pyre was lit and, taking Adaline with him on his horse, rode off into the hills where he remained until darkness came.

Chapter Fifteen

Carson kept himself occupied all during the winter months, trying to ease the ache in his heart that the death of Singing Grass had caused — hoping, too, that Monte Rinehart would return and help him bear his grief. He could talk to him, unburden himself in a way that he could not with other acquaintances. But Monte failed to appear, nor was there any word of him with men coming back from the Northwest. More than once Kit considered the probability that Rinehart had been slain by hostile Indians. It was possible as there was much unrest, even among the friendly tribes who were becoming dissatisfied with the treatment accorded them by the white men and their far-away government.

Late in the spring Kit packed up Adaline and, boarding a Bent and St. Vrain wagon train headed for the States, prepared to fulfill his promise to Singing Grass. He would take the girl, now almost four years old, and leave her with relatives in Missouri — specifically his sister, Mary Ann, who had married a man named Robey. Let them rear and educate her, the funds for which he would gladly supply. A rough, frontier place such as Bent's Fort was not suitable for a motherless child, even under the watchful eyes of Yellow Bird, not when he was gone almost every day.

The family met him as requested, arrangements were made and, after a brief reunion which included a couple of days in St. Louis to see the sights, Carson bought himself a ticket on a steamboat going north up the Missouri that would start him on his way home. That first night aboard, when supper was over, Kit, lonely and dreading the many long days that were ahead for him before he was again on familiar ground, found himself a place at the ship's rail and lost himself in contemplation of the boiling wake aroused by the paddle wheel. A touch on the shoulder and a voice brought him around.

"Are you Kit Carson?"

Kit nodded, studied the speaker, a handsome fellow in the uniform of the United States Army. "I am."

"You will pardon me, but I have been referred to you by certain friends who think you might be in a position to help me."

"Can sure try," Carson replied.

The officer, a lieutenant from his insignia, was probably a year or two younger than Carson and had a sincere, engaging way about him. "I have been trying to locate a mountaineer by the name of Phipps to serve as a guide for an expedition into the Rocky Mountains. I have failed to find him, and I am wondering if you could give me some idea where he might be."

"Could be 'most anywhere," Carson replied. "Maybe I can serve you. I have spent my life in the mountains, and I doubt there is any place that I'm not familiar with."

The young officer thrust out his hand as a smile broke the seriousness of his features. "I am pleased to hear you say that, Carson. My name is John Frémont. Let's go to my cabin and talk things over."

When they had taken chairs in his well-appointed cabin, Frémont said: "My father-in-law is Senator Thomas Benton of Missouri, the leader of the Expansionist Movement." The officer spoke of the relationship, not in a sense of boasting, but simply as a fact. "Perhaps you have heard of him?"

Kit shook his head. "No, I'm afraid not. We don't get much into politics out where I live."

"Well, no matter. I might also add that I am married to the senator's daughter, Jessie. Do you have a wife, Carson?"

Kit waited while Frémont poured brandy from a bottle sitting on the table into the appropriate small glasses. "Was. I'm a widower now."

Frémont clucked sympathetically. "Sorry to hear that. Any children?"

"Got a daughter. Just came from leaving her with my sister and her husband to raise. Live in a town called Boone's Lick."

"I know the place . . . back down the river. Jessie and I have no children . . . fact is, we've only been married a year."

Frémont settled into his chair. "Would you be interested in hiring on as my guide? I've been commissioned to take a survey party into the Rockies by way of the Oregon Trail. The object is to map what is known as South Pass and record the height of the major peaks. I assume you are familiar with the area."

Kit, savoring the excellent brandy, nodded. It was a far cry from the native brew, *aguardiente,* the brandy available in Taos. "Been in and around there for a good many years, trapping and hunting. Truth is, this is the first time I've been away from there and back here . . . to civilization . . . since I ran off and joined a wagon train . . . was in 'Twenty-Six."

"Your qualifications are more than adequate. Are you interested in the job? Pay will be one hundred dollars a month."

Surprise and pleasure rolled through Carson. Not only would he be doing something he liked best — prowling through the mountains, exploring — but he would be getting well paid for it! "Can't think of anything I'd rather do more, Lieutenant."

"The name's John."

"And my friends call me Kit."

"Kit it is. Now, I have friends and equipment waiting for us at Kansas Landing. If it's agreeable, we'll strike out from there, go by way of Fort Laramie. Does that sound practical to you?"

"Best way far as I can tell now, but you never know about Indians. Today they can be friendly, tomorrow they could go on the warpath. I ain't one to run from trouble, but sometimes it's kind of smart to walk around it, just like you'd give a grizzly bear plenty of room."

Frémont chuckled. "We're going to get along fine, Kit! You've got just what I'll be needing . . . a good, level head."

The steamer docked a time later, and the survey party, assembled to begin the long march to South Pass, was waiting. Kit had no sooner stepped off the boat when Lucien Maxwell hurried up to greet him.

"Kit! What brings you here? Figured you was at Bent's Fort."

"I've hired out to Frémont. Aim to guide him to South Pass. I'll ask you the same."

"I'm working for him, too, as a hunter."

Carson was more than pleased to find he would be with Maxwell, also experienced in the mountain and plains country — and where Indians were concerned. John Frémont, he had come to realize on the way to the Landing, was a fine man, filled with enthusiasm for the job that lay ahead, but he suspected woefully short on practicality. Between himself and Maxwell they could perhaps prevent his making many serious mistakes.

Kit met the remainder of the two dozen or so members of the party the next day, among them Frémont's younger brother, Randolph, cousin Henry Brant, and his second in command, Clement Lambert. There was also present a tall, sour-dispositioned German named Charles Preuss who was the chief cartographer.

The company moved out near mid-June, following a trail that took them in a northwest direction until they reached the Platte River. On the Fourth of July they held a celebration where the river forked, Frémont treating the party to brandy and a full ration of food. He announced late in the day that he and Maxwell, with a half a dozen men, would split off and head for Fort St. Vrain on the Platte's south branch where he intended to buy mules. They would then rejoin the main party which he was leaving under the command of Clement Lambert with Carson, of course, continuing as guide as well as assuming Maxwell's chores as hunter.

The company continued on its way to Fort Laramie with no more than the usual incidents until one morning, as they delayed leaving to rest the animals, the sentry called out his warning that several riders were coming in. Carson, taking no chances, suggested to Lambert that he call an alert but a short time later advised the man it was unnecessary.

"Man in the lead's an old friend of mine . . . Jim Bridger," he explained.

Bridger rode in, his dark features lighting up when he saw Kit. Almost immediately he became serious. "Wherefor you headed?"

"Fort Laramie," Carson replied and explained the purpose of the mission.

Bridger clawed at his beard, wagged his head. "Well, you sure better get there fast. The Sioux and the Cheyennes have throwed in with the Blackfeet and are looking for trouble. The word's out that they're figuring to attack the rendezvous next month . . . wipe out every white man there. Kit, was I you,

I'd move these folks right along fast as I could."

Carson nodded to Lambert. "You can believe what he's telling me. Best we break camp and pull out." When Lambert had hurried off, Carson remarked: "I'm sort of worrying about Frémont and Lucien Maxwell now. They took a small party off down the south fork for Fort St. Vrain. You reckon they'll run into trouble?"

"Could be," Bridger admitted. "I ain't been down that way for a spell, but you can bet there'll be a plenty of redskins running loose along the river, all looking to lift a man's hair."

Bridger rode on, and the party resumed the journey to the fort. Kit, bearing in mind Bridger's warning, maintained a sharp lookout during the day for Indians and posted sentries at night while asking Lambert to instruct every man to keep his weapon handy. All willingly obeyed the order with the exception of Preuss, who deprecated the measures taken, saying that he thought the danger from Indians was greatly exaggerated. Such would seem to be the fact as they encountered no redmen, hostile or otherwise, during the remainder of the trek to the fort, a large, sprawling, three-walled affair constructed of adobe bricks and thick timber as were the dozen or so houses built within its embrace.

Looking much like Bent's Fort, it had an open side facing the river and, also like that post on the Arkansas, it was a busy place. It teemed with immigrants, trappers, and Indians, crowding the area while they paused to rest themselves and their animals, traded, bought supplies or, disheartened by misfortune en route, were selling off their possessions in hopes of raising enough cash for passage back to the States.

Frémont and Maxwell arrived shortly thereafter with the mules they had gone to purchase. They had run into a few Indians, Lucien told Kit, but they were Arapahoes and gave them no trouble.

"Just missed an old friend of yours," Milton Sublette, one of the partners in the fort, mentioned to Carson a short time later. "Tom Fitzpatrick."

Kit swore softly. He would like very much to see Broken Hand, ask about some of the men he had trapped with — particularly Monte Rinehart.

"Where was he going?"

"South Pass," Sublette said. "Hired out to guide a party that's on the way to Oregon. Seen some Indian trouble hereabouts, and they was scared to go on without somebody to show them the way."

"The Sioux, the Cheyennes, and the Blackfeet . . . they're the ones stirring up things. Run into Bridger, and he was telling me they'd got together and was making things bad."

Sublette said: "Sioux mostly. They passed the word they wouldn't let no more wagons cross their land. That fellow Frémont, heard him talking. You taking him to South Pass?"

Carson nodded. "He's heading up a U. S. government team that's being sent to survey the Pass and do some map making."

"Reckon I'd best do some talking to him," Sublette said and made his way through the crowded yard to where John Frémont was engaged in conversation with several well dressed men, all obviously just in from the States.

Carson, motioning to Lucien Maxwell to come along, followed the factor to where he halted, waited until the officer had finished — evidently outlining the purpose of the survey party — and then drew his attention.

"Lieutenant, I thought it best to warn you that it'll be unsafe for you and your men to cross Sioux country at this time. Seen some folks killed, their equipment taken."

Frémont brushed at his forehead with a handkerchief. "I can't let that stop the expedition. I have been directed by the government to undertake and complete this project, and I shall do so in spite of all obstacles. Should I fail, those who caused me to do it will be punished by the government."

"That won't be of much help to you if you're dead," Sublette commented dryly.

Frémont shrugged, turned to Carson. "What is your opinion of the situation?"

"I'd recommend laying over here until things quiet down . . . but it's not up to me."

John Frémont again mopped at his forehead. "No," he said, coming to a sudden decision, "we must push on before winter arrives. We'll complete our provisioning here and move out as soon as it's done."

Kit smiled. John Frémont had courage as well as determination, there was no doubt of that. He glanced at Maxwell as the officer hurried off to join Preuss and several other members of his party.

"You still figure to go with him?"

Maxwell smiled. "Hell, I've come this far, might as well go whole hog. Not sure about that lieutenant, though. Can't make up my mind if he's the biggest fool in the country, or the bravest!"

Three days later the survey party, with Frémont riding in the front flanked by Carson and Lucien Maxwell, pulled out, keeping to the North Platte and following its course until they reached the first outcropping of the Rocky Mountains. En route they were unmolested by Sioux or any other tribe of Indians, and they saw no indications that the immigrant party Fitzpatrick was guiding had suffered any attack, although they did come upon a camp site where there was blood-stained clothing.

It was when leaving there that Kit, riding some distance ahead as he made certain there were no hostile Indians about, suffered a nearly serious accident. His horse, picking its way along the edge of a deep, rocky ravine, suddenly began to struggle when the ground beneath its hoofs gave way and sent man and animal plunging ten feet down into the ragged cut. Pain stabbed through Carson as a sharp rock drove into his side just below the shoulder. More pain left him gasping when one of the horse's flailing hoofs struck him in the chest as both fought to regain their footing. It was nothing a man would draw attention to — no more than a bruising experience that left Kit sore for several days after which it was forgotten — and he did not mention it to any member of the party.

Drawing near the long slopes beyond which the towering peaks of the Rockies rose into the sky, seemingly to pierce it, they experienced no more than the ordinary difficulties to be expected — the breakdown of wagons, equipment lost, sore-footed horses, and a developing scarcity of food. Kit led the party up to the pass, a wide, sandy saddle that swung gracefully between two mountains — and not the deep, rock-walled chasm that Frémont had envisioned — and there established a base camp. Snow was already blanketing the higher regions and beginning to sift down and shortly that became a factor — one pointed out to the officer by both Carson and Maxwell as serious — but nothing could deter Frémont. His intention, now that the pass itself had been successfully mastered and duly recorded, was to search out the highest peak and plant the flag of the United States upon it. Thus a number of the party pressed on into the Wind River range, climbing the steep, icy ridges, bucking snowdrifts that continually blocked their passage. Frémont became ill from the cold and the rarefied atmosphere and sent Carson and Maxwell on ahead while he followed at a slower pace.

"Man'll kill himself sure!" Lucien remarked. "He just ain't used to this kind of doings."

Frémont wasn't, Kit agreed — that was

certain, but there was no stopping the man. He pushed doggedly on, a true explorer to Carson's way of thinking, despite an aside of Preuss's who had grown up climbing the high mountains of Europe and felt Frémont was not suited to it and therefore incapable of completing the undertaking. But John Frémont, much to Kit's delight and admiration, was far from calling a halt to what he had begun and eventually scaled the peak he had determined to be the highest and there planted the American flag on its summit.

The return to the plains was no less or no more trying than the ascent into the heart of the mountains, but there was another minor difference of opinions when the journey back to Fort Laramie began. Frémont decided to have a half a dozen of the men, Preuss included, and with a good bit of their scientific records and equipment board the rubber boat that they had brought along and make the trip via water.

"Bad time for that," Carson warned. "River's at flood stage, and it'll be plenty rough . . . could give you trouble. And don't forget about the Sioux . . . they're still around. We ought to keep the party together."

Frémont considered the advice. Then: "Expect you're right, Kit, but I feel I ought to survey the river, get it down in black and white while I'm here so people will know just what to expect."

"Running a good chance of drowning yourself," Maxwell pointed out. "Sure will be a risk."

"Not much danger of us tipping over. This boat I brought along is of India rubber, and it is said it will float under any condition."

Carson let it pass, as he had done earlier when they had disagreed. He had voiced his opinion, and the officer had declined to accept it. So be it. As far as he was concerned, it ended there with no subsequent recriminations or even reference to the matter. The boat was launched, and Frémont with the scientific party aboard headed out into the angry, roily current. Carson, with Maxwell and the remainder of the expedition, began the long trip overland, collecting as they passed the horses that had been left behind for one reason or another as well as any gear that had been set aside during the approach.

They moved much faster since there were now no continual halts to take notes, make maps, and record the flora of the country by Frémont and Preuss as there had been when they were en route to the pass. But they had barely gotten under way when Frémont's boat capsized in the rapids of the Platte, and its occupants had to be pulled from the surging water. All were saved, but many records and much of the equipment was lost. John Frémont was undismayed. The officer looked upon the incident, which could have ended in tragedy, as a great bit of adventure and, because that same bold strain coursed through his own being, Kit Carson understood the man perfectly.

They reached the fort a few days short of a month and a half, all worn, some in tatters, but in relatively good health. Frémont was exuberant. He had accomplished what he had been ordered to do and was anxious to return to Washington and to the acclaim he knew would be awaiting him.

"I owe you more than I can ever repay," he told Kit as he was preparing to move on for the States. "Had it not been for your knowledge of the country and how to survive in it, I doubt my expedition would have been a success."

"Was only doing what you paid me for," Carson said, glowing under the praise.

"You were more than that. You were a wise and good companion . . . and a trusted friend. I shall not forget you."

"Same goes for me, John and, if you ever need a guide for one of your expeditions again, just let me know. Like as not, I'll be around Bent's Fort . . . if I ain't, they'll know where to find me."

Frémont gripped Carson's hand in a firm clasp. "I'll not forget that, Kit," he said and, mounting his horse, joined the party impatiently waiting to head east.

Kit stood quietly near the center of the yard and watched his friend ride out onto the broad plains. They continued straight for a brief time and then turned onto the trail that ran parallel to the Platte. A strange melancholy filled him, and he realized that he was suddenly lonely, that he would miss John Frémont, and Clement Lambert, and dour Charles Preuss, and all the others, but most of all he was going to miss the excitement of leading a band of explorers into country that, while familiar to him, was new and fascinating to them.

"What do you aim to do now?"

It was Lucien Maxwell's voice, coming from nearby. He, too, had apparently been watching the departure of the Frémont survey party.

"Sure don't knew. Feel kind of lost."

"We could head up the river to Middle Park, or maybe go on to Brown's Hole . . . ?"

Carson shook his head. He didn't exactly like the thought of going back to trapping, and besides he didn't particularly need the money that a few bales of pelts would bring. Financially, he was better off — thanks to his job as a guide for Frémont — than he had ever been.

"What say we get back to Bent's Fort? Can make up our minds when we get there," Maxwell suggested.

Again Carson shook his head. "No, go on. Think I'll hang around here, maybe go to work for Sublette. Can't get my mind squared around for some reason."

Lucien reached out, shook Kit's hand. "Reckon I'll see you again someday. Good luck."

"*Buena suerte,*" Kit replied in Spanish as Maxwell moved off to prepare for joining a party that was going up the river.

Carson took the hunter's job at Fort Laramie, but he could find no peace or satisfaction in it. Nothing would dispel the loneliness that was now like a Cheyenne war drum beating a relentless, sullen refrain within him. He was alone despite the dozens of persons he encountered each day, for the ones who counted the most were not among them — his beautiful Singing Grass and their small daughter, Adaline. Monte Rinehart, his closest friend, had simply dropped from sight, and the big adventure with the man he had come to admire very much, John Frémont, was over and done with. There seemed no solution to the stalemate he had reached in life.

Taos . . . ? The idea came to him one morning as he was preparing to ride out. Why not go back to Taos, look up friends there? It could be that Monte had done just that — which would account for none of the mountain men running into him while trapping the streams and rivers. And there was that young Spanish girl, Josefa — the sister-in-law of Charles Bent — that he had met one day at the fort. Several times in the endless hours of past months he had thought of her, recalling her haughty beauty, her saucy charm — the way she had looked at him from her large, dark eyes, the sound of her voice when she had spoken to him. What had Josefa meant when she'd said — in that secret, all-knowing way — that she had heard of him? Had the servants carried some choice bit of gossip — possibly something pertaining to Rosa Lucero and him?

He guessed it didn't matter. Josefa Jaramillo was a *rica*, a member of the Taos aristocracy and not likely ever to have thought of him again, much less become acquainted. But Kit could not shake the idea of returning to Taos from his mind. When

January of the new year came, he packed his gear and struck off on the long trail for the New Mexico settlement.

Chapter Sixteen

Kit Carson rode into Taos late one cold, mid-winter morning. The crisp, homey smell of piñon wood smoke hung in the keen air, and a light dusting of snow lay over the fields and slopes while, on the sacred mountain nearby and other lofty regions of the Sangre de Cristos where the wind howled ceaselessly, it was piled into head-high drifts. Such was ordinary and to be expected, Carson knew, but the fame that had preceded his return was not, and it took Kit completely by surprise when manifested in noisy greetings and welcomes from friends as well as strangers along the street and in the plaza.

Perplexed, but responding with nods and waves, he made his way to Ewing Young's inn where he customarily found lodging and, stabling his animals, carried his gear into the rambling, adobe structure. An old friend, Levi Booker, met him as he came through the doorway.

"Good to see you, Kit! We wasn't sure you'd ever be coming this way again."

Carson, setting his gear down, looked about. "Why not . . . and where's Young?"

"Ewing died. His boy, Joáquin, owns the place now. He's away most of the time, and I work for him."

"I see. I'm sorry to hear that. I liked him. Don't get what you meant about me not coming back to Taos . . . and what's all the hullabaloo out in the street? Folks are acting like I was the prodigal son showing up."

Booker's brows arched in surprise. "You don't know, do you? Well, old horse, you're famous!"

Carson still did not understand. "Famous . . . what for?"

Booker turned to a table placed in a corner of the inn's small lobby. There were several magazines and newspapers from the States scattered about on its dusty surface. Selecting one, Levi Booker pointed to an article in boldface type on its front page.

"Your friend Frémont . . . the 'Pathfinder,' they're calling him. That's his report about the exploring expedition he made into the Rockies with you guiding him."

Kit nodded. "Was me and Lucien Maxwell and a few other men along."

"He mentions Maxwell, but he says he doubts he'd ever made it to that pass and the mountain where he raised the flag if it hadn't been for you, that your counsel and suggestions were invaluable . . . as he puts it. Goes

299

on to say that he thinks you're the best guide in the west . . . as good as Hawkeye."

"Hawkeye?"

"He was a famous guide in the stories about the early days. Frémont just can't say enough good things about you . . . makes you out a real big hero."

Carson was both dumbfounded and pleased. That he and John Frémont had gotten on well was true, but he felt he hardly deserved all of the praise the officer apparently had heaped upon him.

Taking the newspaper from Booker, he studied it carefully. It was from St. Louis, and the article was a reprint of one appearing in a Washington paper. Kit, his education only rudimentary, glanced over the several columns and handed it back.

"Sure does surprise me some," he said. "Had no idea he was going to write all them things about me."

"Well, he did. Article goes on to say that, thanks to you, he was able to open the door to the West like a lot of those senators are wanting, and that it won't be long before a regular flood of folks start coming through."

Carson scrubbed at his beard, long again and in need of a shaving. "Hell, South Pass has been there ever since I can remember, and folks headed for Oregon've been using it right along. I sure didn't. . . ."

"Damn it, Kit!" Booker exploded. "Quit being so blamed modest! Frémont's made you famous all over the country. Thing to do is make the most of it."

Carson grinned, shrugged. "Yeah, reckon you're right. Had myself a fine time with him. He's a right nice fellow and plenty smart and full of gumption. Told him I'd like to go along if he ever takes off on another exploring expedition. Can you put me up?"

"Of course! Just pick yourself a room. Ain't nobody else around."

Kit reached for his pack, hesitated. "You recollect an old friend of mine . . . Monte Rinehart? Seen anything of him?"

"Recollect him, yes . . . seen him, no. Last I heard, he was heading up the Old Spanish Trail looking for you."

Pack over a shoulder, rifle hanging from the crook of an arm, Carson nodded, started for his room. Again he paused. "You know if Charlie Bent's sister-in-law, Josefa Jaramillo, is still around?"

"Sure. Seen her only yesterday. Prettier'n a picture. The Bents have had some trouble. *Padre* Martínez, the priest at the church, has got himself a big hate on for Americans. Wants to drive them out of the country so's the Mexicans can take over again. He got Bent put in jail on a trumped-up charge of some kind. Friends all got together and paid his fine, so's he could get out."

Kit was disturbed by the news. The Bent brothers were special friends of his, and he didn't like the sound of the trouble being stirred up by the *padre*. There weren't many Americans in and around Taos, and they could find themselves in a bad way if Martínez succeeded in arousing the Mexican and Indian population.

"Hearing that, I can't figure why I got all the welcome I did, considering the way things are."

"Well, for one thing, the *padre* ain't around today. Went down to Santa Cruz. And another, not everybody sides in with him." Booker paused as the door opened and a Mexican boy carrying a folded bit of paper entered. Smiling, showing strong white teeth, the youngster stepped up to Kit and handed him the note.

Unfolding the paper, Carson read its contents, and glanced up at Booker in surprise. "It's from Charles Bent. I'm invited to supper at the Jaramillo *hacienda*."

A tremor was passing through Kit. He had no idea why Bent would want to see him — probably had something to do with the fort and Charles's brother, William — but it just could be Josefa would be there, and he would get to visit with her. Would she remember him as he did her? Turning to the boy, he told him in Spanish to thank Bent and say that he would be there at the specified time. The youngster frowned.

"It is from Don Francisco, *Señor* Carson."

Kit looked again at the scrawled signature. It was from Jaramillo. He had misread, or perhaps just assumed, who it had come from. "Got to get myself some decent clothes," Carson said then, as the boy hurried off. "Buckskins are all I own, and I sure can't go parading up there in them. Need to wash up and shave, too."

"You go on to your room, start doing just that," Levi Booker said, looking Kit up and down as he judged his size. "I'll go over to Sol's, buy you some new duds . . . the kind you'll need to wear in polite company. That be jake with you?"

"I'd take it as a favor, Levi, a mighty big one," Carson replied and started again for his room. "I sure want to look my best."

Resplendent and somewhat uncomfortable in white linen shirt, black bow tie, dark broadcloth coat and vest, gray trousers, and glistening boots, Carson presented himself at

303

the Jaramillo residence promptly at the appointed hour. He had shaved off his beard and mustache, and his reddish brown hair was trimmed to neat lines about his face and neck. The freckles, usually visible on his weather-browned face, no longer were to be seen, but his eyes, shadowed by thick brows, were their usual steel blue.

The youngster who had delivered the note opened the heavy plank door at his knock and led him to the main room, or *sala grande*. The entire family appeared to be present. Still wondering just what Don Francisco Jaramillo could want with him, Carson faced them — balding Charles Bent, his wife Ignacia, the don and his plump *señora*, two elderly women who were probably relatives — and Josefa. She was sitting in a chair near one of the deep-set windows. Dressed in white, with much lace and ribbon in evidence, she appeared older and even more lovely than he remembered.

"Kit, it's good to see you again!" Bent said, breaking into Carson's soaring thoughts as he came forward, hand outstretched. "I'd like for you to meet my relatives."

His greeting over, Bent turned and led Kit deeper into the room. Moving from chair to chair, he introduced first the Jaramillos, next his wife, the two elderly women who were visiting aunts, and finally Josefa.

The girl nodded as Kit was presented. Recalling a bit of chivalry noted in the past, he bent forward and kissed her hand, all the while keeping his eyes locked to hers, demurely shuttered.

"Unfortunately Don Francisco's two sons, Luciano and Nicanor, aren't here," Carson heard Bent say. "Perhaps you will meet them later."

"It is good to see you again," he murmured to the girl, ignoring Bent's remark.

"It is good to see you again, Kit Carson," she replied.

The statement was overheard by Don Francisco. "Good!" he echoed scornfully. "She says it is good to see him! All we have heard for months is Kit Carson, Kit Carson . . . !"

"Papa!" Josefa cried in embarrassment and looked down.

The elderly man laughed as the women also lowered their heads in disapproval. He shrugged, brushed at his white goatee and mustache. "Can anyone here say that it is not true? Is that not why we have invited *Señor* Carson to dine with us? It is most fortunate that you have come back to Taos," he added, turning his attention to Kit, "otherwise I fear it would have been necessary to send for you . . . even to the ends of the earth, if I was to have any peace. But come, let us end this conversation and eat."

Kit, as lightheaded as the time when he had climbed to the summit of a cloud-piercing peak, stepped aside. When Josefa, the faint aroma of roses clinging to her, came to her feet, he offered his arm. She took it quickly, and together they moved into the procession led by her father and mother, making its way into an adjoining room where a large oblong table, surrounded by heavy, handcarved chairs had been set with linen, silver, and fine glassware.

It was luxury at its pinnacle, and Kit was lost in contemplation of it but only briefly. The seating began, with Don Francisco and Dona Apolonia taking places at the ends of the table and the others in between. Carson, thoroughly smitten by Josefa and encouraged by what he had heard, made certain he was directly across from the girl. As the servants — all Indian women — began to bring in the food, Bent asked about things up along the Arkansas, saying that he had not been there for a time and adding that St. Vrain — planning to marry one of the Beaubien girls — was expected to arrive in Taos shortly. He then commented on Kit's expedition with John Frémont, speaking in

Spanish that all present might understand, and called on Carson to recount some of his more exciting exploits. This Kit did with relish when he saw the glowing reaction his words evoked in Josefa.

The supper, built around a large, succulent beef roast seasoned with chili, also offered boiled potatoes, onions, turnips, and carrots. There were fresh, still warm Indian bread to be eaten with honey or butter, a side dish of lettuce seasoned with sugar and vinegar, and steaming *tamale* pie served from a tureen by one of the women. It was a feast such as Kit had never enjoyed. When they had all had their fill, Dona Apolonia topped the meal off with *empanadas* — small fruit pies fried in hot grease.

Later, when the men had gathered once more in the *sala* to smoke and enjoy a glass of wine while the women sipped chocolate at the table, Kit and Charles Bent had a few moments in which to talk.

"Levi Booker said there'd been trouble with *Padre* Martínez . . . that he was dead set on driving the Americans out of Taos," Carson remarked.

Bent nodded. "He's doing his best! Managed to have me locked up. Thanks to Don Francisco and some friends, I was bailed out."

"Martínez . . . priest or not . . . is getting out of hand," Jaramillo said, overhearing. "He is becoming worrisome."

"I can see that," Carson agreed. "What about Governor Armijo in Santa Fé? Can't he do something about him?"

"I understand a request to replace Martínez has been made . . . but it will take time. Meanwhile we all have to watch our step. It's not only the Mexicans that he's stirred up but the Indians as well."

"I'm surprised that he was able to put you in the jail," Kit said. "You're well known around here and a member of Don Francisco's family."

"That's probably the only reason I'm alive and here today . . . and you'd best get yourself squared around and in the family, too, or Martínez will be after your hide!"

"Get in the family," Kit repeated. "That mean what it sounds like it does?"

"Right. Josefa . . . she's hoping you'll ask her to marry."

Kit's spirits soared. "Can't say that I haven't done some thinking . . . and hoping . . . about her. But what makes you think she'll have me?"

"Ignacia, my wife. She and Josefa are close, and her little sister told her how she felt. When the word came that you were on your way back to Taos . . . a couple of traders who left the fort a day or so ahead of you, going to Santa Fé, brought the news . . . she became the happiest girl in the province. Ignacia said she'd never seen Josefa so excited. She got busy right then planning for your arrival, persuading her mother to arrange this fine dinner and her father to invite you."

Carson stared in bewilderment. Things were moving a bit fast for him. "Just never dreamed things would work out this way. Hoped, maybe, but . . . well, she's a bit younger than me, and then I'm only a trapper. . . ."

"A famous guide now, and the talk of the whole country according to the articles I've read in the newspapers. But don't waste your time thinking about it . . . go talk with Josefa," Bent said, jerking a thumb toward the patio. "Just saw her go out there, alone. This will be your chance to ask her straight out to marry you."

Kit rose, frowned, glanced at Don Francisco, now dozing. "Best I speak to him first . . . ?"

"Won't be necessary, leastwise not at this time. Have your understanding with Josefa then go to him. He'll be for it . . . Dona

Apolonia will see to that."

Kit and Josefa were married in the church at Taos a month later, the ceremony being performed by *Padre* Martínez who showed his disapproval but evidently feared to challenge the influence and authority of the Jaramillos. Their honeymoon, however, was destined to be a brief one. Settling in with Charles and Ignacia Bent while they awaited the building of a home of their own, word came down from Ceran St. Vrain to Bent that the loaded wagon train they planned to take to the States was ready to depart and that he should come at once. St. Vrain suggested also that Kit be persuaded to sign on as a hunter for the party.

Josefa was tearful when Kit told her that it would be necessary to leave after a few days, but, he pointed out, he was now in the family and must accept his share of responsibility for its welfare and survival. Besides, he wouldn't be gone for long, he assured her, and they could both take heart from that.

Chapter Seventeen

"They're soldiers," Kit said, dropping back to where Bent and Ceran St. Vrain were riding at the head of the wagon train. He had ridden hurriedly on in advance when a large mass, gathered along the Arkansas near its junction with Walnut Creek, had drawn his attention and given rise to the suspicion that they could be running into a large Indian war party.

"Soldiers?" St. Vrain repeated. "U. S. Army?"

"Couldn't tell for certain, but that would be my guess."

"Good chance they're Mexicans," Bent said as the party continued on. "Governor Armijo and his brother are doing considerable trading in the States . . . in fact, I heard something about a large train of freight wagons loaded with goods being somewhere on the trail. Those could be Mexican soldiers sent to protect the train from the Texans."

"Texans? That mean Houston's at it again?"

Bent nodded as the wagons rolled slowly on. "He still wants to take over New Mexico, make his Republic of Texas run clear west to the California border and north to the Arkansas River. He'd have himself a fair-size country then."

St. Vrain spat. "Hell, he'd not stop at the California border if he ever got that far . . . he'd be wanting to swallow it up, too. The man's got grand ideas."

"Houston ain't never got over Armijo's treatment of that jackleg bunch he sent to take us over in 'Forty-One," Bent said. "He's been nipping at the edges of the province ever since. Understand he's now given his approval for another try at making us a part of Texas. Could be what this up ahead is all about."

But, as they drew nearer, it became apparent that the soldiers were American not Mexican, encamped at the Santa Fé Trail crossing of the Arkansas. The dragoons were there, according to their commander, Captain St. George Cooke, to protect the caravan of freight wagons belonging to Governor Armijo of New Mexico and others that was pulled up a mile or so to the east of him. The freighters were afraid to cross the river and continue on their way because a large force of Texans awaited them in ambush.

"How large?" Kit wanted to know, studying the thickly wooded opposite bank of the river just crossed.

One of the train's outriders said: "Two hundred men at least, we've been told."

"Ain't there no way you can continue your escort, Captain?" St. Vrain wondered. "That would solve the problem."

The officer shook his head. "No, my orders were to accompany the train as far as the crossing . . . and no farther. It is up to the governor to assume the protection of his property from this point on. You must understand this . . . we have a treaty with the Republic of Mexico. If I crossed the river into New Mexico, a province of a foreign country, it would be a violation of that treaty."

"I understand. Have you sent word to Armijo?" St. Vrain asked, eyes on Dick Owens who also was serving as a scout and hunter and was now engaging several of the Mexican muleskinners in conversation.

"No, dispatching one of my men would be going against my orders . . . and these wagon train people say they don't have anyone who knows the route to Santa Fé . . . or that could get past the Texans."

One of the Mexicans in charge of the train stepped forward. A slim, dark man, he halted before Kit.

"I am Jésus Cordoba. I have just been told that you are Kit Carson and well experienced in this country. Can you be hired to take a message to Governor Armijo, advising him of our serious predicament and requesting that he send soldiers for our relief at once? We have with us three hundred dollars in gold to pay for such service."

Kit glanced at Bent. "I'll need your permission to do so, Charles . . . yours and Ceran's. And I'd like to have Dick Owens along. That way, one of us is sure to get through."

Bent looked to St. Vrain for agreement and then said: "It's all right with us, Kit, but you best give this some thought . . . those Texans will know what you're up to when they see you heading back."

"Besides," St. Vrain added, "when we left the fort, we'd had reports that the Utes were going on the warpath. Like as not, you'll be running into parties of them."

Carson nodded, waited for Cordoba to produce a written message for Armijo. "I reckon Dick and me'll make it all right . . . and, as soon as we've done it, we'll be straight back."

Bent said: "Expect you will. Take care," he added as Jésus Cordoba appeared with the letter for Armijo and handed it to Carson.

Carson and Owens turned to their horses and swung into the saddles. Both were well armed, each carrying two pistols as well as a rifle, knife, and tomahawk.

"*¡Vaya con Dios!*" Cordoba called after them.

Dick Owens grinned as they rode off. "I reckon we can sure use some of the Almighty's help this time!"

Kit, slightly ahead of Owens, veered his horse toward the brush that lined the river at that point.

"You crossing over here?" Dick wanted to know at once. "Can ford better on up a ways."

"Know that," Carson replied, waiting for his partner to draw alongside. "Figure we best take a look at that Texas bunch, see how many of them there are. Armijo'll need to know exactly what he's up against."

"I reckon that's right. You know where they are?"

"Probably in that bunch of trees about two miles on . . . that place where the Comanches jumped us that time."

Owens nodded. "That's a right good place for an ambush, for dang certain! Them fellows I was talking to back there claims this bunch of Texans . . . they call themselves the Invincibles and some jasper named Jake

315

Snively is leading them . . . has been ordered to kill or take prisoner every Mexican they run into and confiscate their wagons. Sure have got it in for Armijo, for what he done to them other Texans."

"Brought it on themselves, way I see it. They were invading, like that fellow Cooke back there said. I reckon the governor figured they had to be punished. There they are."

Kit had pulled his horse to a stop in the dense brush. Directly across the river, at the extreme east end of a grove of trees, smoke was rising from several fires. Men could be seen moving about restlessly, and beyond them a large number of horses had been picketed.

"How many of them do you reckon there are?" Dick wondered. "Sure looks like at least a couple of hundred."

"That'd be my guess, too," Carson said and swung his horse around. "Let's get out of here before we're spotted."

They moved on slowly at first and stayed well back in the brush and trees. When it was safe to cross the river, they did, then quickly increased the pace of their horses to a full gallop. They maintained a steady run for the next two hundred miles or so, breaking only to rest the animals occasionally and the one time when Owens's horse stumbled and fell, throwing Dick heavily to the ground.

Reaching Bent's Fort, Kit obtained a fresh mount from Charles's brother, William, and prepared to rush on. Dick Owens, suffering from a badly wrenched shoulder, elected not to continue, believing that he would slow Carson down. Also the Utes were said now to be scattered throughout the area, and it would be easier for Kit to slip by them if alone.

Carson rode out only an hour or so after reaching the fort, declining the suggestion that he rest. Snively and his Texas guerrillas, awaiting the wagon train, would not hold back once St. George Cooke and his dragoons moved on.

Pushing his horse hard, Carson went through the pass and on to the plains south of it with no interference. But when he came into the big timber country a day or two north of Taos, he caught the smell of smoke. It could only be a Ute camp. The Indians, cunning as always, had established it on a flat between the trail and the deep, black-walled cañon of the Rio Grande del Norte which lay to the west. From that vantage point, they could keep watch over the trail and pilgrims traveling along it as well as on the river where parties often chose to move their bales of pelts or stocks of merchandise by floats rather than by the much slower pack-train method.

Riding slowly, keeping deeply in the wild growth that bordered the trail, Carson continued until he caught sight of the Ute camp and the sentries stationed on a mound of rocks a short distance from it. Halting then, Kit considered his options. He could not remain on the trail without being spotted by the sentries and to double back and circle around the high mountains to the east would cost him at least two days. He could see but one course left open to him — dismount and, leading his horse, pass by the Utes through the area lying between the camp and the sentries. It could be done, thanks to a wealth of thick ground cover — and if luck was with him.

Carson gave the problem no further consideration. It was the only way he could reach Taos, and then Santa Fé, without losing crucial time. Coming off the bay gelding William Bent had lent him, Kit took the animal's bridle in one hand and began to move silently through the brush. As he drew abreast of the camp, the smell of smoke increased and with it the odors of food cooking in pots suspended over fires. A dance of some sort was under way, the high sing-song of voices and the dull thump of a drum reaching him as he approached.

Pausing, Carson probed the brush around him with careful eyes. He needed to have but one Ute — man, woman, or child — or a dog to take note of him while making his way past the camp, and the fat would be in the fire. He could not see or smell anyone nor hear anything except the activities in the camp and, after several moments, continued. He chose his way carefully, avoiding the denser stands of brush, fearing the stiff branches scraping against his horse or saddle might be heard. He was playing it just right — and luck was walking with him. That thought had come to Kit as he began to draw past the Ute camp and its sentries.

A rustling in the nearby brush wiped that from his mind and brought him to a frozen halt. Rigid, Kit drew his knife and waited. If it became necessary to silence one of the Utes, it had to be done quietly. He saw the brave a moment later — a young, muscular buck, face smeared with paint, sunlight glinting off his copper body, tomahawk and knife hanging from a cord around his waist. The Ute was coming almost in a direct line for him, and there was no doubt in Carson's mind they would shortly be eye to eye. But the brave, when less than a dozen strides away, suddenly paused and, apparently changing his intention, reversed himself and headed back toward the camp. Carson sheathed his blade and moved on, now increasing his pace slightly as he drew away from the sentries and their camp. When he knew the Utes were a safe distance behind him, he went back into the saddle and continued his hard ride.

Kit reached Taos late in the afternoon, both he and his horse completely exhausted. There was no way that he could continue the seventy miles or so on to Santa Fé, the capital of the province where Governor Armijo would be found. Recognizing that fact, Carson rode to the home of the *alcalde* and laid the problem before him. The mayor, immediately shouldering responsibility for the situation, assured Kit he would dispatch a rider with the message to Santa Fé at once, and Kit was to have no worries concerning the matter. Carson, too worn out and hungry to do anything but nod and thank the town official, surrendered the letter, swung his weary horse about, and doubled back to the Bent house where he knew he would find Josefa. She opened the door at his knock. As dead on his feet as he was, Kit was stirred by her intense beauty and smiled as she greeted him with a joyous cry and a quick embrace.

He held her close for a long minute and then, staggering a bit, moved on into the house. "Bed," he muttered. "Need sleep . . . and then something to eat . . . real bad."

At that moment Ignacia Bent appeared, a frown of worry tugging at her features. "Charles . . . is he all right? Has something happened?"

Kit shook his head as Josefa took him with her to their bedroom. Sitting down on the edge of the bed and allowing Josefa to start removing his clothing, he briefly outlined why he had come — and would necessarily have to leave as soon as a reply from Armijo was received. Ignacia was relieved. Josefa, pleased to have her man back if for only a short time, saw to his comfort and undisturbed rest.

Those next days while he awaited word from Armijo were like a second honeymoon to Kit and Josefa. Together they strolled about the town, walked along the creek, visited with the Jaramillos and other relatives and friends. Josefa proudly showed off her husband whose fame had increased even more since his departure — thanks to the continuation of more glowing articles extolling his abilities by John Frémont, printed in eastern newspapers and dutifully copied by the regional press.

The spring days, filled with warm air heavily scented with the smells of many things coming to life after the long, cold winter, moved by swiftly. On the fourth day since he had arrived nearly in a state of collapse a knock on the door brought Carson the word he was awaiting. The messenger — Juan Nuanes — had come from Armijo. He had no written message but with the word that aid had already been sent to relieve the stranded train. The governor had become worried, Nuanes said, when time passed and the train did not arrive.

"He dispatched fifty soldiers to see what was causing the delay . . . and planned to follow shortly with six hundred more men within a few days."

"Then I reckon the men and the train've been saved."

"I fear not," Nuanes said dispiritedly. "The Texans fell upon the first party, and all were either killed or taken prisoner . . . but one man. He said that he was able to mount the horse of a Texan who had been shot from the saddle and escape."

Kit frowned. This attack must have taken place the same, or the following day, after he and Dick Owens had started for Bent's Fort. Armijo's soldiers, understandably taking the shortest possible route to reach Walnut Springs, would have passed farther south and thus missed encountering Owens and him.

"You are returning to the wagon train of Saint Vrain and Mister Bent?"

Kid nodded. "I'm still working for them as a hunter, far as I know."

"Then, if it is agreeable, I shall ride with you. I have business to attend at the fort."

They rode out that next morning with Kit leaving Josefa tearful but with his solemn promise to return as soon as he possibly could. The few days they had spent together had been a time of happiness, and Kit hated to see them come to an end. But on the other hand, it was good to shed the stiff, binding clothes of a gentleman and once again be wearing buckskins and moccasins, in the saddle with his rifle across his lap.

"I shall never become adjusted to life in a town, I fear," he remarked to Nuanes as they rode steadily northward. "Only time I feel free is when I'm out like this."

Nuanes nodded. "And an awareness of danger . . . which is a part of such feeling. There is a saying — *only freedom can satisfy the rebellious heart.* It applies to you in every way, friend Carson."

Kit shrugged. "Maybe so."

"And from such comes courage and bravery. Before making this journey, I was warned of Indians. Had it not been you with whom I was to travel, I doubt if I should have consented to make the trip."

Carson laughed. "I'm afraid you've been reading Lieutenant Frémont's report of our expedition to South Pass! I want to tell you here and now, Juan, all that talk won't for one second stop a bullet or an arrow."

Nuanes gave that a few moments' thought, and then: "Nevertheless, I feel I shall be safe with you. Do you think we will encounter Indians?"

"It's possible. There was a party of Utes camped near the trail when I came down . . . but I managed to get by them. I reckon we can do it again, if we have to."

The Utes were gone. After only a minor brush with a small hunting party, Kit and Nuanes reached Bent's Fort in due time. Kit's first question after Juan Nuanes had taken his leave was the status of the wagon train.

"It's all right," William Bent said, "but no thanks to Armijo. He turned tail when he saw what Snively and his bunch of Texans had done to the fifty soldiers he'd sent on ahead."

"The wagons turn back?"

"No . . . the Texans lost their heads after

hearing that Armijo had backed off and forded the river . . . onto United States soil. That captain in charge of the dragoons camped there moved in quick . . . captured the whole blamed bunch. Last I heard, he was marching with them for Fort Leavenworth, while old Sam Houston was hollering to high heaven about it."

Kit was nodding with satisfaction. "Seems it all worked out just right . . . the wagons got through. Obliged to you again for the loan of a horse. I'll be getting mine now. Aim to catch up with Charles and Ceran."

"No need . . . unless you're just of a mind to. My brother sent back word that they have matters in hand and that you could return to Taos if you wanted."

"That'll suit me fine! Josefa and me. . . ."

"I've got another message for you," Bent continued. "It's from an old friend of yours."

A pleased, expectant smile split Carson's lips. "Monte Rinehart, I reckon . . . ?"

"No . . . John Frémont. Wants you to join him on another expedition. Was here asking for you. Told him I expected you by in a day or two . . . and he said, when you did come, to ride out and talk things over with him. He's camped up the river at the pueblo."

Chapter Eighteen

Kit stood motionless in the doorway of the post, his somewhat round face reflecting a mixture of pleasure and regret. *Frémont had returned — had asked for him!* The officer had indicated that he would do so if the occasion ever arose, and it was apparent he had not forgotten. But there was Josefa to consider. He had actually been with his young bride no more than a few weeks in total since they had married. To make up for that deficiency, he had promised to return to her as soon as his job with the Bent-St. Vrain wagon train was over.

Kit turned to Bent. "Frémont say that he wanted me to go along as a guide and hunter?"

"Didn't give me no details. Big bunch he's got lined up . . . and he's hired on Broken Hand Fitzpatrick, Lucien Maxwell, and a couple of Delaware Indians to keep him headed in the right direction . . . but don't take my word for it. Ride out and talk to him."

"Just what I aim to do," Carson said and, thanking his friend, went to saddle his horse.

★ ★ ★

Carson rode into Frémont's camp the next day around noon. The officer saw him and shouted a greeting as he hurried forward. Catching Kit's hand as the mountain man dismounted, he pumped it vigorously and slapped him heartily on the back.

"Was hoping you'd show up, Kit! I don't think an expedition would be complete if you weren't along with me to share it . . . and this is going to be a great one . . . a humdinger! We're going into the Great Salt Lake country . . . take a look at that lake, then we're going to settle once and for all if there is a Buenaventura River flowing from the basin. After that we head for Oregon . . . it's our final destination!"

Frémont had lost none of his enthusiasm for exploring, Kit saw — and he was immediately caught up in it also. Yet, torn between his promise to Josefa and the exciting prospect of accompanying Frémont on another interesting and possibly lengthy expedition — one in which his old friends Maxwell and Fitzpatrick would also be a part — he felt he ought to demur.

"I have the same bunch of fine men . . . scientists . . . along. Charlie Preuss, for one. They'll all be pleased if you can see your way clear to join us, as they have great confidence

327

in your ability to get us to where we want to go and back again. By the way, meant to tell you . . . I have a daughter now, too. My wife, Jessie, presented me with her not long after I returned to Washington. I understand you have remarried."

"Took a bride last February. A Spanish girl . . . Josefa Jaramillo. She's waiting for me in Taos right now . . . expecting me, in fact."

Frémont sighed heavily in disappointment and looked off into the camp. There appeared to be a vast amount of equipment, Kit thought — even a small cannon — that would have to be lugged through the mountains if they were to reach Oregon. But on the other hand, there were a large number of men — fifty, at least, he reckoned.

Abruptly Carson came to a decision. "Have I got time to ride to Taos, do some explaining to Josefa, and return?"

Frémont rubbed at his smooth-shaven jaw. He had put on a little weight since Kit last saw him, and he was indeed, as the newspaper articles had noted, a most handsome man.

"Kit, we just can't spare the days! You know this country better than I . . . and the same as Fitzpatrick does. He tells me we're going to get caught in deep snow if we don't move out at once . . . not later than tomorrow for sure. Bad weather comes early in the Wasatches and the Uintas, he said, and we need to get through them before we can tackle the Oregon country. Just no way I can hold things off any longer. Can't you get word to her . . . to your wife . . . some way?"

"What I'll have to do," Kit replied. "Fellow at the fort who rode up from Taos with me. He'll be heading back in a few days. Can get him to deliver a letter for me."

"Fine. You go back to Bent's and take care of that . . . and, while you're there, I want you to buy up ten or twelve mules . . . Maxwell wasn't able to get the ones we were figuring on . . . then meet me at the fort on the South Platte. Can save a bit of time that way."

Carson reached for Frémont's hand, shook it. "I'll join you there . . . and, while we've got a minute, I want to thank you for calling on me . . . and for writing all those nice things about me in the newspapers. No way can I live up to them, but I sure aim to try!"

Frémont nodded, his face serious. "You have . . . and you will, never fear."

Kit turned away shortly after that, spent a few extra minutes renewing acquaintances with Thomas Fitzpatrick, Lucien Maxwell, Preuss, Alex Godey, and several others, and then hurried back to Bent's Fort. There he composed a letter to Josefa, explaining as best he could his decision to accompany Frémont and promising to be home soon. Turning the message over to Juan Nuanes who was expecting to depart with a small party of traders for Taos within the week, Kit then outfitted himself with the equipment he felt he would need for the trip, purchased the mules, and struck out for the South Platte. It was a warm, pleasant July day, one filled with the expectancy of an exciting trip.

"We'll split here," Frémont announced several days later when his party had regrouped on the Platte. "Fitzpatrick, I want you to take the major part of the supplies and half the men and head up for the Laramie . . . just as we talked of. I'll take Carson and the remainder of the party and strike for the Great Salt Lake. We'll all meet at Fort Hall."

Carson was pleased with the arrangement. While he held Broken Hand Fitzpatrick in high esteem, they were not likely to see eye to eye as to the best route to be followed in reaching the Great Salt Lake and Oregon. And since he had been with John Frémont before, Kit felt that he knew best what the officer-explorer would prefer to see.

Despite their running short of provisions which necessitated Kit's making a side trip to Fort Hall, Frémont's party broke out of the mountains and had their first panoramic look at the vast Salt Lake pretty much on schedule. Later, as Kit joined them with the fresh supplies he had obtained, Frémont drew him to one side and gestured at the startling white view stretching out before them.

"Carson, have you ever seen so magnificent a sight as that? It seems to stretch far beyond the limits of a man's vision! Tomorrow . . . tomorrow I plan to begin the exploration of the area and have myself a look at that island out there in the center of the lake."

The party moved on early the next morning, reaching a point where the island mentioned by Frémont was directly opposite and some fifteen miles or so from shore.

"That would be a piece of paradise," Frémont observed as he, with Carson and four other men, shoved off from shore in the small rubber boat brought along for such use.

But the island proved to be far from a paradise. There was no fresh water, no lush vegetation, and no game, proving itself to be a singular bit of bleakness. Frémont named it Disappointment Island. After two of the men had carved a cross in the sandstone of the small mountain rising in its center, they made a somewhat perilous return to shore — beating out a violent rainstorm by only minutes.

"Is it going to be safe to pitch camp here?" Frémont asked as the steadiness of the raindrops coming down increased.

"No, move on," Carson replied. "Mud's going to bog down everything if we don't get clear of here in a hurry."

"Then move it is," Frémont said and gave the word to load up.

Kit led the party up the Bear River until they were well beyond the lake and then again struck out across the mountains for the Malade River and on to Fort Hall where Broken Hand Fitzpatrick and the remainder of the party was awaiting them.

Hastily adding more provisions, Frémont pushed on for the Columbia, again leaving Fitzpatrick to follow with the heavy equipment — one piece of which was the cannon which came in for a vast amount of cursing on the part of the men charged with its care. They reached the Dalles on the wild, rushing river and set up camp. Immediately Frémont announced that he, with Charles Preuss and three other members, would continue on by canoe to Fort Vancouver.

It was a surprise move to Carson, but it was John Frémont's expedition, and he made no comment, simply setting himself and the men staying behind with him to repairing equipment and resting the horses and mules while relishing the realization that the return journey to Bent's Fort and Taos was now about to begin. Frémont's orders were to turn back at this point and head east over the Oregon Trail. This meant that as soon as the officer returned from his visit to Fort Vancouver, the return could get under way.

"This year . . . it's Eighteen Forty-Three, ain't it?"

At Broken Hand Fitzpatrick's question, Kit looked up from the bit of saddle mending he was engaged in. "Yeah, sure is."

The old trapper spat, wagged his head. "Well," he said, staring out over the sage flats toward the mountains, "if we don't get out of here mighty quick, it's liable to be 'Forty-Five before we get home! There's a bad winter coming on fast."

"We'll be gone," Carson said confidently.

But John Frémont had other ideas. Returning shortly thereafter with his party and an Indian guide, he called his men together and dumbfounded them all with an announcement.

"I've decided we should continue on to California. With what I've brought back with me, we will have ample supplies, and the guide we now have will take us by the shortest and best trail to Klamath Lake."

"Too late to be heading out across the Cascades," one of the men interrupted, breaking the silence of the others.

"Possibly, but we're well equipped . . . and the weather seems to be holding."

"Well, you can just count me out," the man said. "I ain't going no further."

Immediately a dozen or so of the party assumed a like stand, pointing out that they were hired to go as far as Oregon and then were to turn back for home.

"My plans have changed," Frémont stated coldly. "I have yet to determine if there is or is not a Buenaventura River flowing into San Francisco Bay . . . and that I shall most certainly do."

"Not with me, you won't! And I reckon there's some others that are looking at it the same as me."

"It will be mutiny if you persist on that course!" Frémont snapped, his temper rising. "You forget this expedition is under military auspices!"

"The hell with your military auspices! I'm heading back for. . . ."

Carson raised a hand, stilled the man. "Ain't nobody more disappointed in us not turning back than I am, Zack. I've got a young bride waiting in Taos for me, and I was planning on being with her and maybe getting us a little piece of land and starting to farm this spring. But if Lieutenant Frémont says we're going to go on, then we go on. I ain't about to quit him."

"Can do what you want," Zack said stubbornly. He was one of the recruits Frémont had brought from the States, as were most of those siding in with him. "I ain't going no further."

Carson shrugged, left it up to Frémont from there. As he had said, he was as disappointed as any man at the change in plans, but it was not in him to go back on his word or desert a friend to satisfy his personal wishes.

"Very well, then," Carson heard Frémont say. "I'll provide you with enough food to get you back to Fort Hall. From there, you're on your own."

"And let them take that damned cannon with them!" Charles Preuss shouted, gesturing at the despised bit of artillery — the reason for which even Carson had never been able to figure out. Frémont ignored the cartographer's remark.

"Rest of you . . . be ready to move out in the morning," he said and retired to his shelter.

In the bleak November light the following day the party got under way, taking a rough, difficult route across the Cascades, bucking snow and cold continually until they reached Klamath Lake and the village of Indians nearby. Since they were now committed, both Carson and Fitzpatrick urged Frémont to push on, lose no time as winter was by then upon them. Frémont agreed, and they hurried on, finally reaching the mighty Sierra range that separated California from Nevada. But there was small consolation to be taken from that fact. Snow, in thick, wet flakes, was now falling constantly. Every member of the party was suffering intensely from the cold — and they were again low on provisions, the only answer to which lay with the settlements somewhere on the western side of the towering mountains.

Carson thought he had seen snow, and in deep quantities, but the Sierra opened his eyes and made both him and Broken Hand Fitzpatrick appreciate their part of the country where even the high passes were negotiable during winter months. Searching out a trail that appeared to lead across the great range, the expedition began its ascent — a desperate, back-breaking effort that required creating passage through massive snowdrifts and embankments by any and every means available — until finally they gained the crest and looked down onto the lush, green Sacramento Valley.

Descending, Frémont left Fitzpatrick in charge of the men, most too exhausted to travel, and taking Carson as his guide along with half a dozen other men struck out for Sutter's Fort, somewhere on to the west. Starved, half frozen, and unbelievably weary, the party reached the fort a week later. John Sutter, amazed to learn they had come from the yonder side of the Sierra, took them in, sent a rescue crew for Fitzpatrick and the others, and in general made them welcome and comfortable.

They rested for a time during which they replenished their supplies, repaired gear, and replaced the horses and mules they had lost or been forced to slaughter for meat. Then, expressing their gratitude to John Sutter, they moved on, going down the valley until they reached the Mojave River at which point they turned east.

After the hardships endured on the leg of the journey from the Columbia River to the fort, traveling now was by comparison little short of a lark, marred only by an occasional brush with Paiute Indians. Following a route that took them up to Utah Lake and on to Green River, Brown's Hole, and the Laramie, they then moved hurriedly for the Arkansas.

"Getting close to home now," Maxwell said one day when they were but a short distance from Bent's Fort. "Expect you're lining out first off for Taos and that little bride of yours."

"Just as soon as I can cut myself loose," Kit replied feelingly.

They reached the fort, found preparations made for an Independence Day celebration which was immediately broadened to include their arrival. Kit, despite his determination to get home as quickly as possible, was forced to remain and attend a welcoming dinner for the Frémont party arranged by George Bent.

The delay ended there, however. The next morning Kit — in clean buckskins and moccasins, shaved, hair trimmed, and in good spirits — was preparing to ride out when John Frémont halted him.

"I can't let you go without telling you how valuable your services were to me on this expedition."

Carson smiled. "Always a pleasure to work with you."

"I hope you mean that, Kit. And since I believe you do, I'd like your promise that if there is a third expedition . . . of which there is a strong possibility . . . you will again accompany me as a guide . . . and friend."

"You've got my word," Kit replied and, once more shaking hands with the officer, rode on.

Chapter Nineteen

"I will not hold you against your will," Josefa said. "We have had but a few months together during our marriage, but I shall put that out of my mind."

Carson made no answer, the letter from John Frémont asking him to report to Bent's Fort and take over duties as hunter and guide for a third expedition — this one to California — in his hand. He had been home only since July of that previous year, a period of only nine months in which he had struggled to adapt himself to civilian life — even going to the extent of buying land with Dick Owens and making a valiant effort to become a successful farmer. But it hadn't worked out for either of them. They found the labor boring, their attempts unproductive. When word came from John Frémont reminding Kit of his promise, the urge to draw on his leather, take up his rifle and other weapons again, was overpowering. But he would not permit himself to heed Frémont's summons unless it was all right with Josefa.

"I know," he said. "I've tried to settle down, be like other men . . . become a gentleman . . . but there's something inside me that just won't let me stay put. It keeps cropping up every time I. . . ."

"This I know, my heart," Josefa broke in softly. "You, yourself, are a wild thing. I knew this when I married you, for Ignacia told me how it was with mountain men. I cannot hold you . . . it would be like tying strings to an eagle. You will go . . . and it will be with my love."

Carson wheeled, impulsively gathered her — still so small, so slender and soft — into his arms.

"This will be the last time, my Josefa!" he declared. "That I swear to you!"

She placed her fingers against his lips to still him. "Don't swear if you're not sure."

Kit smiled, drew her close again. "Thank you, but that is how it will be," he murmured. "I have a feeling."

Josefa stiffened in alarm. "You have a feeling of . . . of death?"

"No, not that," Carson said.

He had lately become aware of pain, occasionally in his chest, other times in his side, the result, he assumed, of the bad fall he'd taken with his horse during the first expedition made with John Frémont — the one to South Pass. Weariness, too, seemed to have become more noticeable with the arrival of the past winter, but he reckoned both were to be expected. After all, he was now thirty-six years old, and a man shouldn't hope to remain young and vigorous forever.

"What is it, then?" Josefa pressed anxiously.

Kit saw no reason to tell her of the pains or the fatigue. It would only worry her.

"It is only that I believe this will be John Frémont's last exploration. Thus he will not be calling upon me again and, as there are no beaver left in the mountains, there will be no trapping."

"It will be that you can stay home with me, and we can have our family."

"Yes, my life, that will be the way of it," Kit said in his stilted Spanish and, as they turned to enter the house, added, "You have my promise."

The summer was fast fading when Kit and Dick Owens rode into Bent's Fort and reported to John Frémont. The party was to leave the following day on the expedition — one designed to explore the Great Basin country which they had barely touched on the previous excursion and to search out and classify the various passes through the Sierra Nevada into California as well. Frémont, now a captain, told them the de-

342

tails. He had already engaged Joe Walker, another guide, in Missouri. With Kit and his friend, Dick Owens, signing up, the officer said that he felt the party would have no trouble getting quickly to the areas and particular places that he intended to investigate and map.

"I'd say he's got more'n enough," Owens remarked later when they had moved on. "Seen Maxwell over there by his wagons talking to Broken Hand. Seen Bill Williams, too."

Carson shrugged. "Expect there'll be times when we can use all the help we can get."

Kit reckoned Lucien Maxwell was as surprised as he had been to hear from Frémont so soon. He had made a business trip that previous fall with Lucien and Tim Goodale. While he and Maxwell had talked at length about their experiences with Frémont, Lucien certainly had no idea that a third venture was in the offing as he was then making extensive plans to continue farming on the vast Beaubien-Miranda Land Grant. The German cartographer, Charles Preuss, was not to be one of the party, Kit learned, as he made the rounds renewing acquaintances with other members.

"Kit . . . *mon ami!*"

Carson spun at the familiar voice. A wide

smile cracked his lips as he watched Louie Pineau hurry toward him.

"You are much older!" the Frenchman declared as they shook hands and clapped each other vigorously on the back. "But so are we all, *n'est-ce pas?* How is the beautiful Arapaho wife?"

"Dead," Carson replied quickly and, as Pineau expressed his regret, added: "Married again . . . a Spanish girl in Taos. How about you and Little Bird?"

"We are well. My woman now carries our second child, but my heart is heavy. I have sad news for you."

Carson looked off across the low hills. It would concern Monte Rinehart. He had suspected his old friend had met with trouble somewhere along the way and failed to survive, not having heard either from or about him since that day when he had ridden out of Bent's Fort with his new partners.

"Monte is dead."

"The Blackfeet?"

"No, it was that criminal . . . Seth Grieg."

"Grieg!" Kit echoed, a pulsing anger immediately rising within him. "Was me he swore to let daylight through!"

"And it is possible he will still try," Pineau said. "He has not forgotten."

"How . . . why Monte?"

"I was with him in the Three Forks coun-try. We trap there and down the Yellow-stone. One day we meet these five men. One is this dog Grieg. Another is his partner, Kidder."

"Grieg never had any quarrel with Monte."

" 'Tis true . . . but he makes one. He tells Monte that he knows he is your good friend, therefore he is also an enemy. Monte tells him it is true and that, if he does not have a care with his mouth, he will favor you and kill him. We thought it was settled, and Monte and I continued to work the traps. Monte is slow . . . this you know, Kit. Each trap must be set just so . . . I have told him many times he is like an old woman, so par-ticular is he."

Carson nodded thoughtfully, recalling only too well that trait of his one-time part-ner.

"I was a distance along the stream. I hear a gunshot. For a moment I think it is Monte taking meat for camp. Another moment and I think, *mon Dieu!* Is it that Grieg? I hurry back. Monte is dead, the ball of a rifle through his heart."

Carson's features had become a grim, hard-set mask, and a fire glowed deeply in his pale eyes.

"I go mad, *mon ami!* I search the woods for this assassin, but there is no trace of him and his friends. He has . . . what you say? . . . vanish. But I shall not forget. One day I will meet this Grieg, and it will be his time to die. This I swear on the grave of my mother!"

Carson was silent for a long minute, then: "I'm doing a bit of swearing too, Frenchy. Was no need for Seth Grieg to kill Monte . . . same as there's no reason for him to feel the way he does about me. But that is beside the point now. He has made it a matter of blood . . . and I will have his because of what he's done to Monte."

"That will be possible only if I have not found him before you."

"Best you leave him to me, Louie," Kit said, shaking his hand. "He is a treacherous man . . . and the responsibility of Monte Rinehart's death is upon me. That day on the river when he fired at me and missed . . . I let the matter go. That was a mistake, for it has cost me the life of a good friend. I'll not make that mistake again."

"And for me, also. I shall not turn my back on him when we meet, and it will be my rifle or my knife that talks for me. I am sorry to bring such bad news."

"Don't be. I've wondered about Monte,

and where he was. You sign up with Frémont?"

"No, that is not for me. I go to look for the beaver. They are scarce, but I will find enough to buy my supplies. You go as guide and hunter, I am told."

"Yes. This'll be the third time I've hired out to him."

"Thus you have become, as you wished . . . an explorer."

"Not a real, genuine one yet, I fear," Carson said with a smile. "What do you say to a whiskey or two . . . just for old time's sake?"

Pineau nodded happily. "I say, *bon, bon, mon ami!* Let us go!"

The Frémont party, sixty men strong including a dozen or so Delaware Indians, moved swiftly on its way, making the journey across the Great Salt Lake desert, once thought to be impassable, with no marked difficulty and arriving after a time at the Sierra Nevada. There Frémont split his force, sending Theodore Talbot, his second-in-command, guide Joe Walker, and half the men to locate a pass in the range that was known to Walker. His instructions were to make concise notes pertaining to the route for future use and to continue on into California to the San Joaquin River where he was to set up camp and wait.

"I will follow the Carson River north to North Pass, cross the mountain, and march on to Sutter's Fort," the officer explained. "From there, we will join you."

It went according to plan insofar as Captain Frémont's division of the party was concerned. They crossed the Sierra, strangely devoid of deep snow which had posed such a nightmarish problem that previous December, and reached Sutter's with no problem. Sutter was pleased to see them, offering his full hospitality which Frémont, much to the relief of Carson and the men, accepted. The captain was inclined to push on relentlessly while on the move with little regard for men or animals. While the trip so far had been much less arduous than usual, the miles had taken much out of them. Kit, particularly, welcomed the break. The pain in his chest had made itself felt again several times — usually when he was over-tired — but a bit of rest always put him back in good shape.

Three days later after buying several horses and a small herd of cattle for meat, Frémont and Carson and their half of the party headed up the San Joaquin Valley to rejoin Talbot and the others — camped somewhere on the Tulare Lake fork of the river. Almost at once after reaching King's River, the weather broke, and they encountered heavy snow which began to result in losses among the cattle. By the time they reached the headwaters of the King, none of the herd was alive. Further complicating the situation, Indians began to harass the party, stealing horses and mules and anything else they could get their hands on — and there was still no sign of Talbot. A short time later, with supplies now running low, Frémont ordered a return to Sutter's Fort. Plagued by the Klamaths who attacked when least expected, on foot when the last of the horses gave out, and near starvation after the final mule had been killed and eaten, they finally reached the Fort.

No word had been received by Sutter relative to the Theodore Talbot party, and Frémont began to worry about him and his men, fearing they had encountered Indians in a large force since it was now evident the Klamaths, and other tribes, were on the warpath and preying on travelers in the area.

Obtaining horses and provisions, Frémont directed Kit to lead the party down to San Jose. Reaching there, the officer purchased more cattle and several extra horses and mules and then prepared to cross the mountain known as the Coast Range and press the search for the Talbot party. But at San Jose a message came that the Talbot-Walker group were on the San Joaquin River not too far away. Carson, taking Dick Owens and one of the Delawares, hurriedly went to fetch them. Talbot, it seemed, had grown tired of waiting at the designated point and started down the valley.

There were insufficient supplies available at San Jose and Frémont decided this could be remedied at Monterey, some fifty miles on down the coast. Reaching there, a camp was established while he and Carson, with the American Consul, paid a call on General José Castro, the commander of all Mexican forces in California, to obtain the necessary permits for provisioning the party and allowing its continued passage through the province. Castro, although clearly suspicious, granted Frémont's request.

His expedition equipped and ready once again, the officer prepared to move out, intending to pursue the Sacramento and eventually reach the Columbia. Just as they were about to pull out, Kit called John Frémont's attention to a party of Mexican soldiers led by a ramrod-straight young officer in a gaudy uniform, approaching under a white flag.

"Probably from the garrison at Monterey," Kit suggested, although he wondered why Castro, with whom they had dealt only that previous day, would be sending a detail to confront them.

Frémont, having the same thoughts, beckoned to Kit. "Come with me. I'll need you to interpret."

They proceeded down the slight incline to where the soldiers had halted and took up a position in front of the young Mexican officer.

"Ask him what he wants," Frémont directed.

Carson voiced the question in Spanish and then listened intently to the reply. When it had been made, he relayed the information to Frémont.

"He says he is a lieutenant in the command of General Castro, and that he has a letter for you demanding that you take your force and leave California immediately."

Frémont bristled. "But he gave me permission to continue my exploration of California!"

The lieutenant, so advised, said this was true, but that His Excellency, the general, was revoking that permission. There were too many Americans in California, just as there had once been in Texas, and it was likely the settlers would band together just as they had done in Texas and declare their independence. The general was determined that it would never occur in California.

"Point out to him that we are not settlers," Frémont said, endeavoring to be reasonable. "We are explorers, making new and accurate maps of the country between here and the Great Salt Lake. It is not our intention to overthrow the Mexican government."

"Nevertheless, you are to leave California at once," the officer said. "We have discovered that you are of the American military . . . a captain . . . and such belies your statement that you lead only a party of exploration."

"I may be a captain, but it is of the Engineers and has nothing to do with my being here!"

"Also, my country and yours are very near war. The general does not wish you to be here if a declaration of hostilities is made. I am to warn you that if you do not leave immediately, the general will drive you out!"

John Frémont was a stiff, outraged figure in the face of the threat. "I am not accustomed to such peremptory orders," he stated coldly. "We are a peaceable exploration party not a regiment of dragoons!"

"You are sixty well-armed men, all noted for their ability as sharpshooters. That does not strike the general as a peaceable force."

"Well, damn it all, I can't help that!"

Frémont snapped, suddenly out of patience. "You tell your general that I'll do what I think's best," he added and, abruptly turning his back on the officer, doubled back to where the rest of his party waited.

"We'll move to the mountains," he said, pointing at the low hills a short distance inland, "and fort-up there with the American flag waving over us. Then we'll see what this Castro will do."

Joe Walker slapped his hands together appreciatively. "Was just what I was hoping you'd say, Captain! I ain't never been no hand to run from nobody . . . 'specially Mexicans."

But Carson was of a different mind. "You aiming to fight Castro?"

"Appears we're faced with a case of fight or run," Frémont said, "and I can't see running when I'm in the right!"

Chapter Twenty

The party withdrew to the squat mountain and quickly established a camp on its summit — one complete with log breast-works and an American flag flying over it. While they were so doing, Carson moved in and drew up a battle line some distance west of the mountain. Presently, using Frémont's telescope, Carson watched the Mexican general's preparations with some concern.

"He's lining up artillery."

"I don't believe we're in range," Frémont said, having his look.

Owens took his turn with the glass. "Whatever, we're not going to stand off five hundred Mexican soldiers with sixty rifles," he said dryly, handing the telescope back.

At that moment Castro loosed several of his cannon. The balls thudded into the base of the mountain, stirring up clouds of powder-dry dust. The barrage was brief and was followed by the sight of soldiers drilling smartly behind the line of artillery.

"Trying to impress me," Frémont muttered. "Thinks he can drive me off with a show of power. He might as well learn now that I won't scare. We'll just set tight."

"Castro's not likely to withdraw," Carson said. "Can't afford to. He'd lose face."

"Them Mexes'll lose more than that if they try charging up that hill!" Joe Walker declared.

Kit glanced at Lucien Maxwell and shrugged. It was the Joe Walkers of the world who caused much of the trouble between men.

"Don't fool yourself," Maxwell observed with a frown. "Castro's got artillery . . . along with cavalry and infantry. We might hold them off for a while but not for long."

"You don't see them trying something, do you?"

It was true. There was little activity behind the Mexican lines and, when darkness came, the stalemate still held. Frémont had Carson throw out sentries to make certain no night attack would take them unawares. Kit chose carefully, figuring that men with much experience when it came to Indian fighting would best serve as guards, but nothing developed. Castro made no move that night or even at sunrise the next morning. Frémont couldn't understand why the Mexican officer held off and wondered if Castro feared to attack a party of Americans however small — a thought to which Joe

Walker heartily subscribed.

"Somebody's a-coming!" one of the sentries, stationed half way down the hill, announced in the mid-morning. "Carrying a white flag . . . same as before."

Frémont, with Kit and several other members of the party, hurried forward to see who it was. It might be another representative of José Castro's this time with an offer of peace.

It proved to be a man from the office of the American Consul in Monterey advising Frémont to abandon his position there on the mountain — Hawk's Point — and do exactly as General Castro ordered — otherwise the Mexican officer would attack in force. The demand infuriated John Frémont. He would not comply, he told the courier. He and his men were explorers on a peaceful mission into California and had done nothing to incur the wrath of the Mexican government. Withdrawal was out of the question regardless of the consequences.

The American representative departed. Joe Walker, thoroughly approving of Frémont's aggressive stand, offered to do what he could to fortify their position further.

"Nothing more we can do," Frémont said, "except wait. When Castro makes his move, then we'll know how to react."

The day dwindled by, and night came. Still

there was no activity on the part of the Mexican forces other than the monotonous drilling of the infantry and cavalry and the occasional lobbing of artillery shells. On the third day of this, John Frémont called his men together.

"Prepare to move out. Castro doesn't appear to be anxious to attack . . . and I certainly am not going to waste my time sitting here, waiting."

"That mean you're plain giving up to them Mexes?" Joe Walker asked in disgust.

"No, not giving up . . . just dislike the thought of doing nothing . . . wasting our time."

"Well, I'm not leaving!" Walker declared flatly. "Sooner or later we're going to have to drive the Mexicans out, take over California, and make it a part of the Union. I aim to be here johnny-on-the-spot to help!"

"That's your privilege, Joe," Frémont said, almost wistfully.

When preparations to leave were complete, the captain directed Carson to strike for the Sacramento and head north until they reached Lassen's Ranch where the party would make ready for the homeward journey. Lassen's was achieved without incident, but barely had they arrived when a party of settlers presented themselves to

Frémont and asked for his help.

"There's a thousand or more Indians down a ways holding a war dance. They aim to attack the settlements. You're an officer of the United States Army . . . so we've come to you for help."

Frémont did not hesitate. He called for volunteers to go with him and the settlers to punish the Indians. The response was almost unanimous, and the small army of a hundred or so men, led by Frémont, with Carson, Lucien Maxwell, and Dick Owens at his side, hurriedly advanced on the Indians. The attack was brief and bloody, with the Indians suffering heavy casualties and scattering into all directions. The settlers were elated and wholly satisfied.

"It'll be a cold day in Hades before they think about raiding a settlement!" one of them said. "There just ain't nothing like the U. S. Army to show them savages who's who!"

Frémont remained at Lassen's for a week after that and then, well prepared, moved out — instructing Kit to head for the Columbia River and to do so by the shortest route. The officer had a feeling that trouble brewing between the United States and Mexico was coming to a climax and wanted to be in Washington when, and if, hostilities broke out. The maps and notes that had been made during the exploration would prove of great value to the military. Besides, as a member of the armed forces, he should be there to assume his responsibilities.

Carson did as instructed and conducted the party at a rapid pace over the best trail he, and the other guides, could devise. They reached Klamath Lake in mid-afternoon of the fifth day and halted for night camp — both men and animals in need of rest. They had just set up camp when two soldiers rode in, dust covered, fatigued, horses about done.

"Looking for Captain John Frémont," one announced as he came off his saddle.

Frémont, in his tent, appeared at once. The soldier saluted despite his exhaustion. "Name's Smith, sir. Lieutenant Gillespie sent me . . . or us. I have important communications for you. The United States and Mexico have gone to war. We . . . the lieutenant, me, Tom there, and four others were sent to overtake you."

Frémont began to open one of several letters. "Where's Lieutenant Gillespie now?"

"Back a piece. We was pushing our horses hard, and some give out. The lieutenant sent me and Tom on ahead with the communications."

Frémont nodded to Carson. "Kit, I don't trust the Indians we've seen hanging about. Take ten men and bring in Gillespie and his party."

Kit moved out at once. The Klamaths were a dangerous tribe, and he shared Frémont's mistrust and fear that the soldiers were in jeopardy. But Gillespie and the Marines with him were as yet unharmed when he found them camped beside the trail and returned with them to Frémont's encampment.

Frémont called Kit into his tent a short time later. He was discussing the dispatches with Gillespie.

"I've got letters here from President Polk and my father-in-law, Senator Benton," he said. "Word, too, from some other officials . . . among them my appointment as a colonel. But more important, we are ordered back to California at once where we are to await further orders. Now, I propose we all get some sleep. We'll move out in the morning."

The change in plans was then made known to the men, leaving some happy with the thought of returning to California and taking part in a war for its annexation from Mexico, others displeased with the prospect of not going home. Conversations both pro and con continued for a time around the fires and then died off as the men gradually retired.

Kit, Dick Owens, and Maxwell, however, remained for an hour or so after the others had turned in. Then finally they too wrapped themselves in their blankets — the Oregon night was cold — stretched out near their fire. The camp was dark and silent except for lantern glow inside Frémont's tent where he still pored over the letters he had received — the first since leaving Washington. One of them, he confided to Kit, was from his wife, Jessie, and contained much news about their small daughter.

Frémont's words had stirred Kit, bringing to mind thoughts of his own wife, Josefa — patiently awaiting him in Taos. This would be the last time he'd leave her, he swore quietly to himself. When this expedition was over, he'd return to Taos — and stay there, never again leaving her for any length of time. He and Maxwell had done a bit of talking abut ranching up on the Rayado, a fine valley not far from Taos, and building themselves homes for their families there. It was a good idea — one he certainly would pursue with Lucien once they were back in the Sangre de Cristo country again. It would be wonderful to settle down — this time for good — in a real home, be with Josefa, beautiful, warm, and passionate Josefa.

A dull thump brought Kit from his slumber. Reacting instantly, and instinctively, he seized his pistol and leaped to his feet. Dark shapes were moving swiftly and silently about in the camp, striking with tomahawks, clubs, and shooting arrows.

Carson shouted an alarm but, before it was out of his mouth, other men were up and repelling the attack. In the pale light of the moon Carson could see a mountain man lying dead nearby, his head split open by a tomahawk. One of the Delawares was also down, victim of a like weapon. Another Delaware had snatched up a rifle and triggered it, but the weapon was not loaded. A moment later he went down with several arrows in his chest. By then the camp was a confused milling of Indians and white men. Rifles were cracking, and gunsmoke had begun to hang in the crisp, biting air. Kit, having only his pistol, which he never favored, fired at a brave rushing straight for him. The ball missed as the Indian lunged to one side. Dodging, also, Carson made a grab for the dead man's rifle which lay on the ground close by. A weapon cracked from a step or two beyond him, and Kit glancing around saw that it was Lucien Maxwell — already hastening to reload. The trapper grinned as he rammed powder and ball into his rifle. Carson nodded his thanks, took up the rifle, and began to make use of it. The firing and the close hand-to-hand combat continued for several more minutes and then gradually slowed as the Indians began to withdraw and flee into the night.

Carson, angered and grieved by the loss of lives, was in favor of making up a vengeance party and following the Klamath braves immediately — an idea sanctioned by Maxwell and several others — but Frémont overrode the plan.

"It's necessary we move out for California in the morning by first light. I cannot allow anything to interfere."

"Those Indians have to be punished," Kit protested. "There'll be other white men passing through here . . . immigrants and the like . . . when California is opened up to settlers, and they won't be safe."

"Agreed," Frémont said, "but we'll wait for morning. When we start back, you take a dozen or so men and form an advance party. When and if you spot the Klamaths' village, send back word and we'll advance to help. Meanwhile, I want a burial detail to take care of the dead."

Carson, and the men chosen by him, left well before first light, picking up the trail of the Indians and following it to a village of fifty or more teepees near a fair-size stream. Moving in carefully with his party, several of which were Delawares, he prepared to attack when a dog suddenly roused and began to bark frantically. Immediately, the village came to life. Braves began to appear with their weapons, and both they and Carson's men opened up. The Indians, some with rifles, others with bow and arrows, stood their ground briefly and then gave way.

"Fire every damned teepee!" Carson ordered. "I want this village burned to the ground so that this'll be a lesson they won't ever forget!"

The men set to work at once, applying torches to the shelters and whatever contents that were within. A heavy cloud of smoke lifting into the morning sky brought a smile to Carson's lips.

"I guess that's signal enough for Colonel Frémont," he said.

The fires mounted in intensity, the smoke thickened and, by the time Frémont and the rest of the party arrived, the village was a blackened, smoldering ruin. The officer paused for a time to consider the ashes, made inquiries as to any losses incurred, which were none, and then ordered the march resumed, satisfied they would not again be troubled by the Klamaths.

Carson and the mountain men had their doubts, which proved to be warranted. They encountered small war parties and scouts several times during their hurried passage, and shots were exchanged on occasion. Several mules were stolen, and a considerable part of the supplies were lost, but Frémont permitted nothing to delay him.

They reached Lassen's Ranch, reprovisioned, and pressed on, pointing now for a camp site at the confluence of the Feather and Bear Rivers. Arriving there, the officer sent Gillespie and his men on to their ship, the *Portsmouth*, lying at anchor in Monterey Bay.

"I shall remain here and await my orders," he told Gillespie. "You will relay that information to your commander."

Chapter Twenty-One

"I'd sure like to be heading back," said Able Green, one of the Frémont party, as he sat in front of his shelter, cleaning a rifle. "I just don't hold with all this here expansionist business. Let the Mexicans keep California."

"And New Mexico?" Kit asked, repairing the strap of his bullet pouch nearby.

"New Mexico, too. Only country worth a damn to a man is north of the Arkansas. You can have everything else left over, far as I'm concerned."

"That part of the country's filling up with people," Owens said. "Fact is, they're getting so danged thick a fellow can stir them with a stick!"

It was the third day of the camp at the forks while Colonel Frémont awaited orders — from whom, Carson was not exactly certain — and the men were becoming restless. Many occupied themselves with hunting for meat, others for Indians who seemed to be non-existent in the area for the time.

"Riders coming!"

At the warning of one of the sentries posted by Carson, the camp came to an alert.

Kit, with Owens and several others, separated and took advantageous positions about the clearing.

"Friends!" called out the leader of the party, some thirty or forty horsemen, all in civilian dress.

Frémont, out of his tent at the first alarm, moved into the open and waved the riders in. The leader dismounted a few moments later and presented himself.

"Name's Harkness. We're settlers . . . and we've banded together against the Mexican army . . . General Castro. We aim to take over the military post at Sonoma before he gets there."

Frémont gave that consideration. Then: "How many men do you have?"

"Only forty or so now," Harkness replied, "but there's more throwing in with us. We need a hundred at least to do what we want and, you being a military man and your men all good rifle shooters, we're here to ask you to help us."

Frémont nodded thoughtfully as he stared off into the distance. The day was already warm, and most of the men had their coats off with shirts open down the front.

"I can see no reason not to help," Frémont said finally and then paused, as if listening to a mockingbird back up on the slope somewhere. "However, it will have to be on a voluntary basis. I am military, but my men are not."

Turning, the officer swept the camp with his glance, his erect figure silhouetted against the open sky, dark, bearded face solemn as he spoke. "Men, I ask for volunteers for this mission. It will be one that doubtless entails combat with soldiers of Mexico. Those of you wishing to participate will form a group on my left."

Kit started to join the immediate move. Frémont halted him. "Carson, it will be necessary that you remain with me. I may have need for a courier."

Thirty of the exploration party joined with the California farmers who were calling themselves the Bear Flag Rebels. Thus reinforced with men and equipment, they rode on. Two days later a messenger arrived with word that the fort had been taken along with several prisoners, and that the United States and Mexico were now truly at war. Frémont immediately ordered the remaining members of the expedition to strike camp and led them on a hurried march to Sonoma. At the post, which he found well supplied and equipped militarily, he took charge, ordering the captured prisoners taken to Sutter's Fort and held there while he reorganized the post and awaited his orders.

Almost immediately a warning came that General José Castro, infuriated by the bold move of the Frémont-aided rebels in taking over Sonoma, had dispatched one of his captains, Joáquin de la Torre, with a large force of soldiers said to be around six hundred to retake the post and drive the Americans out of California.

Mustering every man possible, John Frémont prepared to turn back de la Torre's advance, his determination and that of the men in his command doubled by the report that the two couriers he had sent north to warn settlers of impending danger had been caught and executed by the Mexican captain.

The first head-on clash was brief. Under the deadly accurate volleys of the mountain men and settlers, de la Torre's forces gave way and began a retreat south toward Yerba Buena with the Bear Flag Rebels nipping persistently at their heels.

"They're gone," Kit reported to Frémont when the pursuit finally came to an end. "Abandoned a lot of supplies and horses. Word is they crossed the bay at Yerba Buena and lit out for the Pueblo de Los Angeles."

"Expect that means he intends to join with General Castro there," Frémont said.

"They'll combine, reorganize their forces, and then march back up the coast with the idea of driving us before them. Somebody once said that the best defense is offense. I think I'll see how true that is."

Taking a small force but leaving Sonoma well garrisoned, Frémont and Carson rode out for Sutter's Fort. Reaching there with no opposition, the colonel placed the fort under military command in charge of one of the Bear Flag Rebel leaders. Then, moving fast, he led his party to Monterey which, word had advised him, had also been taken over by an American naval officer, John S. Sloat, who had raised the Stars and Stripes over the settlement. Reaching there, Frémont presented himself and made his report. Sloat's rebuff was apparent, and he made it clear that he did not particularly approve of the Army man's activities ashore.

Kit was mystified. He could see no reason for the naval officer's attitude and could not imagine any conflict of interest. He reckoned it was his friend's enthusiasm for getting the job done. He was fully in agreement with John Frémont's plan to have the navy transport him and his men to San Diego, at which point he would lead his men up the coast to the Pueblo de Los Angeles where Castro and de la Torre were consolidating and preparing to march north. Sloat was in the process of turning over his command to another commodore — Robert Stockton — and had no time to listen to the idea. Biding his time until the proper moment, Frémont laid the plan before the new officer.

"It must be done at once," he said when he had finished. "We can't let Castro build his forces up to the point where he can simply overwhelm us by sheer numbers. We still have no army. I have only my mountain men, the California Volunteers who call themselves the Bear Flag Rebels, and of course whatever Marines and sailors you can provide."

Stockton, young and aggressive like John Frémont and making no secret of his admiration for a man who with a small band of followers had successfully routed the tyrants occupying California, saw the need and advantage of such a move immediately. He called in Captain Samuel Dupont and directed him to take his ship and transport Colonel Frémont and the one hundred and fifty men in his command to San Diego.

It was a rough voyage, and Kit, never one for traveling on water, disliked every moment of it, but he made no complaint. Going by ship saved much valuable time and would place them below Castro and his army and thus provide the Frémont forces with the element of surprise. They landed four days after embarking and quickly ran into problems. Kit, sending out small details to buy horses, found animals scarce and was finally compelled to report the failure to Frémont.

"We can do nothing without them," the officer said. He had hoped to mount his men at once and move out. Delay could be costly as spies could warn the Mexican general of their presence. "Send men farther out into the country, impress upon them the importance of getting animals quickly . . . even if it becomes necessary to commandeer . . . or confiscate."

Carson did as directed and three days later the Frémont force, all mounted, began the move up the coast for the pueblo. Stockton, meantime, as had been agreed, was coming in from the rear with an estimated four hundred men with plans to land at the port of San Pedro — at which point the two forces would combine and move on Castro. Frémont led his volunteers to within three miles or so and sent Dick Owens and several other men ahead to determine the situation. The delay in finding horses had caused him to arrive much later than scheduled, and he was unsure where matters stood.

Owens returned in a short time. "The Mexicans are on the run . . . scattering in every direction," he reported.

"Any sign of Stockton?"

"Nope. Kind of got a hunch he's already heading for the pueblo."

It was most likely the fact. Arriving at San Pedro and not finding Frémont, the naval officer had probably delayed a short time and then moved on. Holding back no longer, Frémont gave the command to advance. As they drew near the settlement, what Dick Owens had reported became evident. Mexican soldiers could be seen fleeing frantically. Then, from over to the left, Carson and the rest of the men caught sight of a solid plateau of United States sailors and Marines marching smartly toward the pueblo.

"Stockton's men!" Frémont shouted and ordered a trot.

The two forces met, joined, and together entered the settlement, but their anticipated prize, General José Castro, was not to be found. He and his officers had fled into Mexico, leaving behind a large amount of arms and ammunition.

"We've done it!" Frémont shouted, openly exuberant as he and Stockton clasped hands. "California is now a part of the Union!"

The naval officer nodded and then, raising his hand for silence, said: "That is true . . . and the nation can thank you and your men for making it possible . . . and to show my country's appreciation I, as Military Governor of the State of California, hereby appoint John Frémont the Civil Governor and turn the territory over to you."

A cheer went up at that, and Kit, vastly pleased at the honor he felt John Frémont so richly deserved, was the first to step up to his friend and congratulate him.

"Just want to say good luck, Colonel, and wish you the best."

Frémont nodded and then frowned. "Are you planning to leave now that we've got the job done?"

"Aim to head back to Taos . . . me and some of the other men. We're sort of anxious to get back to our families."

Frémont, moving away from Stockton and several junior officers taking plaudits from the growing crowd of Angelenos in the square, shook his head. "Kit, it'll be all right for the others to go, but frankly I still need you."

"For what?" Carson asked bluntly. "I'm not in the Army, and I'm sure not a politician."

"For courier duty . . . a man I can depend

on to carry my dispatches to Washington. You're the only one I can rely on absolutely to see that my papers are delivered. It's a most important job and, while I can't order you to accept the assignment, I sincerely hope you will."

Carson stirred resignedly. He had looked forward to going home, to rejoining Josefa and resuming the life together they had never really begun.

"Whatever you say, Colonel," he replied after a time. "Was sort of set on returning to Taos, but if you figure you need me that bad, then I'll stay."

"You'll not regret it, Kit . . . and I'll see that you are well rewarded for your loyalty to me . . . and the country. As for Taos and your wife, you can stop there on your way back to Washington."

Kit smiled. "That's something."

"There won't be time for you to lay over. The dispatches you'll be carrying to the President and Congress, telling what we have accomplished here, must reach Washington as soon as possible . . . within sixty days at the most."

"Can make it, I expect, by using mules. They've got more bottom than horses when it comes to hard riding."

"I'll leave all that up to you, Kit, same as

375

it will be your choice who you want to ride with you."

"Lucien Maxwell, for one . . . and some of the other boys who figure the job with you is over. Like to take a couple of the Delawares, too. They'll come in handy if I run into hostiles."

"Whatever you want. Important thing is to get the dispatches to Washington fast. Folks back there don't know yet that California is a part of the Union, that we've driven the Mexicans out. I might add that those dispatches will mean much to you also."

Carson frowned. "In what way?"

"I have written a full report of your value to me and the California conquest and recommended to the President that he commission you a lieutenant. In that way, I can express to you my thanks for being not only the best guide any explorer could ever have but a good friend and wise counselor as well. When you have delivered those dispatches in Washington, you will receive the praise and acclamation due you."

Carson had fallen silent, overwhelmed by John Frémont's lavish words. Finally he smiled. "Said it before, Colonel, that I think you're laying it on a bit thick, but I reckon I can bear up. When do you want me to leave?"

Frémont extended his hand, took Kit's into his own, and shook it firmly. "I want you to know that I've meant every word I said. Now, as to leaving, be ready the day after tomorrow. Stockton and I will have the dispatches finished by then."

Carson, with Lucien Maxwell, several mountain men, a few of Frémont's survey crew, and a half a dozen Delaware Indians for a total of sixteen persons in the party, set out for Washington on the specified day. In the interest of traveling fast, they had provisioned light, planning to supply themselves with meat en route, but luck was against them. Game was scarce, and they soon found themselves in a bad way. Hardship, adverse conditions, and difficult circumstances were not unfamiliar to Kit and the other men, and they made the best of it until they reached the Gila country where there was game and numerous small creeks which not only furnished them with badly needed water but fish as well.

Several days later they came onto an Apache Indian camp and were able to replenish further their depleted larder with cracked corn, dried venison, and meal. The chief, accepting gifts offered by Carson in exchange for the food, invited him and his men to spend the night in the village.

"We are the friends of the white people," he declared.

"And we are friends of the Apaches. We wish them no harm." They were speaking in Spanish, the tribe's favored tongue.

"That is good. Where is your true home?"

"In a place called Taos . . . to the north of here."

"Taos," the old Apache repeated. "I have heard of it. I have also heard the white people have a new chief . . . a new governor who lives in a fine, large palace in Santa Fé."

Kit glanced at Maxwell. Many changes had apparently taken place in New Mexico, too, while they were away. Armijo was no longer governor — for one.

"Do you know how the new governor is called? Have you heard that?"

"It is said to be Charles Bent. Do you know him?"

A flood of pleasure rushed through Kit. "I do know him. He is of my family . . . my brother-in-law."

The chief nodded solemnly, unimpressed by Carson's joy and that of Lucien Maxwell at hearing of Bent's new status. "It is said that a great general with a large army drove the Mexicans out and placed this Charles

Bent in charge, and that this army now comes this way."

A general . . . ? That could only mean that Washington had dispatched military forces to aid Frémont in consolidating control of California, and the officer had remained long enough in New Mexico to effect a take-over there also.

"This great general . . . have you heard what he is called?"

"No, only that he is very powerful, that he has many soldiers to do his bidding."

The following morning Kit and his party pressed on. They were still woefully short of food and must depend on available game and the corn obtained from the friendly Apaches, but always as before they made do. The news that Charles Bent was now governor of New Mexico — a territory of the United States rather than a province of Mexico — had come as good news and filled Kit with pride as well as an increased urge to reach Taos as soon as possible, congratulate Bent, and visit with Josefa and the rest of the family.

Reaching the Rio Grande del Norte, the party was again fortunate in obtaining food supplies from two of the settlements along its bank and then set out in earnest to reach Santa Fé and Taos — they were not certain in which town they would find Bent since the capital was the former, while Charles Bent's home was in the latter. They rode north at a steady pace, following a trail along the eastern slopes of the Black Range Mountains and on through the San Mateos, making excellent time. Then one morning, not long after daylight, Kit saw several men on horseback approaching from the east. In the distance one looked familiar — being dressed in buckskins and a flat-brimmed hat; the three other riders appeared to be soldiers. As they drew closer, Carson and Maxwell both let out a yell. The mountain man was Broken Hand Fitzpatrick.

They met, exchanged greetings, and Kit learned that Fitzpatrick was serving as guide for the great soldier leader the Apache chief had spoken of — General Stephen W. Kearney. He had just taken over New Mexico for the Union and was now on his way to California to accomplish the same chore.

"Too late!" Kit said. "California's already in the Union. John Frémont, and a Navy man, Commodore Stockton, have already done it! Frémont's the governor."

Abruptly the soldiers with Fitzpatrick wheeled and doubled back over their tracks toward the main body of Kearney's force, just coming into view from beyond a roll in the land. They had camped that night in

Socorro, a settlement on the river, Broken Hand said, and had just gotten under way in the march to the coast.

"It true Charles Bent's the new governor of New Mexico?"

"Sure is," Fitzpatrick assured him and cut his horse about. "We best quit this palavering, and get back to the general. He's mighty testy . . . and he'll sure be wanting to talk to you about California."

Kearney had halted his force, dismounting, and was standing off to one side with several of his aides when Carson and his party, accompanied by Broken Hand, reached him. The army, Kit noted, was fairly large — several hundred men at least, both infantry and cavalry along with numerous wagons loaded with supplies. Kearney himself was a stern-faced man with deep set, piercing eyes and a hard, unsmiling mouth. He merely nodded when Kit presented himself and offered his hand.

"I understand you are lately from California," the officer said.

Carson nodded. Usually a fair-minded man, he took an instant dislike to Kearney. "I am. California is now in the Union, thanks to Colonel John Frémont and Commodore Stockton. I am on my way to Washington with dispatches to the President and Congress advising them of it."

Kearney's lips had tightened as he listened. It was evident he had planned to be the one driving the Mexicans back to Mexico and raising the American flag over California as he had done in New Mexico. "By whose authority did Frémont accomplish that? From whom did he receive his orders?"

At the officer's question, Carson shrugged. "Expect he did the job on his own, General," he said dryly. "Was there on the spot when it came time to do it. Now, if there's nothing else I can do for you, me and my men will be pushing on. The Governor wants. . . ."

"Governor? Governor of what?" Kearney cut in, face coloring with anger.

"Governor Frémont . . . of California. Was appointed that by Stockton. He's given me sixty days to get my dispatches to Washington, and I ain't got any time to spare, so if. . . ."

"Neither Stockton nor Frémont had the authority to do what they have done," Kearney said, ignoring Kit's words. "And you are relieved of your duties as courier. I will appoint another man to proceed with the dispatches to Washington . . . I need you as my guide to California."

Anger lifted within Kit — anger and a surge of disappointment. If he complied with

Kearney's arbitrary order, he not only would miss seeing Josefa but be denied the honor of delivering the first dispatches from the new territory to the nation's capital and receiving the recognition Frémont had planned for him. "I reckon I'll just have to decline that order, General," he said coolly. "I'm under my promise to Governor Frémont to personally deliver these dispatches, and I aim to do it. You've got John Fitzpatrick guiding you. He'll get you there."

Kearney's deep voice had taken on the quality of iron. "You, sir, will do as I order!"

"I'm not in your army, General."

"Perhaps not but you are in possession of government dispatches, and they come under my control. I direct you to hand over that pouch to John Fitzpatrick. He is capable of fulfilling the delivery."

Carson turned, placed his back to the officer, and nodded to his friend Lucien Maxwell. "I'll be riding on tonight. You're welcome to come with me."

Lucien looked down, shook his head. "Don't do it, Kit," he said quietly. "You'd not get far. That brass button and braid will have half of his army on your tail before you get a mile . . . then you'd for sure be in the soup."

Carson shifted his attention to the soldiers,

spat. "If I couldn't lose that whole bunch of greenies before I got to the river, I'd shuck my skins and call it quits."

"You could for sure," Maxwell agreed in the same low, cautious voice, "but he'd put your name up as a deserter or something, and the Army'd be dogging your tracks from this day on. And you got to think of your wife."

Carson was silent for a long minute and then came back around. Taking the strap of the dispatch case from around his neck, he handed it to Kearney. The officer disdained the offer, motioned for Fitzpatrick to take it. Broken Hand complied, making no show of hiding his reluctance.

"I'll drop by and tell your wife what happened when I get to Taos," he said. "Sure want you to know this ain't my idea."

Kit smiled tautly. "Know that . . . you don't have to tell me. And I'll be obliged if you'll tell Josefa I'll be home just as soon as I can get shed of the Army . . . which will be plenty soon far as I'm concerned!"

Chapter Twenty-Two

It was early November and Carson, ignoring the route Kearney's aides had selected as the shortest way to California's San Diego, followed one, while much rougher, involved quite a few less miles. They reached Warner's Ranch, set as a primary goal by the general, but upon arriving there sooner than anticipated, thanks to Carson, Kearney ordered the march continued on to Stoke's Ranch, some distance farther on.

Going into camp there, the officer, disturbed by reports of a large force of Mexican guerrillas operating in the area, sent word by Stokes to Stockton at San Diego to send an escort. With his command badly worn from the forced march, ill and in no shape to fight, Kearney, a realist, felt he needed reinforcement. The response came in the form of thirty-five men led by Kit's old friend, Alex Godey, and now Captain Archie Gillespie. His command thus strengthened, Kearney ordered a resumption of the march.

Godey, drawing Carson aside upon hearing the order, said: "Best you warn your general friend that there's a band of what we call *Californios,* maybe a hundred or more, on down the way. He'd be smart to hold off two, maybe three days before going on . . . till they pull out."

Kit relayed the information to Kearney. "Would these be Mexican army regulars under General Castro?" the officer asked.

"No, Godey says they're called *Californios* . . . men still loyal to Mexico."

"Guerrillas," Kearney said disdainfully and, turning to an officer standing nearby, said: "Lieutenant Hammond, take four men and investigate the report that a party of Mexican guerrillas are in the area ahead."

Hammond saluted, called off the names of a quartet of cavalrymen, and rode out. He returned within an hour, reported there was a large force of men quartered in an Indian village some ten miles ahead. Kearney, again taking stock of his men's physical condition, dispatched Alex Godey at once to San Diego for additional reinforcements.

Kit, while not being asked for his opinion on the situation by Kearney, nevertheless approved the general's decision and made it known while talking with Archie Gillespie and a young naval officer he had taken a liking to, Edward Beale.

"We're in no shape to go up against a bunch of loco guerrillas. From what Godey told me about them, they're like the Black-feet Indians . . . they'll fight you right down to their last breath."

"Fanatics," Gillespie said.

"Reckon that's a good word for it. They figure California should stay a province of Mexico and are willing to do anything they can to get it back. Ain't no doubt in my mind that we need reinforcements."

But when the third day passed and no troopers had arrived from San Diego, General Kearney decided he would delay no longer and ordered an attack. It began in the dark of night with a three pronged charge on the Indian village. The *Californios,* armed with razor sharp lances as well as rifles, stood firm for a time and then fell back. Kearney pressed the advantage and pursued them. The *Californios* played the game for a time and then, suddenly, reversed themselves and threw a deadly ring of steel about the smaller parties.

"Hell out there!" one of the more fortunate dragoons who had managed to escape reported to his lieutenant. "Captain Moore's dead. So's most of his command. Same for Captain Johnson. And the general . . . he's been hit. Ain't sure how bad. Them Mexicans ain't doing much shooting . . . just use them goddamn lances . . . a-stabbing and sticking like they was spearing frogs!"

Carson, in the thick of the swirling confusion, struggled to assist the few officers remaining to reorganize a stand. The soldiers were at a distinct disadvantage, being mounted on mules and tired horses that were slow to react to commands. He heard Kearney call for the two howitzers they had dragged across the mountains and through the cañons at such labor and saw the officer in charge of them, with his crew, hurry up. Before he could get the pieces set, a dozen *Californios* swept in. The gunners all went down, pierced by lances. A rope snaked out of the smoky haze and dropped about one of the cannons. Before anyone could intervene, it was dragged off toward the enemy's position.

Kearney, not badly wounded, astride a mule, sent out the call to retreat and led the movement for a large, ragged stand of rocks in order to regroup. A burial detail was designated and, while they took care of that grisly chore, the company surgeon did what he could for the wounded. The remaining troopers, near exhaustion, rested for the night.

Shortly before first light, Lieutenant Beale, one of the few officers left alive in the command and himself slightly wounded, roused

Kit from the nap he was taking. "The general wants to know where the nearest water is. Says we can't stay here."

Carson gave the area a mental review. "It'll be about a day's march."

Beale nodded and faded back into the gloom. An hour later the call to boots and saddles sounded, and the badly battered force moved on. Kit, now riding well ahead of Kearney, dropped back when summoned by the officer.

"Take a detail and see if you can sight the enemy," Kearney directed, no longer disdainfully referring to the Mexicans as guerrillas. "I must know how large a force we are up against, and what they are planning . . . if possible."

Carson, electing not to take a detail of men, rode off at once. Avoiding the open as much as possible, he hurried to close the gap between the dragoons and the *Californios*, retreating steadily for some mysterious reason. Within ten miles Kit caught sight of them and halted in surprise. Their number had increased considerably during the night, and he reckoned that now, with the reinforcements received, the *Californios* would total near two hundred fighting men. Kit, the coolness existing between him and Kearney still prevailing, returned and made his report, pointing out the size of the Mexican force and stating that, for reasons unknown, they were continuing a retreat.

"They have something in mind, that's certain," Kearney said. "I want three men out ahead of the troops. They are to advise me immediately if the Mexicans halt."

The order was carried out, and the column moved on throughout the sharp, clear day. The *Californios* did not stop but simply maintained a position a safe distance away, while occasionally throwing out flankers who would appear on the crests of nearby hills, observe for a time, and then disappear.

"We should be getting near that water you spoke of," Beale said late in the day as he rode beside Kit. "The general's wondering about it."

"Getting close, all right," Carson said, and pointed to a cluster of trees a quarter mile or so on down the valley along which they were traveling. "Expect we'll make it about dark if. . . ."

Abruptly yells broke the quiet of the fading afternoon. A line of *Californios,* sun glittering against their poised lances, surged over the top of a ridge several hundred feet distant and came on at full gallop. Kit and Beale wheeled and rejoined the main force, now hastily forming ranks. The oncoming riders split into two groups, and Kearney, ordering his dragoons to fall back to a more advantageous position on a rock-studded hill to their left, gave the order to fire at will.

The hail of lead slowed the *Californios*, allowing Kearney's men time to entrench themselves among the boulders and thick brush. It became clear then to Carson what the Mexicans had had in mind. They had permitted Kearney to lead his men into more open country in search of water and then had launched an attack that effectively stalled his march.

Another hill a short distance to one side, again to the left, came suddenly to life as rifle fire broke out on its slopes. The Mexicans had sent a small party to it and were endeavoring to catch the Kearney forces in a crossfire. Immediately the general sent two of his officers with a number of dragoons to drive off the *Californios*. The move was a success, and the soldiers quickly took possession of the hill.

"The couriers General Kearney sent out last for San Diego have both been captured," Beale said when he and Kit had moved off to the side in hopes of getting a better look at the Mexican forces. "Be no reinforcements coming now for damned sure. No point in telling you we're in a bad way . . . down to eating mule meat and almost out of water."

The day wore on, evening came, and then the night, filled with strong moonlight, claimed the hills and flats. Kearney had a close watch maintained, but there were no attempts made by the Mexicans to invade the camp or mount a charge.

"I guess they've got us right where they want us," Beale said. "Can take their sweet time about making their move."

"And that'll be after we're half dead for need of water and grub," a nearby trooper added glumly.

But Stephen Kearney had other ideas. After the morning mess, such as it was, had been finished, he called his officers, Carson included this time, to his tent.

"We're pinned down here . . . with only the worst to look forward to," he said, his sharp, hawk-like features grim but showing no sign of defeat. "I propose to advance. Come what may, it will be better than remaining here."

Carson felt his estimation of the officer rise. The general was a brave — and a daring — man, and Kit agreed wholeheartedly with his idea. The other officers concurred and at once began making preparations to put the order into effect.

There was immediate activity on the part

of the *Californios* at the movements. Mounted men with lances and foot soldiers carrying rifles began to form a line to block the departure. Kearney, observing this through his field glasses and recognizing the futility of endeavoring to break out of the pocket in which he now found himself, called a halt.

"I will not lead men into a death trap," he told his officers. And then: "We have but one course left open to us . . . get a man to San Diego and send help."

There was no response to the statement. It had already been tried, the men making the attempt having failed to get past the *Californios*.

"I figure I can make it, General," Carson said, studying the country to the south.

Like the surrounding area, it was devoid of heavy brush and large trees, offering only scattered clumps of mesquite, snakeweed, broom, creosote bush, and cactus, with occasional windswept piles of rock and sand.

"You'll never get by their sentries either," Davidson, one of the officers, said.

Kearney frowned. "I'm inclined to believe that. What makes you think you can do it, Mister Carson?"

Kit smiled wryly. It was *Mr. Carson* now! He shrugged off the stir of anger. Considering the treatment accorded him earlier by Kearney, he was little inclined to do anything for the officer other than in the direct line of guide duty and would as soon leave it up to the man to get himself out of the difficulty he was in as best he could. But there were others to think of — good men who would die unless reinforcements could be procured.

"My line of work," Carson said dryly. "Can be done after dark . . . and by crawling."

"Crawl! Two miles, perhaps even three? That's how far you'll have to go to get past their sentries."

"Can leave it up to me," Kit said. "It'll be smart to take a man with me. If one of us gets caught, he can keep the Mexicans busy while the other one gets away."

"I'll volunteer for that duty," Edward Beale said at once.

Kearney looked inquiringly at Kit for confirmation. He nodded. He liked the young officer and reckoned he'd be as good a man to have along as any.

"We'll move out when it's dark," he said.

The moon again was bright, but there were a few clouds in the sky occasionally to mask it, thus making it fairly easy to leave the camp. After the first hundred yards or so, during which they had proceeded on hands and knees, Carson signaled a halt.

"Guards ain't far ahead. From here on and for quite a ways, it will be tricky going," he whispered. "Take off your shoes, tie them to your belt. Don't want them scraping against a rock. And if you've got anything on you that might jingle, or make a sound . . . get rid of it."

Beale, showing both excitement and nervousness, did as he was directed and then, crouching lower, they continued. To Kit it was like the days back in Sioux or Cheyenne country when it became necessary to slip past waiting Indians — or lose one's hair. They drew abreast the first guard, a man sitting on the ground near his horse, lance laid out beside him. Although he was no more than ten yards away, they moved by without disturbing him.

The second was not so easy. He was not alone and was sitting on his saddle, conversing with a friend, also mounted. Brush scraped against Beale just as he and Kit, flat on their bellies, crawled past the pair. Instantly one spoke.

"Did you hear something?" The question was in Spanish.

"There was a sound . . . a rabbit, perhaps."

Carson and Edward Beale lay frozen, scarcely breathing as they rode out the tension-filled seconds. Kit's hand was on his knife — the only weapon he dared use should it become necessary.

"Perhaps. There are the small things that come out at night . . . mice and such. This woman of whom you speak . . . ?"

Kit held the young lieutenant motionless until he was absolutely certain there was no danger of detection and then, slowly and carefully, they resumed their tedious crawling. They covered only a dozen yards when Beale muttered a curse. Carson halted, turned to the officer.

"Lost one of my shoes . . . and stuck my hand in some damned cactus," Beale whispered.

"I'm having about the same luck," Kit muttered.

Somewhere along the way his shoes, tied together and affixed securely, he thought, had worked loose and were also lost. Moving toward a large mound of rock looming up in the night, Kit gained the formation, paused, and carefully raised his head to look at what lay before him and Beale. More of the same rugged country — and for that he was grateful since it was affording needed cover. There was also a last sentinel.

"One more man to get by," he advised the officer as he settled back down. "You making it all right?"

"Got no choice but to make it," the lieutenant replied. "I sure as hell don't plan on staying out here."

Kit grinned and, dropping flat, began to crawl once more. Around them the land seemed to have grown brighter, as if the moon and stars had become stronger. A coyote barked somewhere off in the distance, and small animals appeared in the scrubby growth around them, hesitated briefly, and then scurried silently away as the men approached. Insects, disturbed from the plants and low desert flowers upon which they had clustered, sprang alive in small clouds to buzz and drone about Kit's and Beale's heads.

They pressed doggedly on, sweating out every inch, cursing silently the sharp rocks that gouged at them, the stiff, resisting weeds and plants that scratched and drew blood from the exposed parts of their bodies, until at last they had made it past the last of the guards — a restless man on an equally restless horse — and were a long hundred yards beyond him and the sprawling camp of the *Californios*.

"Thank God . . . we can get up and walk!" Beale said and started to rise.

Carson seized him by the arm, dragged

him back down. "Wait. The night's pretty bright, and a man with good eyes could see us. We'll stay on hands and knees till we get to the next wash or pile of rocks."

The officer muttered an exhausted reply, but he followed Kit's order and now, forsaking their prone positions at last, they began to make their way to another rock and sand mound at a crouch. Reaching it, Carson led the way to its far side and only then drew himself erect.

Beale, visibly shaken by the ordeal, followed suit. For several minutes they stood there in the pale light, stretching and twisting to relieve their cramped muscles as they listened to faint sounds coming from the distant Mexican camp. Both were scratched and bleeding, and neither had shoes. Their clothing was ragged and stained, and only Carson's buckskin breeches had withstood the sharp rocks.

"Sure glad that's over," Beale said in a faltering voice. "Was hell . . . 'specially laying there, waiting and wondering if those two soldiers had heard us."

Carson nodded. He was only then beginning to breathe easier — but the mission was far from over. They still had many miles of rough country to cross.

"Can figure on it being just like this all the

rest of the way to San Diego . . . sand and cactus. And the desert's wide open. We've got to be as far from those *Californios* as we can, come daylight. Sure don't want any of them spotting us . . . not after we've made it this far."

They struck off at once, Carson in the lead, picking the best path available, one as devoid of sharp rocks, cactus, and other punishing impediments as possible. With the arrival of daylight, it was possible to pick a more comfortable trail through the sandy washes when they were at hand. Both men were suffering not only from foot discomfort and their innumerable cuts and scratches but from the cold which seemed to penetrate to the marrow of their bones. The sun, coming out finally, brought some warmth, but it was well beyond noon as they trudged slowly across the desert floor that the chill wore off.

Late in the day, Carson caught sight of Stockton's encampment and sent up a yell to attract the guards. Several hurried out to meet them, two taking charge of Edward Beale who collapsed when it became apparent the nightmarish journey had ended. They carried him to the shipboard hospital. On the verge of exhaustion himself, his side paining him considerably, Kit waved off all offers for similar treatment and had himself conducted to Stockton's office.

The naval officer, astounded at Carson's appearance, greeted him and repeated the sentry's suggestion he report to sick bay aboard the *Congress*, anchored off shore.

"Best you get troops on the way soon as you can. Kearney and his men are in a mighty bad fix," he told Stockton and went into further details relative to the situation.

Stockton immediately called to an aide. "Prepare to take a company of men into the desert at once . . . a hundred and fifty, all well armed . . . to relieve General Kearney." He paused, glanced at Carson. "How far is he?"

"About a day and a half's march."

"You heard him, Lieutenant," Stockton said and then brought his attention back to Kit. "Now, old friend, you're going aboard my ship and get yourself fixed up . . . and some sleep."

"Not going to argue with you about that any more," Kit replied and drew himself wearily out of the chair into which he had sunk. "Just you show me the way."

Chapter Twenty-Three

Early in the spring Kit, weary of inactivity, approached John Frémont with the request that he be allowed to resign his somewhat nebulous position and return to Taos and his Josefa. Although matters had undergone swift changes in the new territory that winter — the rescue and arrival of Stephen Kearney and his tattered Army of the West, the futile attempt of Mexican General José Castro to reoccupy the Pueblo de Los Angeles and his subsequent surrender to Frémont, the power struggle between the three dominant figures on the scene — Frémont, Stockton, and Kearney — for control of California, Kit had found himself only on the fringe of the arena, and life had become dull and meaningless.

Frémont, busy at a desk piled high with documents and papers, shook his head.

"It's out of the question, Kit. Fact is, I was just about to summon you," he added and handed a leather case to Carson. "This is for Washington . . . dispatches for the President and the War Department. Lieutenant Edward Beale . . . I think you know him . . .

will be going with you, carrying dispatches also, for the Navy Department. Pick yourself ten men and move out immediately. General Kearney's sending his messages by boat. We would like ours to reach Washington first."

"Expect I can manage that," Kit said.

"There will be replies which you will wait for. When they are in hand, return with them in all possible haste. They will be of great importance to me."

"I understand," Carson said, and frowned. "Lieutenant Beale . . . he's been a bit under the weather. You think he's fit enough for the trip?"

"I assume he is, else Stockton would not be entrusting him with his dispatches. I don't think you'll have any problem."

"Glad to hear that," Carson said and, shaking Frémont's extended hand, returned to his quarters.

Carson rode out early that next morning with Beale, who was still far from well, and the men that he'd picked to make the journey. They ran into the usual minor problems, during which time Beale gradually improved, but faced nothing major until they reached the Gila River where a large band of hostile Indians was encountered. Mindful of the time that could be lost should they get involved in a skirmish, Kit carefully maneuvered his party away from the warring Apaches and pushed on, reaching Santa Fé with no further difficulty. There he was met with shocking news as he and his men rode into the Plaza, and halted for the night.

"Kit! Kit Carson!"

Carson turned toward the inn. John Solomon, one of the Taos merchants with whom he did business, was hurrying toward him.

Extending his hand in greeting, Kit said: "There something wrong, Sol?"

"Plenty . . . or leastwise there was! It's all over now." Solomon paused, looked around carefully as if to make certain there was no one to overhear him. Alarm lifted within Carson.

"Josefa . . . something happen to her?"

Solomon shook his head. "Nothing bad the way you're maybe thinking. But there's been an uprising in Taos by some of the Mexicans and Indians. Charles Bent was murdered."

"Murdered!" Kit echoed. "Josefa . . . ?"

"Josefa's all right. Had a bad time of it, but she and the governor's wife weren't hurt. Josefa's two brothers were both killed."

Kit spun to Edward Beale. "Lieutenant, I'm going to get myself a fresh horse and ride on to Taos . . . I've got to see my wife. You can lay over here like we planned and join me later."

"I'll go with you, Kit," Beale said. "Where can we get fresh mounts?"

One of the men in the party said, "I'll take care of that." He hurried off toward a livery stable.

Carson turned back to John Solomon. "You aiming to go on or stay the night here?"

"Had figured to stay, pull out in the morning, but I think I'll go on with you and your party. I'd feel safer."

An hour later Carson, Beale, Solomon, and four more of the men who'd come with them from California were moving out of Santa Fé into the teeth of a sharp, snow-tinged wind. Taos was some seventy miles distant.

"I want to know what happened," Kit said, sidling his horse in close to that of Solomon's. "Knew there was trouble brewing with *Padre* Martinez stirring things up against the Americans. Was doing it back when Josefa and I got married."

"Nobody knows for sure if the *padre* was behind the rebellion. Lots of rumors about it saying he was. All broke loose just this past January . . . the seventeenth, I think it was. The governor had just come up from Santa Fé to visit with his family. I'm not too certain who he brought with him, but I think it was the Jaramillo boys. Anyway, when he got home, everything was all right. Guess you know your wife is still living with them."

Kit nodded. "Has ever since we got married. Going to build our own house if I ever settle down." There was a note of bitterness in his tone that did not go unnoticed.

"Tom Boggs's wife, Rumalda . . . Bent's daughter . . . was there, too. The governor had been warned about threats on his life from the bunch that were peeved over General Kearney's appointment of him . . . an American . . . as governor, but he didn't put any stock in it. As you said, there've been grumblings against us Americans for years. That morning . . . was the eighteenth . . . Bent woke up to a lot of yelling and somebody pounding on his front door and hollering for him to come out. He sent the women into a back room and had them . . . your wife and Rumalda Boggs . . . start digging a hole in the adobe wall . . . just in case things got bad, and they needed to escape."

"What about Ignacia, his wife?"

"She wouldn't go . . . stayed with him. Anyway, the governor opened the door and stepped out. He figured the people in the mob were his friends . . . they always had been . . . and he could calm them down by

405

talking. Instead they grabbed him . . . and scalped him right then and there. He managed to get away from them, bleeding bad . . . I seen all this from the roof of my store. Before he could close the door, some of them in the bunch started shooting at him . . . bullets and arrows . . . and he dropped dead. Then come the worst. His wife had to stand there and watch them crazies hack his head off and then was told to stay there in the room with the body unless she wanted some of the same for herself."

"Josefa see that?" Carson asked tautly.

"No, she and Rumalda got away and were hidden by a neighbor. The Jaramillo boys were caught . . . in the stable, I think somebody said . . . and both killed."

Carson's features were grim as they rode on through the late afternoon crispness. Beale, on Kit's left and listening as John Solomon recounted the tragic incident, laid a hand on his friend's shoulder.

"I'm sorry to hear about this. . . ."

"My wife's all right, and that's what counts with me," Carson replied. "Hate to hear, though, about what's happened to Charles and the boys." He turned back to Solomon. "There anybody else murdered?"

"Every American they could find . . . about twenty men, I think it was. They'd kill them, drag the bodies into the plaza, and throw them into a pile."

"Wasn't there anybody around who could stop it?" Carson wondered.

"Not at the time. They raised hell in town all that next day then went to Arroyo Honda and some of the other settlements . . . killing any American or anybody that favored them. Some of us got together . . . I'd gone to some Mexican friends who didn't go along with Martinez's kind of thinking and stayed under cover . . . and, when we got a chance, we sent runners to Charley's brother at Bent's Fort and to the Army in Santa Fé, telling them what had happened.

"Expect it was a terrible shock to the governor's brother . . . and to Ceran Saint Vrain, too. Ceran right quick got himself a small army of volunteers and headed for here. In Santa Fé, Colonel Price mounted several hundred men and started north with them and a couple of cannon. He met Saint Vrain and his volunteers, and they moved in on the killers. Was a man named Montego . . . you might know him . . . at the head of the bunch. Called himself a general. He'd got together close to five hundred men . . . Mexicans and Indians. They made a stand in a cañon, but Saint Vrain and his volunteers and Price's dragoons drove them out.

407

A lot of them run for Taos and hid in the church. Guess they figured they'd get protection there. But it didn't work out that way. Colonel Price brought in his cannon and bombarded the church until finally they knocked some holes in its six-foot walls. There was quite a fight after that . . . hand-to-hand combat . . . before Montego's bunch surrendered."

"There many killed?"

"Somebody said Price and Saint Vrain lost only seven men, and had fifty or so wounded. Montego got a hundred and fifty of his gang killed and twice that wounded."

They had reached the mouth of the black-walled cañon through which the Rio Grande del Norte flowed and, as darkness was beginning to close in, Kit led the party to higher ground where it would be easier for the horses to make their way.

"That end it?" he asked when they were again moving steadily northward.

"Was a trial held. Ignacia pointed out the Indian who had scalped the governor and some of the others who she saw cutting his head off. Your wife was with her and told what she had seen. This Montego, he had the guts to be wearing the governor's coat at the trial, was convicted right quick, and he and five of his bunch were hung there in the plaza. A couple of days later about a dozen more got the same treatment."

"It must have been terrible for all of you," Beale said, "having that mob running wild in the town, hunting out your friends . . . killing."

John Solomon, drawing his greatcoat tighter about his lean frame, swore quietly and nodded. "Was, for a fact. Had made up my mind that my time had come . . . but I got lucky. They didn't find me, and I had friends who kept me well hidden until Montego and his gang moved on."

"Charles . . . the governor . . . did they come for his body and throw it onto that pile in the plaza, too?" Kit asked, apparently reviewing Solomon's account of the murder.

"No, left it there with Ignacia. Then early next morning some friends slipped in and took the body away and buried it . . . leaving some food and heavy clothing for his family. The day after that, I think it was, Ignacia was able to leave the house. It was a terrible time for her . . . for all of the women and children."

"I keep cursing the fact that I wasn't there," Carson said, almost to himself. "I should have been."

"Kit," Edward Beale broke in, "I expect your wife could use your comfort. If you'd like to stay over, go ahead. I'll take the dispatches on to Washington."

Carson glanced at the young officer. He had all but completely overcome his illness, it would appear, during the past three weeks or so since leaving California.

"Obliged to you, Lieutenant," he said. "There's nothing I'd like better, but my orders were to get these packets to Washington as fast as possible . . . and I reckon that's what I'll have to do. Josefa's all right, it seems, so I'll spend only a day with her while we all rest up and then ride on. With a little luck, I can have a bit of time with her on the way back. Shouldn't take long in Washington."

However, it didn't work out exactly as planned, as Kit discovered in what was his first brush with high-level politics. After a brief reunion with Josefa during which he gave her his promise to return home as soon as the mission was completed and remain there — a husband in fact, not only in theory — he rode on with his party. Reaching St. Louis, he and Edward Beale went to the home of John Frémont's father-in-law, Thomas Benton, who insisted that Kit stay with him and Mrs. Benton while in Washington. Jessie Frémont was living there also, he said, and Kit could deliver in person the letter that her husband had given to him for her. There would be other advantages to such an arrangement, Benton pointed out. He could see to it that Kit received the acclaim due him from Congress and the War and Navy Departments and could also arrange for a long overdue appointment with the President. Edward Beale was also hopeful that Carson would spend some time with him and his parents in his Washington home so that he could be properly thanked for what he had done for the young lieutenant — saving his life, Beale maintained.

In Washington, Carson settled it by dividing his time between both parties while being whisked from committee to committee, bureau to bureau, and department to department of the government where he gave first-hand reports on the California situation. Kit was also summoned to meet with President Polk. After the usual pleasantries were passed, the tall, sad-faced leader of the country asked Carson for his opinion of political matters in California.

"If you're meaning what do I think about John Frémont and what he's doing out there," Kit said in his blunt, straightforward way, "why, I don't think you'll ever find a better man to be governor of the territory. I know there's been some that's bucked him,

but I was there when it all took place . . .
taking it over and driving out the Mexicans
and making it a part of the Union . . . and
I know he did what he figured was right."

The President listened quietly and nodded
solemnly. "I shall bear your thoughts in
mind, Mister Carson. Now, I have a duty to
perform. Upon the recommendation of
Colonel Frémont, I am commissioning you
a second lieutenant in the Mounted Rifle
Regiment. You will receive an official confirmation later."

Kit had all but forgotten about the promised commission. He thanked the President
and then left in the company of Jessie
Frémont to whom he had become attached.
For several days after that, while he awaited
the dispatches that were to be carried to California, he spent his time at the Frémont
home regaling Jessie with accounts of her
husband's exploits and making it clear that
John Frémont was one of his favorite persons.

Eventually all was ready — dispatches for
both Frémont and for Sterling Price, Military
Commander in Santa Fé, a long letter from
Jessie to her husband, and certain naval
documents for Commodore Robert Stockton. Kit struck out for Taos together with
Beale. The long delay in Washington while

he waited for the return dispatches had wiped out all possibility of spending any time with Josefa, but he pressed hard nevertheless, hopeful of having at least one day with her. At St. Louis, Edward Beale became ill again and was forced to turn back. Kit continued on by himself to Fort Leavenworth, in Kansas territory, where an escort of fifty heavily armed men awaited him.

"Why?" he asked of the post commander. "I know the trail same as I know my name."

"No doubt, but the Comanches are on the warpath and running wild. My orders from Washington are to see that you get safely through to Santa Fé. You're an important man, Lieutenant Carson."

Kit was both flattered and skeptical, but insofar as the Comanches were concerned, the officer's statement was accurate. At Pawnee Rock he and his escort went into night camp near a large wagon train being conducted across the plains by a number of volunteer soldiers. The Comanches attacked at sunrise, capturing two dozen or so horses and scattering the cattle. Carson and his party were able to save some of the cattle, but the Indians got away with the horses — inflicting no injuries on the soldiers from Leavenworth but wounding several of the volunteers.

The remainder of the journey into Taos was uneventful and, although he arrived there several days later than anticipated, his reunion with Josefa was no less warm.

"You will return to me as soon as you have finished this mission?" she reminded him as he prepared to leave.

Holding her close, Kit said: "Such is my hope, but I cannot be sure. I am now a lieutenant in the Army, and I must follow orders. But I believe Colonel Frémont will permit me to resign and return to you."

"But if he does not . . . how long will you be gone?"

"That I cannot say, my heart. A year, perhaps even longer."

"Then I shall come to California, too. I will not live as a widow."

Carson gave that thought, nodded. "It is an idea, and I would like nothing better than to have you with me. Wait until I get there and, if it is to be my post, I will come for you."

Thus it was left. Kit resumed the journey to Santa Fé where he delivered the dispatches destined for Colonel Price, released his Fort Leavenworth escort, hired on a dozen or so men to replace them, and continued on his way, his thoughts brightened by the possibility of at last having a life with

Josefa. The party moved fast until they came into the area of the Virgin River. There a large encampment of Indians blocked the trail. Before Carson could swing aside, several braves rode forward to meet them, all professing friendship but in the same breath demanding guns and ammunition.

Kit, in no mood for dalliance, turned the braves away, but only after it became necessary to shoot one. The main body of the tribe fortunately did not hear the gunshot and a further, more serious confrontation was avoided when Carson, familiar with the surrounding country, led his party quickly into the brushy hills. They were troubled no further by Indians, but they did suffer from a lack of food when a part of their provisions was lost, forcing them to slaughter a mule or two for meat.

It was fall when Kit and his men, gaunt and worn, rode into Army headquarters in Los Angeles. He went at once to the commanding officer, expecting to find either Frémont or Stockton, and was confronted instead by a stranger in the uniform of a major.

"I'm Lieutenant Carson," Kit said. "Was looking for Commodore Stockton or Governor Frémont."

The officer considered him with a frown

415

and shook his head. "We've been expecting you. Stockton has been called back to Washington, and your orders are to report to Colonel Mason in Monterey."

Kit, no soldier at heart, was short on military courtesy and the privileges due rank. "My dispatches are for Governor Frémont . . . not some colonel that I don't even know."

The major stiffened. "You'll do as you're ordered, Lieutenant!" he said coldly. "And as for your Governor Frémont, he was ordered back to Washington also . . . to face a court martial."

Chapter Twenty-Four

"Court martial!" Kit echoed. "What in heaven's name did he do?"

"Seems he overstepped himself here in California, did a lot of things without proper authority."

"Sounds like something I once heard General Kearney say. He the one behind it?"

The major's face was stern. "You know better than to say a thing like that, Lieutenant! Now, suppose you mount up and be on your way to Monterey."

Carson, having no particular respect for military formalities or protocol, shrugged. "I reckon it is all Kearney's doings, all right. He didn't much like Colonel Frémont being here ahead of him, driving the Mexicans out, and making California a part of the Union. Was I asked. . . ."

"You weren't, Lieutenant!" the senior officer snapped. "Now . . . move! And get out of that mountaineer outfit you're wearing and into a regulation uniform before you present yourself to Colonel Mason."

Kit, somewhat lean, a bit stooped, but with the same sharp blue eyes, reddish hair, and freckles that showed through the bronze applied by years of weather, good and bad, shrugged indifferently and, foregoing the customary salute, wheeled and returned to the stable. Obtaining a fresh horse, he headed up the coast for Monterey with his dispatches.

Riding into the post some five days later, he was met at the commanding officer's headquarters by another lieutenant who introduced himself as William T. Sherman and conducted him to an office where a hard-faced officer sat behind a table upon which were mounds of papers.

"Colonel, sir," Sherman said, taking the dispatch case from Kit and laying it on the table, "this is Lieutenant Carson . . . the man we have heard so much about. He has just ridden in with the dispatches from Washington."

Mason, acting as Military Governor of the territory, considered Kit evenly. "So you're the famous Carson Frémont wrote so much about," he murmured.

"I was with the colonel," Kit said quietly.

"So I understand," Mason commented dryly and, reaching for the dispatch case, opened it and dumped the contents on the table. "Well, you may be surprised to know that he is in Washington right now, facing a

418

court martial for his high-handed activities here."

"Was told that in the pueblo," Kit said, anger stirring through him. What right did a man like Mason — who perhaps had spent his military time behind a desk — have to speak of John Frémont in such a derogatory manner? Could it be said of him that he had accomplished even a tenth of the things for his country that Frémont had? "Far as I can see, the colonel didn't do anything that wasn't for the good of the Union," Carson finished.

Mason's shoulders moved slightly. "The court martial will decide that, Lieutenant Carson. Now, you will return to the Pueblo de Los Angeles tomorrow. Report to Captain Smith of the First Dragoons, and he will assign you to your new post. I suggest you get into uniform before you leave."

It was in Kit's mind at that moment to resign from the Army. He didn't like what was happening to John Frémont, as good and decent a man as he'd ever met, and he had taken an instant dislike to Mason under whose command he found himself. But in some vague, roundabout way, Carson felt an obligation to remain in the service out of a sense of loyalty to John Frémont — who most certainly would be cleared of all charges at the court martial and returned to his rightful position as governor of California. One good thing, he would be putting in his duty at the pueblo and that placed plenty of miles between him and Mason. Sherman followed Kit out onto the parade, laid a hand on his shoulder.

"Don't take the colonel's words to heart. He doesn't like it here . . . didn't want the duty in the first place, but like all of us he does what he's told. You sit tight down there at the pueblo. I expect he'll be calling on you to carry dispatches back to Washington before long."

Carson nodded. "What I do best . . . and I'm obliged to you, Sherman, for your words," he said and extended his hand.

The young officer gripped it firmly. "Like to say I enjoyed reading about you in Frémont's reports. He claimed you were the best guide and scout in the country. I feel it's a privilege to meet you, Kit."

Carson grinned self-consciously. "The colonel had a habit of laying it on thick."

"Doubt that! According to him, he wouldn't be alive today if it weren't for you."

"Expect that goes both ways, Lieutenant," Kit said. "Been a pleasure meeting you."

Carson didn't wait until the following day to leave but, getting a fresh horse, rode out shortly after dark. He reached Los Angeles in due time, reported to Smith, the captain of the First Dragoons, who saw to it immediately that Kit was issued a uniform and then assigned him to take charge of the two dozen men at Tejon Pass, stationed there to keep Indians from escaping the area with stolen horses and cattle.

Settling into the monotonous routine of sentry duty, Carson wrote a letter to Josefa explaining why he was uncertain when he would return to Taos and outlining why it was neither wise nor practical for her to make the long and dangerous journey to join him in California just yet. He expressed as best he could his love and desire for her, along with his hope that they would be together again soon. There was no one heading east at the time and the letter to Josefa was pigeon-holed at the post to await the departure of a military detail or a party of pilgrims going in that direction. It could be there for days — or even months, the sergeant advised Kit, and it came to him, when he thought about it, that in all likelihood he would eventually be the one to carry the letter to Taos when, and if, he was sent to Washington with dispatches — which could be well off in the future.

But the order came sooner than expected.

Kit, despising the inactivity of sentry duty, received the command with joy. Slinging the dispatch case over a shoulder which contained among other communications word of a large gold strike at Sutter's Fort, he lined up two dozen or so men and another lieutenant, George Brewerton, and moved out.

"Rivers will all be high this time of year," he told the officer as they rode on. "Have to raft them, most likely."

"Is there no other route we can take to avoid crossing the Rio Grande . . . and this Green River you spoke of?"

"No, we have to follow the Old Spanish Trail," Carson said.

They encountered problems in Utah when they attempted to cross the Rio Grande del Norte, but no lives were lost, only some of their supplies. The Green gave them no trouble, nor did the Indians, and in better than expected time Kit led his men into Taos. Sending them on to Young's inn, he hurried to the home of the Bents and Josefa. Their reunion again was brief as he had dispatches for the commander at Fort Marcy in Santa Fé, after which he was to continue on to Washington.

"Will you remain with me in our home when you return from Washington this time?" Josefa asked in a hopeless tone as she voiced again the time-worn question put to him before. She had laid aside the letter he had written to her some eight months previously and now delivered by him to be read after he had gone.

"I have that hope, but there is no way to know for certain," he replied. "One thing, they have not treated John Frémont as I think they should. If he is found guilty of doing wrong, and discharged from the Army, then I certainly will resign."

"And if that does not come to pass?"

Taking Josefa into his arms, Kit pressed a farewell kiss upon her lips and said: "Only then will I be able to decide. But this is true, you are my life, and I want to be with you . . . and I shall be . . . as soon as it is possible."

In Santa Fé Kit found himself with another reason to quit. Delivering the dispatches marked for Colonel Edward Newby, then in charge of Fort Marcy, he was informed by the officer that Congress had failed to confirm his appointment as a lieutenant, and he was accordingly denied officer's pay.

One of the men with Kit overheard and swore deeply. "Was I you, Carson, I'd chuck the whole blasted thing right here and now . . . and let them get their dispatches to Washington the best way they can."

Kit gave that thought. The refusal of the military committee, or whoever was responsible, to confirm him as an officer was a disappointment and would be so to Josefa and their friends as well. Probably he should do as the soldier had suggested — resign and let Newby arrange to get the dispatches delivered. It would be easy — he was no longer in the service of the Army. But Carson could not make himself see it that way. He had been entrusted with the dispatches and, in a sense, that meant giving his word to see that they reached their destination.

"The Comanches still on the warpath?" he asked, masking his disappointment as he took up the dispatch case and hung it on a shoulder.

"Bad as ever," Newby replied. "Been reports of parties as large as three hundred watching the trails. You best take a different route east . . . if you know one."

"There's a couple I recollect," Carson said and, discharging all but a dozen of the men who had accompanied him from the Pueblo de Los Angeles, started back for Taos.

His mind was made up now. He would discharge his duties as a courier and then resign, permitting his return to Josefa and civilian life. He scarcely knew his own wife, he realized. It would be good to settle down with her, try ranching or farming — and raise a family.

With the small party he had purposely chosen, Kit rode north, circling the country where the Comanches were carrying out their raids and angling toward the Platte River. Reaching it, he followed its irregular course down to Fort Kearney and from there traveled to Fort Leavenworth. It was a fairly quick and simple trip then to Washington and the fulfillment of his obligation. But, upon the discharging of it, he was made aware of his worst fear — John Frémont had been found guilty by the court martial and, faced with receiving a dishonorable discharge, had resigned. Kit hurried to the Frémont home and expressed his sorrow and indignation at the unfairness of the court's decision.

"No more unfair than the refusal to approve your lieutenancy," Frémont declared. "It would seem we are both out of favor, old friend."

Pressed by some deep-seated urgency, Kit spent only a brief time with his acquaintances in Washington and then headed back for home. He did pause in Missouri long enough to see Adaline and speak with relatives, before he pushed on. He would return by way of Bent's Fort. He'd not had the opportunity to express sympathy to William Bent on the death of his brother, Charles — and he'd like again to see Ceran St. Vrain. Too, there were others he'd enjoy meeting once more — Broken Hand Fitzpatrick, Jim Bridger, Dick Owens, Bill Williams, Alex Godey — the little Frenchman, Louie Pineau. He wondered if Louie had ever caught up with Seth Grieg and squared up accounts for the murder of Monte Rinehart.

Monte . . . ? He wished the big New Yorker was one he could look forward to seeing again, but that was impossible. How long ago was it when he met Monte? A summer's day in Taos, he was certain of that — and there was a fandango that led to trouble for him. The summer of 'Thirty-One, that's when it was — and it was now 1848. Seventeen years! It was hard to believe.

A lot had happened in that time, Kit thought. Besides major expeditions into the mountains, the troubles with Indians — there was his meeting with Singing Grass. Singing Grass . . . ! He could picture her now as she was that day when he had gone to bargain with her father, standing straight, dark eyes wide and soft as a young doe deer, black hair long and shining, firm young breasts thrusting proudly and challengingly from her satiny upper body. She had presented a vision he had never forgotten, one that remained in a back corner of his mind even after all these years of marriage to Josefa.

Josefa . . . ! So cool, so utterly beautiful — and she was nonetheless so today. He recalled clearly that day at the fort when he first saw her stepping down from a carriage, the impact of her beauty carrying the force of a rifle ball striking him. She had deserved better than he had given her, had certainly got the worst of their marriage, for out of the five years that they had been husband and wife, he had spent less than a fifth of that time with her. But he would make it up to her now. He was finished with the Army. There was but little beaver trapping, and there'd be no more Frémont expeditions. He would settle down in Taos, as he'd always planned, and put his mind to other things.

Why was he rambling so? The realization dawned suddenly on Carson — all those thoughts about the old days, of how it had been, memories of friends — some dead, some missing, others perhaps still around. He shrugged, grinned tautly. The Arapaho people said a man about to be covered by the Dark Shadow experienced a swift review of his life and of his friends and loved ones. Was this happening to him?

He shrugged again, shook off the idea, and glanced ahead. They had been on the trail for days, and now Bent's Fort stood in the distance. He'd spend the night there with his men — the ten he'd brought from Santa Fé — and then leave early in the morning for Taos where he would discharge them with instructions to proceed to Fort Marcy at Santa Fé. Then he would be done with the Army, once and for good.

William Bent was pleased to see him, was touched that he would take the trouble to swing out of his way to express his condolences. George Bent felt much the same. St. Vrain wasn't there, and most of the trappers with whom he was acquainted were missing, but he did encounter Joe Walker and Alex Godey, along with four or five others.

At the stable with Kit, enjoying a bit of reminiscing and a drink of good whiskey, Godey said: "What're you figuring to do now, old hoss? You settling down?"

Old hoss. Monte had always called him *old son.* The similarity of the words stirred Kit, held him quiet for several moments. Then he nodded. "Yeah, settle down. Going to get myself a place of some kind in Taos, maybe raise horses or cattle. Lucien Maxwell and me have done some talking about building ourselves fine homes and going together on something . . . likely will do that. I've had my time of roaming . . . what I want now is my wife and my home."

Alex nodded sagely. "That's what we all best be doing, I expect. Things are changing around here . . . and I ain't sure it's for the best. Could be I'll light out for California. Sort of took a liking to that country."

"Seemed a mighty fine place to live, all right," Kit agreed as they moved out of the animal shelter and started for the store. "Ain't sure I could ever leave Taos for good myself . . . and I doubt if I could get my wife to, either."

Carson broke off abruptly as they reached the corner of the post. A squat, burly individual, evidently headed for the stables, was suddenly before him.

"Grieg!" he shouted as their eyes locked.

He realized then, in that brief fragment of a moment as he reached for his knife, that what the Arapaho people said was true: a man about to meet death swiftly remembered everything! But it did not necessarily follow that he must die, that he must simply surrender his life. It was his right to fight.

"Goddamn you!" Grieg shouted and swung his rifle in a blurred arc.

The stock caught Carson in the side, sent him stumbling from the force of the blow —

and filled him with soaring pain. But, cat-like, he caught himself, spun, and hurled himself at Grieg, who now threw away his broken rifle and clutched his knife. Carson, head low, drove into the man, into the murderer of his best friend, a surging hatred lending strength to his charge. Grieg's breath exploded in a gusty blast. He went down hard with Kit pinning the hand holding the blade to the ground while he struggled to escape Carson's knife seeking his throat.

A dozen men had gathered quickly at the scene, but there was no yelling, no shouting of encouragement to either contestant. They recognized the fact that a man was to die, either Kit Carson or Seth Grieg, and there was no cheering.

Suddenly Grieg's resisting hand gave way. Kit's knife plunged downward as restraint to it ceased. A bright red splash of color showed where the razor-sharp point nicked Grieg's jaw. And then the blade was pressing into the leathery skin of the man's neck.

"Rinehart . . . he was my best friend . . . like a brother to me!" Kit gasped as he sucked for breath. "I've been hoping for the chance to cut you . . . for a long time . . . ever since you . . . shot him in the back!"

"Hell, Kit, he ain't nothing but scum," Carson heard a voice say — William Bent's, he thought. "Not worth dirtying your knife with."

Carson, straddling Grieg, relaxed slightly as tension began to drain from his taut body. He reckoned what Bent said was the truth — and killing Grieg wouldn't bring Monte Rinehart back.

"There's been too many killings," Bent continued in a sad voice. "My brother, all those other folks down Taos way, the ones that've died in the hills . . . maybe it's time to stop killing . . . white men as well as red."

Carson hung motionless for a long breath, knife still poised, and then suddenly drew back. "The hell with you," he said and, rising, turned away.

"Kit . . . look out!" Godey shouted a warning.

Before Carson could wheel, a pistol shot echoed across the compound. Completing the turn, he saw Grieg, hand upraised with knife ready to strike, but there was a mass of spurting blood, and he was sinking to the ground.

"That son of a bitch was going to get you in the back, Kit," a man said angrily, holding a smoking pistol. "I wasn't about to let him get away with it!"

Carson smiled tautly. Rubbing his side where Grieg's blow had fallen, he found the pain that had plagued him periodically through the years was reawakened. He thanked his benefactor, a man named Conwell.

Bent overheard. "What I said is still the truth, Kit. Don't let what happened change your thinking. We've all got to turn to Christian ways if this part of the country's ever to amount to anything . . . and us killing off one another is the first thing that must be stopped."

"That Grieg was a back stabber . . . a back shooter. He had it coming," someone said.

"No doubt," Bent replied, "but we ought to have law to handle his kind. And I reckon we will one day. It's just that we've got to start some place . . . and soon. When are you pulling out, Kit?"

"Morning," Carson answered.

"Well, before that, let's set around and have a few drinks . . . just for old time's sake."

"Yeah," Godey said. "Old times that're sure fading fast."

The journey from the Arkansas to Taos was the most pleasant Kit could recall and as he rode steadily south, he regaled the soldiers accompanying him with incidents that had occurred in the past and pointed out the many things that had always interested him. But they weren't too attentive. California men all, they were accustomed to the more lush growth of the coastal territory, and each was anxious to report to Fort Marcy in Santa Fé where they expected to receive orders that would direct them to return home.

As for Kit, he was lost in the beauty of his New Mexico — the rugged grandeur of the mesas and bluffs, the deep green of the junipers that dotted the plains. The smartly erect pines and firs marched, like soldiers, up the long slopes and were already showing banks of white along their crests. There were the groves of golden aspens trembling in the slight breeze while, high above the roily river that cut its path through a black-walled gorge, a chevron of geese was making its way south.

The land lay quietly, as if slumbering, girding itself for the winter soon to come. Leaves of the lesser brush had long since changed to flaming reds or a bright yellow, as had those of the cottonwoods, always among the first to forsake the green of summer. In the crisp air was the tang of what was to come, a sharp, clean smell. As they drew nearer to Taos, the odor took on a thread of wood smoke, of piñon burning in the fireplaces that were a part of every home. Home . . . ! Home meant Josefa. She would be waiting for him just as she had for all those years. But the waiting was over now . . . for both of them.

Epilogue

FEBRUARY, 1868

The ride, first by stagecoach and then by train to Washington, had been long and tedious. Kit Carson, at the behest of several Ute chiefs who considered him a good and trustworthy friend, had agreed to accompany them to the nation's capital where a treaty setting forth their reservation boundaries was to be signed. He was in no condition to make the journey. The injury sustained in a fall years before had developed into a major problem. The surgeon at Fort Garland had told him frankly he could do nothing for him beyond administering doses of laudanum to lessen the pain and suggested that he consult doctors while in Washington.

This he would do, Kit assured Josefa when he boarded the stagecoach at Fort Lyon, but he also had in mind to see again his old friend and fellow argonaut, John Frémont. Frémont, made aware of Carson's coming, met him at the railroad station and immediately took him to his home. There followed several days during which Kit discharged whatever duties were required of him by the Bureau of Indian Affairs and the Ute chiefs, the renewal of friendships with soldiers he had known, trappers and mountain men now in politics or government service, traders to whom at times he had sold his bales of beaver skins and who had become important sutlers engaged in supplying military installations or Indian agencies.

When all that was done, he and Frémont were left with time to be together to relive the hours when they had fought their way through snowdrifts at South Pass, had their first look at the Great Salt Lake, and Disappointment Island where they almost drowned, the California Expedition, and the subsequent taking over of the Mexican province for the Union.

"Still get a thrill when I remember raising the flag there at Monterey," Frémont said, as they sat before a roaring fire in his Washington home. "And I still think what we did there was right."

"Same here," Kit agreed. "That court martial was wrong. You did what had to be done . . . what any man in your position would have done. Tried to make that clear to the President that time when I saw him, but I think he had his mind already made up."

"There wasn't much he could do . . . but he did favor the generals who were running things at that time."

Carson settled deeper into his chair, seeking a bit of relief from the pain that now reached well up into his chest. "Was hoping you'd be elected to the Presidency yourself when you ran in 'Fifty-Six. Did what I could for you up Colorado way."

Frémont frowned. "Colorado? You've moved from New Mexico?"

"Yes. I was appointed Indian agent at Fort Garland. Then, when my health began to go bad, I resigned and moved my family to a little place on the Purgatoire."

"The Purgatoire," Frémont mused. "I remember how the trappers always called it the Picketwire. Your health? I've noticed you appear far from well. Have you consulted any doctors about it?"

"Only the Army surgeon at the Fort. He told me to see a couple when I got here, see what they think. I was figuring maybe you'd recommend. . . ."

"Of course! Tomorrow I'll put you in touch with our family doctor here in Washington. And if you don't like what he tells you, I'll get word to Jessie . . . she's in our home in New York . . . and have her arrange for you to see the best physician there."

Kit shook his head. "Don't want to put you to a lot of trouble."

"Trouble!" John Frémont echoed. "After all we've been through together . . . the things you've done for me and my family . . . why, I'll never be able to repay you enough!"

Frémont rose, laid another log on the flames, now beginning to dwindle in the ornate marble fireplace. Outside the night was raw with the wind whistling shrilly around the corners of the house.

"At times like this," Frémont said, resuming his chair, "I think of the days when we were in the high Rockies, or the Sierras when the snow was up to the bellies of our horses, and we were low or out of provisions and all but ready to quit. It was you, Kit, who stood by me at such times and gave me strength . . . in fact, often figuring out a way to survive. I've told Jessie many times how invaluable you were. I just wish there was more I could have done for you."

"You did a-plenty," Carson said quietly. "To me, a man's friendship counts most. Besides, there were all those fine things you wrote about me in the newspapers and books."

"I was never able to really say what I wanted to. There just weren't the words. . . . Do you ever see Lucien Maxwell? I remem-

438

ber hearing that the two of you were building homes somewhere near Taos."

"See him occasionally. We were in business together for a spell, but I was never much of a hand at it . . . not like Lucien. We sort of split up when I moved to Fort Garland."

"I see. Well, if you run across him again, give him my regards. Now, I want you to get some rest. Tomorrow you're going to see my doctor."

It was a tumor — a serious matter, Frémont's doctor stated after the examination, and one likely soon to be fatal. Kit accepted the diagnosis with his customary stolidness, but Frémont was not about to give up his old friend so easily. He got word to Jessie in New York and sent Kit there for further consultation with the city's best. The reports were the same. Carson would be fortunate to survive the long journey home. Physicians in Boston and Philadelphia concurred.

"I reckon that's the word," Kit said when the last report was in. "And I reckon I'd best be heading back. Josefa will be worrying . . . and" — he added in a bit of grim humor — "it'd sure kill her if I happened to die before I got home."

The Frémonts understood and immedi-

439

ately arranged passage on a train that would take Kit back by way of Cheyenne, Wyoming. They considered it a better and more comfortable route. At the railroad station, Jessie Frémont bade Kit farewell and returned to her carriage so that the two men could be alone. As they awaited the train's departure, they spoke again of the old days, of both the good and bad times they had weathered together. All too soon came the locomotive's warning whistle and the call for all departing to get aboard. The two clasped hands for a final time, Kit with tears in his heart, Frémont's showing in his eyes.

"Godspeed, Kit," Frémont murmured as he turned away.

"Vaya con Dios," Carson replied in his soft voice and, entering the coach, took his seat. *"Vaya con Dios, amigo."*

Kit Carson died that year on the 24th of May in Colorado.

About the Author

Ray Hogan is an author who has inspired a loyal following over the years since he published his first Western novel, EX-MARSHAL, in 1956. Hogan was born in Willow Springs, Missouri, where his father was town marshal. At five the Hogan family moved to Albuquerque where Ray Hogan still lives in the foothills of the Sandia and Manzano mountains. His father was on the Albuquerque police force and, in later years, owned the Overland Hotel. It was while listening to his father and other old-timers tell tales from the past that Ray was inspired to recast these tales in fiction. From the beginning he did exhaustive research into the history and the people of the Old West and the walls of his study are lined with various firearms, spurs, pictures, books, and memorabilia, about all of which he can talk in dramatic detail. Among his most popular works are the series of books about Shawn Starbuck, a searcher in quest for a lost brother who has a clear sense of right and wrong and who is willing to stand up and be counted when it is a question of fairness or justice. His other major series is about lawman John Rye whose reputation has earned him the sobriquet, The Doomsday Marshal. "I've attempted to capture the courage and bravery of those men and women that lived out West and the dangers and problems they had to overcome," Hogan once remarked. If his lawmen protagonists seem sometimes larger than life, it is because they are men of integrity, heroes who through grit of character and common sense are able to overcome the obstacles they encounter despite often overwhelming odds. This same grit of character can also be found in Hogan's heroines and in THE VENGEANCE OF FORTUNA WEST (1983) Hogan wrote a gripping and totally believable account of a woman who takes up the badge and tracks the men who killed her lawman husband by ambush. No less intriguing in her way is Nellie Dupray, convicted of rustling in THE GLORY TRAIL (1978). Above all, what is most impressive about Hogan's Western novels is the consistent quality with which each is crafted, the compelling depth of his characters, and his ability to juxtapose the complexities of human conflict into narratives always as intensely interesting as they are emotionally involving.

The employees of Thorndike Press hope you have enjoyed this Large Print book. All our Large Print titles are designed for easy reading, and all our books are made to last. Other Thorndike Press Large Print books are available at your library, through selected bookstores, or directly from us.

For information about titles, please call:

(800) 223-2336

To share your comments, please write:

Publisher
Thorndike Press
P.O. Box 159
Thorndike, Maine 04986